A Novel

CW01496991

EVIL CAST UPON HER

By Brian Greenall

PROLOGUE

To know that you are rotten through and through and to continue to do the things that make you that way is either stupid or evil.

Stupidity can be in many forms. Not knowing how to get out of a situation can perhaps be forgiven. Not wanting to accept the way you are can also be forgiven. Even just giving up on yourself because you see no way out of the life you have, can be forgiven. Stupidity or simply lack of knowledge or understanding are things that we all suffer from occasionally.

Evil is different. Very few of us are actually evil. We may, now and then, have rotten thoughts or even carry out isolated rotten deeds but we have the boundaries within us to ensure that they do not continue unchallenged.

There are however some people who are just born EVIL or have EVIL cast upon them. It is up to each individual to decide which category they or others fall into.

DEDICATION

I dedicate this book to everyone who read my first book and especially those who provided me with feedback.

A special thank you to my wife Orietta who has read all of my work over and over again searching for grammar and punctuation errors, of which there were many in my earlier drafts. She also encouraged me when I was ready to turn on the TV or play a computer game instead of writing. Finally she provided the artistic talent for the book cover and helped with the whole 'self publishing' cycle.

CHAPTER 1 - ME, 2007

I pull the car over to the curb and stop. I look at the slumped body in the passenger seat next to me and I wonder where the hell I am. I know that I am in the inside lane of a dual carriageway in Stevenage but having driven without thinking for the last five minutes I am not sure exactly which road this is. I thought I would be able to stay cool but I panicked and now I need to recover my composure and get out of here.

I check the rear view mirror and see that the road is empty behind me. It's what I expect for this time of the morning. I push the button for the warning lights, get out of the car and shut the door. A quick look around tells me that there is no one about so I run across the road, jump over the central barrier and then up the bank and over the fence into a playing field. I take another good look around and then march along a gravel path past a children's play area and into a car park.

It might be June but the air is cold and I pull the collar of my coat up as I turn into a small road leading towards a large supermarket on the edge of the town. I could really do with a hot drink, I think as I approach the supermarket. My mind is still not completely clear and it isn't until I reach the big sign at the entrance that I realise my mistake. I have been too busy thinking about what has unfolded during the last few hours and now here I am searching for a coffee over four hours before the 10am Sunday opening time.

I need to get away from here but I am worried about the car so I retrace my steps until I reach the park. From here I can see the car across the road and I note that the warning lights are still flashing and the passenger is still sleeping. Thankfully there are no other cars on the road at this time on a Sunday morning. I pull my collar up as high as I can both as a defence against the cold and to hide as much of my face as I can in case I encounter anyone.

I am worried about what to do next and where to go but I turn right and head towards what looks like a row of shops and as I reach a roundabout I note the road name. It is the start of the high street and I see a telephone box ahead of me on the other side of the road. I race over and dial 999. After telling the operator that the car parked on Martins Way has a dead woman in the passenger seat and a box of incriminating evidence in the boot, I hang up. I know that the woman is not dead but I need the police to arrive before she wakes up.

I turn left and hurry along with my head down until I reach a large modern church. Here I enter the church garden, cut through the grave yard and I am about to go through the gate into a field at the back when I notice a woman in a bright yellow coat crouching by one of the graves. She looks up at me and smiles. Then she winks at me as I pass and as I rush through the gate I find myself winking back at her then wondering what the hell I am doing. I look back through the gate but she has gone.

Once in the fields I begin to run and it takes me ten minutes before I reach a gate that opens up onto a small road. Where to go now, I think, left or right. Luck is on my side as a car comes around the corner and stops beside me.

I am beckoned into the back seat and as I climb in I can relax for the first time in many hours.

CHAPTER 2 - ANDY, 1990

Andy was having a great evening. No, better than great, fantastic. He had woken up feeling lonely and depressed that this weekend would be as boring as every other weekend he had endured since he moved to Luton. But that had changed when he met Paul in the cafe that morning.

Andy knew Paul from work and although they had hardly ever spoken Andy respected Paul. Paul had the charisma and confidence that Andy lacked and even though they had both only worked at the warehouse for six weeks Paul had already become a favourite among the staff and was always the centre of attention. Andy on the other hand was a loner who found it difficult to make friends.

Paul had sat down at Andy's table with a tea in his hand.

"Mind if I join you?"

Andy had nodded and looked down at his mug. He had always had trouble making eye contact with people and never knew what to say.

"You look like you could do with some cheering up. Fancy coming to a party in Watford this evening? A couple of the girls from work will be there and Jessie has promised to bringing along a few 'pick me ups' if you know what I mean. A few beers, a few pills and all your worries will be behind you. Come on Andy, come and join in tonight, it's going to be great."

"I've got nothing better to do so I suppose I could."

"That's the spirit, can you pick me up here at about 7:30 tonight then, you have got a car haven't you?"

"Yes, I can do that."

"Great!" And with that decided, Paul finished his tea, got up and left the cafe.

Andy had worried all day that the invitation might just be a joke or that Paul just needed a lift. He was in two minds as to whether to turn up but with the alternative being yet another Saturday night in watching TV he decided to go.

Paul was waiting for him when he arrived and they headed out of town to the party. Paul's navigation skills where not brilliant but they found the address eventually and having parked the car they made their way to the nearest Pub.

"Far too early to go in to the Party." Paul had said. "We can go back around 11."

After three pints Andy was starting to relax. It was easy with Paul because Paul did about 90% of the talking and all Andy had to do was nod and smile and laugh where appropriate. Paul ordered another couple of pints and announced that after these they should make their way to the party.

When they entered the party Paul immediately made his way over to Jessie and Andy followed. When Paul grabbed Jessie and started dancing to the 1980s pop blaring out from the speakers Andy gravitated to the corner of the room and found a chair.

After about 20 minutes Paul came over and told Andy to follow him to the bathroom where he handed over a couple of yellow pills and told Andy to take them. Andy had no idea what they were but did as he was told. Then they returned to the living room.

After that Andy remembered very little. He could remember dancing, he could remember kissing an unknown girl and he remembered staggering alone to his car. Now he was driving along a country lane with no idea where he was going, he could feel his face contorted into a wide smile. He had a bottle of beer in his right hand and as he took a bend in the road he nearly hit the bank at the side. He dropped his bottle and took hold of the steering wheel with both hands, laughing out loud at the near mishap. He looked down at the beer bottle on the floor and as he leant forward to try to retrieve it......... he died.

His car had drifted across the lane and hit head on a car coming the other way.

Andy and the two passengers in the other car all died instantly.

The repercussions of this fatal accident would be felt by many for years to come.

CHAPTER 3 - LOUISE, 1990

Louise was an intelligent, polite, friendly young girl who had many school friends and of whom great things were expected. Her teachers believed that she would do something special with her life. She had already passed all her GCSE exams with flying colours and now she was focused on her A levels.

At 18 years old she was a key member of the County ladies youth football team and she was captain of the schools athletics squad and the netball team. She had had offers from a number of top football teams to join them but she was very focused and wanted to be a lawyer. She saw sport as a release but not as a career.

Although Louise studied hard to achieve her results she was also aware that many of those around her had to work twice as hard to achieve lesser results. She knew that having loving parents, who were both lawyers themselves, a stable home and the security that this offered were invaluable but she also knew that she was gifted.

She had been told many many times throughout her life that she was special and she knew that this was true. Everything was easy for her.

Louise was very popular in school especially with the boys. She knew that she was attractive and she was not shy of flirting with boys and men alike. She loved to party and most Saturday nights she and her closest friends could be found in one of the fashionable clubs in town.

This particular Saturday night she was at Sizzles, a new club with a huge dance floor and she was dancing with friends when a boy of roughly her own age caught her eye.

He was standing at the edge of the dance floor watching the dancers and drinking from a bottle.

As she watched him she knew that they would be together by the end of the evening. She was confident that she would be able to capture him for herself for tonight. Her confidence was borne from the fact that she always got the man she wanted.

Louise was athletic, dark haired and beautiful. She could have been a model if she had wanted to. In fact she knew that she could be anything she wanted to be.

Tommy, the boy she was watching, was strong looking but in a rough and ready fashion. He wore tight fitting clothes which showed his muscles and Louise could imagine him being a mechanic or a farmer not an intellectual or studious type. She was a good judge of character, she believed.

By midnight Louise and Tommy were drinking together at a table in the corner of the club. They were both laughing and under the table Louise's hand was resting on Tommy's knee.

Both knew that they had found a partner for the night and that in the morning they would go their separate ways such was the nature of relationships these days. Both were happy with this unspoken agreement.

A young man, obviously quite drunk and presumably not having registered the size of Tommy approached from the dance floor and asked Louise for a dance. Louise declined but the young man was persistent.

"Come on, one dance won't hurt you." He slurred and took hold of her hand. Louise laughed. She was used to this sort of attention and she knew how to deal with it. However, before she could reply Tommy stood up and reached across to the young man. He grabbed him by the shirt collar and shoved him backwards where he fell in a heap then quickly got up and shuffled away.

"Thank you but you didn't need to do that, I can deal with people like that myself." Said Louise, a little annoyed by the intervention.

'You're welcome." Replied Tommy with a smile. "Shall we get out of here? My place is only about 15 minutes up the road."

"Yes, let's go." Louise answered. Louise signalled to her friends that she was leaving and smiled at the somewhat crude hand signals she got from them. Nothing new there she thought.

They left the club and hailed a taxi.

CHAPTER 4 - SERGEANT SHORWELL, 1990

The police at the scene of the car crash were devastated to find three bodies. The young man in the Ford Fiesta had not been wearing a seat belt and had gone through the windscreen on impact. It was certain that he had been on the wrong side of the road and had caused the accident. They guessed that he had been speeding and was probably drunk or high at the time of the crash.

The other car was a Mercedes-Benz C class and the two bodies in the car were obviously a wealthy middle aged couple.

After the scene had been secured and the road closed the bodies were removed from the cars and laid on plastic sheets in the road. Sergeant Janice Shorwell searched through the pockets of all three dead and found identification and telephones.

She now had the unenviable task of contacting next of kins.

She decided that the middle-aged couple deserved to be dealt with first as she was sure that they were not responsible for the accident. From the wallet taken from the drivers pocket she had determined that Mr Micheal Whitwell and his wife, Geraldine lived at 9 Westview Drive, Northwood, just 15 minutes up the road from the accident. She found a photo of the couple with what Janice assumed was their daughter taken outside a villa in a hot Mediterranean country. She couldn't determine which one.

Janice bit hard on her bottom lip and told herself that she was the best person to break the news to the daughter despite the sickness she could feel brewing in her stomach.

She called PC John Kingston over and together they made their way to her car and headed to Westview Drive. It was 9:30 Sunday morning when they got out of the car and knocked at the door of number 9. There was no answer. After a few minutes of looking around the house and determining that no-one was home they returned to the car and Janice called the station to report.

Whilst still on the phone a car pulled up in the road and a young girl climbed out of the passenger seat. Janice recognised the girl from the photo, hung up and got out of her car. She was not sure if there was anything in her face that gave away the fact that there was bad news but on seeing her the young girl seemed to shrink in size and she put both hands to her face.

Janice noticed that the driver had not got out of the car and asked PC Kingston to invite him into the house. She asked the young girl to let them in and while she sat and explained what had happened only a few hours before, PC Kingston made some tea.

Louise was devastated and collapsed on the sofa. Tommy went to her but was shaken off. He sat in an armchair not knowing what to do. Eventually Louise sat up and looked first at Sergeant Shorwell and then at Tommy.

Tommy had only known Louise for less than 12 hours but he could see that behind her eyes she had changed. He got up and moved to the sofa where he put his arms around her. They stayed like this for a long time until Janice handed them both a cup of tea from the tray that PC Kingston had bought in.

Sometime later having determined that Louise was over 18 and that she was happy for Tommy to be there with her,

Sergeant Janice Shorwell and PC John Kingston left the house.

Louise had lost the two most important people in her life and could only seek protection in the arms of Tommy, a boy she had only met the night before. Her mind had stopped working the minute she heard the news and she needed this virtual strangers arms around her.

CHAPTER 5 - ELIZABETH, 1990

The days that followed the car crash had a profound effect on both Louise and Tommy. They had been thrown together in a tragedy and neither of them were able to cope with the fall out.

Louise had gone into complete breakdown and refused to speak to anyone but Tommy, and then only a few words. Many of her friends, teachers and even her one remaining family member, her aunt Elizabeth, tried but failed to get through the fog that surrounded Louise. There was no recognition in her eyes and they were black and empty.

Tommy had seen his life change overnight too. He had fought off the urge to just walk away and he did his best to help Louise where he could. Although he tried, he did not have the skills or experience to deal with the turmoil that had followed that one night of excitement they had shared. He quickly came to realised that Louise had become totally dependant on his support and although he found it strange that he was the one she turned to when she had so many friends, he also liked the idea that this beautiful girl had chosen him. He was very quickly becoming besotted with her and vowed to himself that he would be there for her, whatever she needed.

The funerals were going to be the second most stressful situation Louise had had to deal with in her young life, the first being the news a few days earlier. However, Louise didn't deal with it in any practical sense. She had been too upset to think about organising the funerals and this odious task had been taken up by aunt Elizabeth. Tommy had helped as best he could too but Louise had just shut herself away in her room, only appearing for an occasional meal or to collect another bottle of vodka from the drinks cabinet.

Elizabeth was Louise's father's elder sister and upon realising the frail state of her niece's mind had taken charge of everything. She arrived with a suitcase of belongings and announced that she would take over the funeral preparations. She was an organiser and a practical lady but she had never married or had children herself and lacked the more inter-personal and caring skills required to get through to Louise. She tried to understand what Louise needed but was unable to help in anything other than a practical nature. Instead, the course of action she took was to involve the family doctor.

Dr Brook had been the family doctor and a family friend for as long as Louise could remember. He was reaching the end of his career now and was looking forward to a retirement that would see him and his wife travel the world. They had planned in detail the countries they would visit, the food they would eat and the sites they would see. He was a happy and outgoing man and was renowned for his bedside manner and his positive and infectious personality. He had dealt with a few health problems in the Whitwell family over the years including Mrs Whitwell's miscarriage a couple of years after Louise was born, the diagnosing of the broken leg Louise had as a toddler when falling 4 feet from her tree house in the garden and the administering of stitches to a wound in her head when she had tried to do a cartwheel in her bedroom, aged seven. He had also spent many an hour in Louise's father's study drinking his whisky and discussing the woes of the world.

Having practised medicine for over 35 years Dr Brook was not easily shocked. He had seen pretty much everything from terrible terminal illnesses to embarrassing sex-play accidents. He was able to provide the support and strength to many and to suppress his amusement to others and he had always thanked God that he was a healthy and happy man.

When he knocked on the door to Louise's bedroom he felt a dread that he had only experienced a couple of times in his life. He knew Louise well and was shocked by the news of her parents death and by the worrying words spoken to him by Elizabeth. When there was no answer to his knocking he quietly spoke through the closed door to Louise. He fought back the urge to open the door and enter uninvited and instead asked to be allowed in. He then waited patiently until eventually he heard the sound of feet on the floor and the door opened.

It had been four days since the news of her parents death and Louise had spoken only a few words to Tommy and Elizabeth since then. She had stayed in her room alternately crying, drinking and sleeping although the former took up most of her time. She had neither washed nor groomed herself during that time and Dr Brook was faced by a sight that made him wince. He could smell the room from the landing and he could smell the alcohol on Louise's breath.

Doctors have to deal with death often and they will tell you that no two reactions to a family death are the same. Dr Brook had never seen anyone in all his years that had reacted the way Louise had. Over the next two days he spent many hours in the house and in particular in the bedroom with Louise. He held her hand, he talked to her for hours and he prescribed drugs to help her sleep and numb the pain a little. Tommy popped in from time to time and Elizabeth waited downstairs for updates on the health and state of mind of her niece.

On the Friday afternoon before Dr Brook left the house he sat at the dining room table with Tommy and Elizabeth and tried to explain the concerns that he had. He had been unable to get through to Louise in any meaningful way and he explained that the shock of her parents deaths had left Louise completely lost and numb. This in itself was not completely unusual but he had sensed in Louise a degree of loss that he had rarely seen. He was extremely worried about her lack of response to him and he suggested that he would like to admit her to hospital so that her health could be monitored more closely.

Elizabeth and Tommy looked at each other and knew that the doctor was right. Tommy was in no position to have a say in the matter and he acknowledge this and left the decision to Elizabeth. Elizabeth asked Tommy if he would leave the house for a couple of hours while she spoke privately with the doctor and he was happy to oblige. He got up, picked up the small rucksack of his belonging that he had collected from his flat a few days earlier and left the house.

Tommy drove back to his flat, parked the car and walked to his local pub. He had been a fairly regular drinker in the pub until this last week and acknowledged a few of the faces as he went to the bar. It was 6:15pm and the bar was starting to fill up with those wanting a drink or two on their way home after a long weeks work. Tommy was in no mood to talk though and took his pint to a table in the back bar. He sat down and took a long draw on his pint before allowing himself to think about the last week.

Tommy was quite a loner. He had a couple of people that he would probably call friends but he preferred his own company and would often go out to a club, pub or bar on his own, hoping to meet a young lady or just to have a few drinks and listen to some live music. When he met Louise he was glad of the company for the night but didn't think any further than that. What happened the following day had changed his life. Now he was at a crossroads. He could either just walk away or he could continue to support Louise until she was better and see if they had any sort of future together. He definitely liked her very much but now that she was going into hospital and her head had been messed up, he was not sure he could cope. He had promised himself that he would look out for her but that was nearly a week ago and a lot had happened since then.

Tommy got up, ordered another pint and returned to his table. He wondered how long it might take for Louise to recover fully and move on with her life. Even if she did, would it be the type of life he could be part of? He was aware that she was beautiful and that she was clever. She would probably go on to be a lawyer like her parents and he couldn't see that he would live up to her expectations. Elizabeth had told him just how bright Louise was and that she was destined for a top university and a fantastic career. He did not feel that she would want an out of work labourer around for long.

After getting a third pint and a whisky chaser Tommy decided that he would ask Elizabeth to help him write a letter to Louise explaining that he hoped she got well soon but that he had to move on with his life and she should do the same. He didn't much like himself for this thought and decided that he would wait until after the funeral and after Louise was in hospital before asking for Elizabeth's help in composing something appropriate.

As he rose again to get another drink his phone rang. It was Elizabeth saying he could go back now, Dr Brook had left.

Tommy apologised and said that he had been drinking and would call in the following morning. He had made his decision and deep down he knew that it was the correct decision for him although he was not sure it was best for Louise. He returned to the bar and ordered another pint.

CHAPTER 6 - TOMMY, 1990

Tommy woke and slowly opened his eyes. He knew immediately that he was hung over and he could feel his head pounding. He was in his own bed for the first time in a week and he realised that the last time he had slept here he had had Louise by his side. He gingerly sat up and looked around. His small bedroom was about a third of the size of the guest room he had been using all week. He needed a shower but unlike the house he had been staying in he only had a small hose hanging from the tap in his bathroom and his rucksack with his toothbrush was still in his car. These were not major problems in the scheme of things but in this moment he saw them as mountains to climb and so he lay his head back down and closed his eyes.

He awoke again an hour later and with a concerted effort he fumbled his way to the bathroom, relieved himself and showered. Once downstairs and with a cup of coffee in his hand he thought again about the last week. He retrieved his rucksack from the car and compared his tiny rented flat to the luxury house Louise would be inheriting. No, he was not jealous. How can you be jealous of someone who has just lost both parents? After finishing his coffee, eating a couple of slices of toast and cleaning his teeth he made his way back to Louise's house.

Elizabeth opened the door to him and immediately collapsed into his arms. He picked her up with ease and took her into the living room. He assumed she was in her 60s or 70s and she had quite an austere personality so he was surprised at how light and insignificant she felt. He settled her on the sofa and went to make her a cup of tea.

When he returned she was sitting up and she welcomed the tea, took a sip and then turned to him with tears in her eyes. She explained how she had discussed with Dr Brook the options open to her and eventually decided that she would not be able to look after Louise herself so had agreed that the best place for her, at least for a little while was the hospital. Dr Brook had agreed to make the arrangements and had gone up to Louise's room to explain the situation. A while later he had returned to the dining room and told her that although Louise had said nothing and shown no recognition of what he was telling her, it was for the best.

Tommy sighed and said that he would like to go up and see Louise. When he got to the landing though he had second thoughts and descended the stairs, returning to where Elizabeth was still seated. He explained the thoughts he had had last night and asked her to help him after the funeral. She seemed to understand and said she would help him write his letter to Louise.

They sat there together for a couple of hours discussing the funeral arrangements, Louise, her parents and anything else that came to mind. Neither of then really knowing what else to do. Finally, they were both relieved when the door bell rang and Tommy got up to answer it.

Dr Brooks stood in the doorway and behind him Tommy could see an ambulance in the driveway behind his car. He knew that now would be a very difficult time as Louise was coaxed from her bedroom and into the ambulance. Dr Brooks took charge and went up to see Louise. When eventually they came down the stairs together Tommy realised that Louise had been given a sedative of some kind and he watched helplessly with Elizabeth as Louise was helped into the back of the ambulance. She had passed them at the bottom of the stairs and there had been no recognition in her eyes at all. Both Tommy and Elizabeth had tears in their eyes as the ambulance with Louise and Dr Brook in the back reversed out of the drive and disappeared.

It was Saturday morning and there were 3 days until the funeral. Tommy had another cup of tea with Elizabeth and then went home.

CHAPTER 7 - DR BROOK, 1990

Elizabeth knew that she had done her best to arrange the funeral but that because Louise had been in no position to help there was a possibility that many friends may have been missed off the guest list. She had spoken to the Law office where her brother and sister-in-law worked and to a couple of friends and neighbours who she knew and asked that they spread the word to anyone who may want to attend. She had also put a small notification in the local newspaper. Even so, she was absolutely amazed with the amount of messages she received from those wishing to attend. She decided that there were likely to be in excess of 100 people at the church and she had cleaned the house and prepared food and drinks accordingly. She had also written a eulogy and planned to read it at the funeral.

She had been very very busy and had been grateful for Tommy's help. At the advice of Dr Brooks neither she nor Tommy had visited Louise in hospital but he had kept them up to date with her progress. He had reported that she spent most of her day either sedated or sleeping and that as yet there was no response to any questions asked of her.

Tomorrow, the day of the funeral, Dr Brook would bring Louise to the house before the funeral and Tommy and Elizabeth would be able to see her for the first time in 4 days.

Elizabeth had sent, via the doctor, a suitcase of appropriate clothing and makeup for Louise to wear.

Tommy was outside cutting the grass lawns and Elizabeth was making a pot of tea when the phone rang. It had rung many times in the last week and Elizabeth knew that each call was going to be as difficult as the last. She answered the phone and nearly collapsed on the floor when she heard the voice at the other end of the line.

"Auntie, it's me."

Elizabeth nearly fainted. She sat down on the sofa without replying, her mind telling her that it was her imagination.

"Auntie, it's Louise, I hope I haven't given you a fright. I am not sure where I've been for the last week but it seems I have just come out of a dream. I want to do a reading at the funeral tomorrow. Auntie, are you there?"

"Yes, yes, I'm here, I just can't believe it's you. You sound so coherent. How are you feeling?"

"I woke up about an hour ago and for the first time since last Sunday I realised I had things to do. The nurse told me the funeral is tomorrow and I want to say something there. I will write it now. I'm sorry I have not been around to help with the planning etc, is everything ok?"

"Yes, it's all organised." Elizabeth was now in floods of tears. "I am so glad to hear your voice, wait I'll call Tommy in to have a word with you."

"No, not now. Tell him I'll see him tomorrow, I've got to go now, love you."

With that, the line went dead and Elizabeth slumped into the chair. After a while she got up and called Tommy from the kitchen window. It took a couple of shouts for her to be heard above the sound of the lawn mower and Tommy signalled that he would be in in a minute.

It is no surprise that at the loss of both parents a child would feel the end of the world had arrived and that the future was impossible. It is also no surprise that the brain is a

28

miraculous organ and defies logic on a regular basis. However, Elizabeth was stunned by how Louise sounded on the phone and Tommy found it both astonishing and unbelievable in equal measure. He made Elizabeth repeat her story of the phone call over and over looking for explanations or looking to see if the stress of the last week had got to her and she had cracked, like her niece had.

He reserved judgment until he could speak to Dr Brook and having sat with Elizabeth for a while in silence he rose and headed back into the garden. His own head was now spinning and he tried to review his thoughts. Just over a week ago he had told himself that he would be there for Louise, a few days ago he had decided that he would be better off going back to his 'old' life away from the crazy situation he had found himself in. Now, he didn't know what to think and that scared him. Life had always been a struggle for him but a struggle that affected him alone and he had coped comfortably with that. If Louise was now 'back in the land of the living' did he really want to leave her or did he want to hold her tight and look after her? He didn't know the answer and so he started up the lawn mower and finished cutting the grass.

By the time he had finished, Elizabeth had prepared a snack and after a quick wash Tommy sat at the dining room table opposite Elizabeth and asked her to once again go over the brief details of the phone call. Before she could start her mobile rang and she looked at Tommy before she picked it up and saw that it was Dr Brook calling. She had tried a couple of times to call him since the call she had from Louise and she was glad that he had called her back. She answered the phone and after listening for a few minutes she, for the second time that morning, nearly fainted.

What Dr Brook had told her was heart-breaking. She again looked at Tommy across the table and then she passed over the phone and burst into tears without saying a word.

CHAPTER 8 - FUNERAL, 1990

It was the day of the funeral and no-one knew what to expect.

Elizabeth had slept very little and was drinking tea at 6am in the kitchen when Tommy came down the stairs. He too had not slept and he gratefully took the cup of tea that Elizabeth poured for him as he sat down. Neither said anything. They had discussed everything for hours the previous evening and now there was nothing else to say.

Dr Brooks was at home but both he and his wife were also sitting at their dining room table in silence with a tea in their hands.

The turn of events from the previous day was on everyones mind and it was only Dr Brooks who could come up with any vaguely viable explanation and even for him, a doctor for over 35, he found it unimaginable.

Dr Brooks was not at the hospital when Louise had awoken from her dream-like state. He had been called and told that Louise was coherent, asking questions and had insisted on using the telephone. After his last appointment he had driven to the hospital with his customary smile back on his face, delighted by what he had heard. Louise was the daughter of a very close friend who had died recently and he felt a special bond with her. He had seen her grow up and become the wonderful girl she was and he had seen her decline over the last week or so and he had been affected by this more than he had expected. Now, he would be able to help her to full recovery and this buoyed his spirits. However, as he entered the ward and turned the corner towards the nurses station he had a terrible sense of dread and a shiver ran down his spine.

The two nurses were in deep conversation and he could see beyond them that the door to Louise's room was open and that it was empty. The tall Nigerian nurse caught site of the doctor and she moved to intercept him.

"Doctor, there has been a change and Louise has been taken for a brain scan and some other tests. Please let me explain what has happened."

The nurse led the doctor to a small room and then she explained the events of the day.

That morning had started like each of the previous three mornings with Louise being given her morning medication followed by her breakfast. She had not responded to any conversation and had only taken a couple of mouthfuls of food before turning towards the window and refusing anything further. The nurse had left the room and continued with her duties. Around 10:30 she had noticed that the door to Louise's room was closed and as she opened the door she saw that Louise was sitting up on the side of the bed, looking out of the window. This was the first time she had seen Louise sitting up and she said so to the back of the young girl. Louise immediately turned round and asked if she could use the telephone.

For the next hour or so Louise chatted with the nurses and also asked for a pen and paper. The nurses were happy to see Louise in this state and called the duty doctor who, after a quick bedside examination and a longer discussion with Louise, declared that she should be allowed to make a phone call and that her GP, a personal friend, should be contacted. All was looking very promising and after Louise had made two phone calls she started writing on the paper provided. She then ate all of the lunch she had been given. It was at this stage that Dr Brooks had been contacted.

An hour later Louise had left her room and approached the nurses station. She had asked for a couple of aspirin as she had a headache and she had then returned to her room to sleep.

Some time later the nurse had checked in on Louise and found that she was awake but completely unresponsive to her questions and comments, just like she had been first thing that morning. She was shivering even though the room was warm and her eyes were again black and empty. Again the nurse had called for the duty doctor. They were at a loss as to her sudden relapse and were now very concerned about her health. An hour ago the doctors decided to carry out a number of tests and that was where Louise was now.

Dr Brook slumped in the chair and took out his telephone so that he could update Elizabeth on the sudden relapse.

After calling Elizabeth and talking to Tommy he had waited for a couple of hours before he could talk to the hospital doctors. He has seen Louise wheeled back to her room and put into bed and the doctors had explained to him that there was no sign of any damage and that they were baffled by the sudden 'awakening' and the equally sudden relapse. They repeated the text book lines that Dr Brook had himself used many times about the brain being a complex and mystifying organ and that they just had to wait for any further signs of improvement.

When Dr Brook left the hospital he felt drained. He knew that he was getting too old for the job and thought of the retirement that awaited him. He called Elizabeth to update her and then he called his wife. He needed to get home and relax and he needed his wife to be there for him.

Now it was the next morning and he was still shocked by the previous days events. He was not looking forward to the day ahead, not that anyone would expect him to as two of his best friends were being buried.

Elizabeth was the first to recover from the malaise in the Whitwell household as she quickly turned on her organisation mode. She cooked Tommy a good breakfast and then ushered him up the stairs to get showered and dressed. At eight o'clock she called the hospital but nothing had changed overnight.

Everything had been prepared for the hoards of people expected to come back to the house after the funeral and after washing up and making one last check of all the food and drinks, Elizabeth went up to prepare herself for the funeral. She had nearly three hours before the cars would be arriving and she felt that she needed a long soak in the bath.

Tommy had showered and was laying on the bed in his boxers with his eyes closed. He was trying to picture how the day might go and how it could bring to a close his nightmare of the last 11 days. He was still, almost by the hour, changing his mind from 'walking away from it all' to 'staying and supporting Louise come what may'.

He had never met Mr and Mrs Whitwell and so had no opinion of them other than that they appeared to be model parents. He felt that he knew Elizabeth far more than he knew Louise and although they had worked together during this difficult period and perhaps build a mutual respect for each other he was not sure that he actually liked her very much. She was very austere and bossy and she had a way of making him feel quite insignificant. On the other hand, she had worked wonders with what she had to do and perhaps he was premature in his judgment. He had after all only seen her at her most stressful. Tommy was not very good at seeing things in black and white so he often deferred making any decisions.

Did he want to put this whole nightmare behind him and leave after the funeral?

Did he want to stay and support a girl he hardly knew but for whom he seemed to have developed a deep affection despite the circumstances? Did he dislike Elizabeth? He really had no answers.

At 11:30 both Tommy and Elizabeth were dressed and waiting for the cars to arrive. There was going to be the hearse with the two bodies plus a car for the two of them and Louise. Louise was expected to arrive along with Dr and Mrs Brook at 11:45 with the funeral cars due about 30 minutes later. Tommy was getting nervous and wasn't sure how he would react when Louise arrived. He walked up and down the living room until Elizabeth told him to stop and then he jiggled about from one foot to the other. Elizabeth sat patiently on the sofa and jumped when the door bell rang.

Tommy answered the door and Dr Brook helped Louise into the house, followed by Mrs Brook. Tommy smiled, said hello and introduced himself to Mrs Brook.

Elizabeth rose from the sofa and took Mrs Brook's hand as Dr Brook lowered Louise into a chair. "Would anyone like a drink before we leave for the church, I think I could do with one." She said looking around the small group. No one wanted to join her in a drink so she sat back down again. Perhaps it wasn't such a good idea after all.

Dr Brook started a conversation about the weather with Elizabeth and Mrs Brook and Tommy stood staring at Louise. She had been cleaned up and dressed at the hospital and she looked as beautiful as ever except for the blankness in her eyes. She sat looking down at her feet and said nothing.

35

Everyone was relieved when the cars arrived and they no longer had to sit in silence or make small talk.

The Whitwell's had been a very popular couple and there were indeed over 100 people at the funeral. All was going well until Elizabeth got up to read her eulogy.

Elizabeth was not used to public speaking and she was pretty nervous in front of such a large audience. She had written the words herself and she could just read them out verbatim without having to improvise so that had calmed her a little. She moved up to the microphone and starred out at the people in front of her. She knew that after today she would see very few of them ever again and that also made her relax a little. Taking a deep breath she began.

"It is lovely to ...erm... to see so many of you here today to show your respects to Micheal and Geraldine and to celebrate their lives."

The first sentence went well except for that small stutter but Elizabeth's eyes were steaming over and she was having trouble reading her notes.

"My ...erm... brother and his wife, were ...erm... not... erm... ready to leave this...erm... world but ...i'm sorry, I seem to be having trouble reading my notes. My brother and his wife...erm... "

Dr Brook rose from his seat and joined Elizabeth, taking her now shaking hand in his and looking out at the crowd of mourners.

"It has not been an easy time for any of us." He began. "When I first heard the news of the terrible accident....."

That was as far as he got as another member of the crowd stood and walked to the front. It was Louise and the church went even more silent than it had already been.

"I think it would be best if I speak about my parents. I know them better than anyone and I had prepared a speech but I seem to have lost it. I can remember it well enough though and I want to tell everyone what wonderful people they were."

Louise then gave a heartfelt, warm and above all sincere eulogy for her parents. She explained how they had nurtured her, inspired her and loved her. How she in turn had worshipped them and how much they would be missed, not just by her but by everyone her parents had come into contact with during their lives. She joked about some of her fathers habits and how her mother would rebuke him for smoking in his study, which he always denied. She praised the strong woman that her mother was and the affection that they had for each other. After 20 minutes she turned to Elizabeth and thanked her for the work she had done in organising the funeral then she went back to her seat. She looked at the young, handsome man sitting next to her and smiled.

"I need to get the fuck out of here now, and I need a drink." She whispered to Tommy. She took hold of Tommy's hand and led him out of the church.

CHAPTER 9 - DISAPPEARED, 1990

Elizabeth sat on the sofa facing Sergeant Shorwell. It had now been over a week since the funeral and no one had seen or heard from either Louise or Tommy since they had walked out of the church. They had obviously been back to the house while everyone was still at the funeral as a note in Louise's handwriting had been found by Elizabeth on the kitchen counter next to the kettle. It had simply said that she and Tommy were going away. Nothing further.

Dr Brook was also sitting on the sofa next to Elizabeth.

Sergeant Shorwell had been contacted five days earlier by Elizabeth and she had commenced an investigation although she had pointed out that as no crime had been committed and both Tommy and Louise were old enough to do whatever they wanted she had her hands tied a little. The evidence of Louise's state of mind and fragility, provided by Dr Brook had helped her to convince her superiors that time should be spent on this case but she knew that at any moment she might be moved on to something else.

"We have found out that Louise withdrew a very large sum of money from the bank on the corner of Darwin Street at 1:50pm on Wednesday, just minutes after they had left the funeral. She and Tommy were then seen first by a neighbour, entering Tommy's flat at about 3:30pm and then by a friend of Louise's, on foot on the high street heading towards the train station at approximately 4:45pm. The witness believes they were both carrying ruck sacks. Although there is CCTV at the station no record of them entering the station can be found and there have been no sightings since then.

They obviously don't want to be found. At the hospital Louise made two phone calls the day before the funeral. As you know one was to you Elizabeth but the other one was to an unregistered mobile number which we cannot trace. The number is now no longer in use." Sergeant Shorwell reported.

"Tommy's car is still parked outside his flat and if they both had rucksacks we can assume that they have packed, albeit quickly, some personal clothes and belongings. I know you are not familiar with what Louise has but can I ask you again to think about anything that may be missing from the house."

"It's not my house. I have only been here for a couple of weeks or so and I will be going home again on Friday. I do not know what could be missing, if anything. I hope nothing has happened to Louise, she is obviously not well and not thinking straight." Replied Elizabeth with a quiver in her voice.

"How could they have avoided the CCTV at the station?" Asked Dr Brook.

"We don't know for sure that they were going to the station, just towards it. We really have no more information than that at the moment. I will keep looking for them as long as I am allowed but at the moment we have no further leads."

Dr Brooks reiterated his concerns about Louise's health and asked to be kept 'in the loop' with any further developments. He was due to retire at the end of the month and two weeks later had plans to travel to Canada. That was the first stage of a planned five month trip around central and southern America and Oceana and he hated the idea that he was leaving at such a difficult time but the trip had been planned months ago and couldn't be cancelled or rescheduled easily.

Elizabeth explained that she would be going back to her own home in Oxfordshire and would update the doctor with any significant news.

Unfortunately, they all agreed, there was little more that could be done at that time.

CHAPTER 10 - BAZ 1990

Louise watched Tommy as he concentrated on driving through the torrential rain storm that had abruptly started about an hour ago. He squinted slightly at the windscreen as the wiper blades whipped back. He had not spoken since the rain began, concentrating on both his driving and the map. Actually he had said very little since they left the funeral a few hours earlier.

Louise had surprised everyone at the funeral, including herself. She was not very aware of what had happened to her since the police woman had told her the news of her parents deaths. She clearly remembered the night before that she had spent with Tommy, she remembered seeing Auntie Elizabeth at the house and she remembered the telephone conversations she had had with Baz and Auntie Elizabeth. Everything else up until the moment she got up to speak at the funeral was vague and foggy.

She was not sure where the words that she spoke at the funeral had come from either but now her mind was clear and focused. She knew that the second call she had made from the hospital would not be traced and she had told the person on the other end of the line to destroy his sim card and replace it after she had finished giving her orders, as if he needed to be told. She had told Baz, her drug dealer of choice, what she needed and explained when and where she needed it. She also explained how she would pay for it.

Louise was not a regular drug taker and rarely did anything more than smoke a joint or two but she had been introduced to Baz when she was fifteen and had built up an unlikely friendship with him. He was in his early 50s with long hair and a waistline that got bigger every time she saw him. He had once told her that he had been a Hell's Angel in his youth and had killed a man in a fight when he was 19. Louise didn't know whether this was true or not but she had questioned him relentlessly about it and the story seemed to ring true. She had been fascinated by it and as she got to know Baz better she had come to realise that he was far more than your average drug dealer. He provided services far more varied and in some cases extreme. He had his own network of clients and employees and had once boasted to her that he could get anything for anyone if the price was right.

In turn, Baz was impressed with Louise. He knew she was very clever, he had not failed to notice that she was beautiful and he was impressed with her confidence. Not many people would dare to ask Baz half the questions Louise did. He also knew that she came from a wealthy family.

Baz had provided the car they were now in, together with a full tank of petrol, an atlas of the British Isles, a few complementary joints, a bottle of vodka and a carrier bag filled with some snacks. He had been parked outside the station away from prying eyes and Louise had paid him in cash. He had looked closely at Tommy and made sure that Tommy had noticed. Baz was unaware of the events of the last couple of weeks but he had developed almost a paternal feeling for Louise. He felt she was in some sort of trouble but believed she was more that capable of looking after herself. He got out of the car, passed the keys to Tommy and got into the car behind where a young man was waiting and they drove off.

Louise and Tommy were now driving through a storm on their way to Southampton.

Louise had, she assumed, planned this all in her head during the periods in the last week that she could not now remember. She was aware that they would be catching a ferry to Cowes but not aware of what would happen after that, so she assumed that her planning stage had only reached this far. She searched her brain to see if there was anything relating to what she might want to be on the Isle of Wight for but came up blank.

When they had first left the church Tommy had asked what was going on and whether Louise was feeling better. She had simply replied by turning round and kissing him hard on the lips. Then she had told him they were going away together for a while and that she needed to get some clothes and belonging and after that he should do the same. He had asked where they were going but she had just smiled, winked and carried on talking about what preparations were required. The smile had done it for Tommy. He knew then for certain that his indecisions about the future during the last week were over, he would follow her to the end of the earth if she asked him.

Tommy was both confused and amazed firstly at the clarity and sparkle of Louise and secondly at the organisation that had gone into todays plan. How had she done it? Even for a big strong man as he was he had been pretty nervous when he saw Baz. No introduction was made but Tommy had noticed the look that Baz had given him and he could see that Baz was not someone you got on the wrong side of. He would make sure he looked after Louise.

When they arrived at the ferry terminal their car had already been registered and they were directed straight to lane eight. Tommy pulled the car up behind the large Mercedes in front and turned off the ignition.

He looked at Louise and his heart melted. She was smiling back at him and the look in her eyes told him that she was happy. Happy to be there and happy to be there with him. He needed the toilet and Louise said she would get some coffees while they waited for the ferry to arrive.

When he exited the toilets he saw Louise chatting to the young man serving the coffee. She was smiling and flirting with him and Tommy felt a pang of jealousy run through him. He put this to one side and went over to help Louise carry the two coffees and the two pasties that she had bought back to the car.

By the time they had eaten the extremely hot pasties and finished their coffees the ferry had arrived and was unloading the cars, vans and lorries from the island.

Louise had been to the Isle of Wight a couple of times before and as Tommy drove up the ramp to board the ferry she told him that judging by the few cars in the queue the ferry would be half empty. She was right and they had no trouble finding seats with a view out of the front of the ferry. It had stopped raining by the time the ferry left the terminal. They sat in silence watching the other boats out of the window and the other passengers on the ferry. Tommy closed his eyes and relaxed back in his chair.

It seemed like only minutes had passed when he was awoken by an announcement over the tannoy telling all passengers to return to their cars. He looked to his right and saw that Louise was not there. He jumped up from his seat looking around him as he did so. No sight of her. What should he do, he wondered. Wait for her to return or go looking for her? He decided on the later and headed down the aisle towards the toilets. He couldn't go into the ladies so he asked an old lady if she wouldn't mind going in and asking for Louise. Louise was not there. He was getting worried now and panic was setting in. He decided that he should return to the car and wait there.

Cars were beginning to roll off the ferry and Tommy knew that the cars in front of him would be starting their engines soon. He was panicking a little until Louise eventually opened the passenger door and got in.

"Where the hell were you?" He shouted as he let out his frustration.

"Calm down darling," she replied, "I just went for a little walk up on the open deck to get some fresh air. When I returned to the seats you were gone and I assumed you would meet me here."

"I'm sorry, I was just worried about you. These are far from being normal times and I panicked a bit." Tommy apologised. He was angry with her but didn't want to show it. A little misunderstanding that would soon be forgotten.

Louise, without knowing why, directed Tommy out of Cowes and towards Newport. She then told him to follow the sign posts until they reached the small village of Brighstone. As they arrived in Brighstone it was beginning to get dark and they were aware that they had nowhere to stay so Tommy suggested they go to the local pub for a drink and try to find somewhere for the night. Tommy was fully aware of the looks they got as they entered the pub. He knew that none of the locals drinking at the bar or dining at the tables were looking at him and as he followed Louise to the bar he could see why. She was as beautiful from behind as she was from the front and he was her boyfriend. He believed he was a very luck man.

As luck would have it the pub had a number of holiday rooms for rent and Louise booked them in for four nights. She also ordered a couple of meals from the menu and a couple of glasses of wine.

Tommy was not a wine drinker but decided that it was easier to drink the wine than to argue his case for a beer. He went and found a table in the corner and Louise settled up the payment of the bill and joined him.

The food was good but they were both too tired to stay long in the bar. After finishing eating they were told where their room was and they retreated there for the night. Once in the room and with the door shut behind them Tommy realised exactly how tired he was. It had been a long day and a lot had happened. He would save all his questions for Louise until the morning he decided.

Louise was also knackered and after a quick shower she got into bed and waited for Tommy. Tommy got out of the shower and looked at himself in the mirror. He was a little nervous about sharing a bed with Louise again, mostly because of her recent deterioration in health but also because he was completely shattered and needed sleep. Luckily, when he opened the bathroom door and moved into the bedroom he could see that Louise was already fast asleep. He climbed in beside her and soon he too was asleep.

CHAPTER 11 - BRIGHSTONE, 1990

Tommy woke early the next morning and surveyed his surroundings. Louise was asleep beside him. The room was small and slightly stuffy, neither of them had thought about opening a window before they had climbed into bed. The room had tea and coffee making facilities and Tommy rose, took a peep inside the kettle, filled it up from the bathroom tap and plugged it in. There was a small TV on the wall but he didn't really want to watch anything at this time of the morning so he quickly washed, donned some clothes and ignoring his need for coffee he stepped outside the door which led down a small path to the pub garden.

Everywhere was quiet and he couldn't even hear any cars. He decided that a quick walk along the High Street would wake him up and prepare him for the morning coffee. He was back in the pub garden within six minutes as the village High Street seemed to consist only of one shop, one cafe/ newsagents and the pub. Both the shop and the cafe were already open even though it was only 7am but there was no one else about.

'Bloody Hell, we're in the middle of nowhere." He muttered to himself.

As he entered the room he glanced over at the bed and saw that Louise was still fast asleep. He remembered the state she had been in over the last week and quietly went over to check that she was breathing well. Her breathing was strong and regular so he took the three steps to where the kettle was and made himself a coffee. He then stood his pillows up and sat down on the bed with his back to the headboard. As he drank his coffee he watched Louise and marvelled over her beauty. Even in the half light of the room she seemed to shine.

It was another hour before Louise stirred and a further 45 minutes before she was fully awake, showered and dressed. By then Tommy was feeling hungry and he suggested they walk the 50 metres to the cafe for breakfast.

"No need." Said Louise. "We have a hamper full of snacks in the boot of the car, we can have something from there." She waited to see what Tommy's response would be.

"Erm, OK, I suppose but I was hoping for something hot." He replied.

Louise burst out laughing.

"I was only joking, the pub provides breakfast so we can go through and get a good old English breakfast and some good coffee. I'm not keen on that powdered stuff."

Tommy sighed and smiled at Louise.

"We need to talk too. I have so many questions and we need to make some plans...." Only one of them said. It could have been either of them, until "... and after breakfast I need to find somewhere to buy some face cream, my skin is terrible." was added. Tommy did not use face cream and he certainly hadn't seen a need for Louise to use any either.

Once sat at the breakfast table and with a large plate of food in front of each of them, Louise started with the questions. She asked about what had happened since that terrible Sunday morning news, she asked about Auntie Elizabeth, she asked how she had ended up at the hospital and she informed Tommy that she had very little memory of anything during that period.

"And yet you were able to give a very moving speech at the funeral and plan this whole trip."

Tommy had many questions of his own but he now realised that there would be no point in asking Louise many of them due to her obvious lack of knowledge or memory about the time they had known each other. He did have one question though.

"Who the fuck was that scary fat guy who gave us the car yesterday?"

Neither of them were really satisfied with the answers the other had given but they turned to the question of what to do next. Louise was adamant that they should stay away from their lives before 'D' day as she had started to refer to the Sunday she received the news about her parents as. She wanted to 'vanish' and she wanted to take her time getting to know Tommy better. Everything about her life before 'D' day was irrelevant now and she only had eyes for the future. She would eventually write to Elizabeth and ask her to sort out the sale of the house, her parents will and all the other issues that arose but for now she felt that she had grieved enough, though she couldn't remember it, and she wanted to have some fun.

Tommy was concerned that Louise wanted to hide from everyone and everything but decided that he would go along with her wishes at least for a while. When he mentioned money including claiming his benefits and paying his rent Louise told him not to worry and reminded him of her desire for them to remain off the grid and electronically invisible. She had enough cash to last them for a while and had booked into the room at the pub under a false name.

Louise had been to Brighstone before. Four years ago she had stayed in a small cottage in the village with her parents.

Her parents had fond memories of the village from when they were at University and soon after they had first met. They had taken a week off mid-term and 'run away' to the Isle of Wight, staying in a tent in a farmers field between Brighstone and the coast, walking the many footpaths along the coast and up in the forest and both completely forgetting about University for a week. Louise remembered the way they spoke about the island and in particular about this village. Perhaps that was why as they had driven off the ferry she had directed Tommy there.

Over the next three days and nights Tommy and Louise settled into a pattern. Evenings were spent in the pub, mornings were for sleeping off the night before and for breakfast. Luckily the breakfasts were served right up to 11am otherwise they would have more often than not missed them. In the afternoons they explored the village and the surrounding area.

Louise loved the peacefulness of the village. She loved the little gift shop and the museum and she loved the steep climb up to the forest where she had walked before with her parents. She loved sitting in a meadow making notes about their trip and about Tommy, in her diary. All these places remind her of her parents and she felt a calmness there.

Tommy did not have the same feelings. He had only ever been on holiday once before in his life and it had been a week during October half term in a grotty Southend BnB with his Mum when he was thirteen. He had hated it. He had never known his father and had been bought up by his mother. They had always been short of money and although she had done the best she could as a single parent they had struggled. She was a weak woman who was always ill and could never hold down a regular job for very long. When she died Tommy was seventeen.

50

Tommy had moved away from Highbury after his mothers death and had rented a flat in West London where he had found a job with a removals company. That job had lasted only two years before the company went broke and he had been on the dole ever since. He had only ventured outside the M25 for work and that one holiday to Southend. Now he was in the country taking hikes up hills and walking for hours just for the fun of it. He didn't find it fun.

What he did enjoy were the evenings in the pub with Louise.

They had quickly become quite popular with the locals. Tommy played pool and darts, Louise socialised and they both drank heavily knowing that they only had to walk about 50 metres to their bed.

The landlady had been paid up front in cash for their stay and Louise had also set up a tab for their drinks, having handed over a couple of hundred pounds in advance. This meant that Tommy could go to the bar and get a drink anytime without it being obvious that Louise was paying for it. This was important to him as he did not want to be seen as a free-loader, even though he was.

Nearly everyone seemed very friendly and Tommy noticed that all eyes where always on Louise. In addition to her beauty she had a very charming and confident nature and she was not afraid to use her charm on the men in the bar. Tommy had notice that drinks were often being bought for Louise and that she would thank the buyer with a kiss on the cheek.

Tommy was quite a jealous man and on their last night had asked a particularly insistent young man, named Ben, to back off after Ben had turned his head while Louise was trying to kiss him on the cheek. He had grabbed Louise with his hand on her shoulder and held their lips together while Louise was trying to part from him. Afterwards he had laughed with his friends and Tommy had overheard him say a couple of rather unsavoury things. Ben was no older than Tommy but was at least a stone lighter. Tommy had grabbed the man by the throat and almost lifted him off the floor. He was angry and squeezed hard until a couple of other locals pulled him away.

"Stay away from her and if I ever hear you make comments like that again I will not be stopped so easily" He gnarled.

Louise took him by the arm and they moved to a table in the corner. She was smiling and her eyes were like they were on fire.

"Thank you. The bastard deserved that, you should have knocked his lights out. That was so exciting though. Wow." She was reacting very different to the last time, during their first meeting, when Tommy had stood up for her.

The rest of the evening passed without incident and they returned to their room a little earlier and slightly less drunk than they had the previous days.

"Have you ever killed anyone Tommy?" Asked Louise.

"Of course not, what a daft question. Why are you asking that?" Tommy asked as they climbed into bed.

Louise snuggled up to Tommy and was silent for a while.

"The look in your eyes was murderous when you grabbed Ben by the throat. What would you have done if they hadn't stopped you?"

"I was already calming down when they grabbed me. I only wanted him to think I was going to hurt him." Tommy put his arm around Louise and pulled her close. "Don't worry, I know how to control myself."

Louise turned over and away from Tommy and said goodnight. She starred out of the window and before she fell asleep she realised that a tiny part of her was disappointed that Tommy had not killed Ben.

The following morning they had their breakfast and Louise settled up with the landlady. They had very little to pack and by 11am they were in the car and ready to leave.

"OK, Next stop Ventnor." declared Louise.

"Where's that?" Tommy asked.

"No idea, just follow the road signs, it is on the coast and it is where Mum and Dad had their first honeymoon."

"Their first? You mean they had more than one?"

"Oh yes, they were still students when they married and could only afford a short break in England. A few years later, just before I was born, they had a second honeymoon in Rome."

"I suppose that's where we'll be off to next then is it?" Joked Tommy.

And as Tommy started the car and headed out of the car park Louise whispered mostly to herself "Invisibility Tommy, electronic invisibility, no passports."

CHAPTER 12 - COWES, 1990

For the next ten days Louise and Tommy moved from place to place on the Island. They drank in many of the Island pubs and mixed with the locals and the tourists alike. Most mornings were spent quietly getting over the heavy drinking session of the night before and the afternoons were spent having a pub lunch, a few drinks and usually a walk.

Tommy was getting used to the walking and was actually starting to enjoy it. They could find places where they were alone together and Tommy liked that. Although they had only made love the once, the day they met, Tommy was not worried. He knew Louise had some healing to do and he did not push her. He had no idea of the extent of the mental problems she had in the period between 'D' day and the funeral but she had been in good spirits since then and he was convinced that she was getting better every day. She would want him soon enough.

On the evening of the last day that they planned to spend on the Island they were in Cowes. They had booked a ferry in the name of a friend of Baz' for 1:30pm the following day and had decided to spend the evening in a small pub near Cowes Harbour. They had decided that tomorrow they would return to the mainland and travel west to Devon and Cornwall and continue their current life style until the money ran low. They had no plans for what to do after that.

That evening they had a nice Indian meal in a restaurant and then walked up to the pub. It was still before 9pm but the pub was crowded and noisy. Tommy was not certain but the volume seemed to reduce as Louise walked in and again he noticed that many eyes were focused on her. This had happened in pretty much every pub they had walked into and although he was getting used to it, it still irked him.

By 11pm they were both pretty drunk. They had been drinking more and more and quicker and quicker each day, urging each other on and laughing when either one of them couldn't keep up. When the pub finally closed and they were ushered out of the door neither of them knew which way to go to the BnB they had booked. They argued about it, laughed about it and then headed east along the road back towards the Indian restaurant, arm in arm. Tommy hoped that the sight of the restaurant would remind them of the way back. Louise didn't really seem to care either way.

As they rounded the corner and saw the restaurant ahead of them a call rang out along the quiet street.

"Hey, wanker, remember me?"

They both turned to see where the voice had come from and out of a side street strode Ben and a few of his mates. Tommy felt his anger rise immediately and took a few steps back towards the group of young men. Tommy was confident that one on one he would beat any of them but there were four of them and he had Louise to think about too.

He sobered up quickly and turned to Louise.

"Lets just head back to the BnB it's that way, we don't want any trouble now." He said.

Louise too had sobered at the sight of the little gang but her reaction was very different to Tommy's. She looked around and picked up a half-brick from the side of the road. Tommy was too slow to stop her and she threw it as hard as she could towards the men. To Tommy's surprise she hit one of the men who was not looking towards them on the back of the head and he collapsed onto the road.

"Come on Louise, let's get out of here." Tommy pleaded and grabbed for Louise's arm. Again he was too slow and Louise strode purposely towards the men.

"Come on then you bunch of little shits show us what you've got." She yelled towards the group.

Ben and his remaining two standing friends seemed to be indecisive for a second and Tommy charged forward past Louise and punched Ben in the face. Ben went down, his nose squirting blood and before he could see clearly again Louise was on him. She punched, scratched and kicked at him with ferocity and he rolled himself up into a ball on the floor. Tommy was now on to Ben's mates and he floored the first one before rounding on the second.

"We d,d,d, don't want any t,trouble mate." The one remaining man stuttered and backed away. Tommy stopped and surveyed the scene.

Ben was on the floor and Louise was still aiming kicks at his head, one of the men was sitting on the curb bleeding profusely from the gash in his head caused by the brick. Another was now standing but didn't look like he had any fight left in him and the final one had backed away and was now tending to the one with the gash to his head.

A sorry bunch they looked and Tommy turned his attention to Louise. He wrapped his arms around her and pulled her away from Ben. She swore at him and struggled to get free and Tommy was surprised by her strength but he held tight.

He led her up the road all the time watching the four men. They were regrouping and watching the retreating couple but Tommy knew they would not be launching an attack. Ben was an absolute mess and Tommy could see that in addition to what looked like a broken nose Ben was missing a couple of teeth and was limping heavily. It had all happened so fast and Louise was still fighting to get free of his vice-like grip.

They turned right and then left into the street where the BnB was and then Tommy felt it was safe to let Louise go. She had continued her swearing right up until Tommy released her and now she went silent. She look hold of Tommy's arm and looked up at him. Again he saw the fire in her eyes and a shiver went down his spine.

"That was bloody brilliant." She said. "We certainly showed them. God, I'm buzzing. You were great, where did you learn to punch like that? Did you see me kick Ben's teeth in? He deserved that, the creep."

Tommy listened but he didn't feel the same. He could fight but he wasn't really a fighter. Sure, he would stand up for himself and for Louise but because of his size he had rarely had to fight like he did tonight, a look was usually enough.

"You only threw two punches and both hit home. You should take up boxing, haha. I really wanted to smash Ben into little pieces. Wow."

The following morning Tommy woke later than usual and saw that Louise was already washed and dressed and was scribbling in her diary. It was 9:45 and they had already missed breakfast. They also had to be out of the room by 11am.

"Can you put the kettle on while I jump in the shower." He asked.

He only took 30 minutes to shower, dress and put his dirty clothes into a carrier bag. He drank the coffee Louise had made him and ate a couple of the biscuits she had retrieved from the hamper in the car.

They were ready to head for the ferry, well, two ferries actually. The first took them from West Cowes to East Cowes and lasted all of 10 minutes. The second would take them to Southampton and would take an hour.

Tommy had decided while he was in the shower that when they were settled on the second ferry he would raise with Louise the changes that he had noticed in her recently. He had no idea what she was like before 'D' day but he had noticed that since the funeral she had gradually become more wild. Twice in the last fortnight he had stepped in to defend her honour and he had been happy to do so but each time he had seen something in Louise that he wasn't sure he liked. She had a dark side to her and he had a feeling that before long someone would get seriously hurt. He hoped that it was not him but he knew that unless she changed she would put him in some very difficult situations.

It was another cold, windy and rainy day and so the inside deck of the ferry was crowded, no one was up on the outer decks in that weather. There was no opportunity for Tommy to raise the issues he wanted to without someone listening in so he waited.

Only once they were in the car, away from the busy Southampton roads and heading along the A36 did Tommy broach the subject of Louise's mental health, her apparent appetite for violence and the problems that could be caused if she continued on the path she had started on the day of the funeral.

He waited and waited for a reply but Louise remained silent, instead staring out of the window to her left almost as if she hadn't heard him. He leaned over and put on the radio and decided that he was back where he had been on the morning of the funeral...undecided.

CHAPTER 13 - EXETER, 1990

It wasn't until Tommy pulled the car up in front of a hotel in Exeter over two hours later that Louise spoke.

"I'm sorry Tommy, I don't want to explain myself to you. I just want to enjoy myself and forget about the world I came from, just for a little bit longer."

And that was it. All the explanation that Tommy was going to get.

"I'm not sure I want to continue like this. I have come to love you over the last couple of week but you scare me sometimes and eventually we will have to go home and sort out our lives. You have so much to live for." He told her but she was not listening again and after rummaging in her handbag she handed a wad of notes to Tommy and told him to book a room in the hotel for three nights and to again use false names.

Tommy sighed and did as he was told. He had tried to tell Louise how he felt but his speech had fallen on deaf ears and he was at a loss as to what to do next.

After quickly getting settled into their room, taking a shower and dressing for the hotel restaurant they descended the stair and went to the hotel bar. It was quite a posh hotel and Tommy felt a bit under dressed and uncomfortable. Louise as always looked beautiful and led the way. It was early and the hotel bar was virtually empty . They found a table by the window, ordered some drinks and booked a table in the restaurant for 7:30. Louise was feeling happy and she chatted openly to Tommy about her childhood and her parents. She asked Tommy about his patents and was genuinely sad when he told her about his upbringing.

"Tonight you will feel like a king." She declared. After dinner we will find a pub, have a few drinks and then return to our room early so that we can spend some quality time together, if you know what I mean. I feel the need to make you smile. I have neglected your needs and I want to put that right. She smiled at him, leaned forward and as she kissed him she ran her hand up his leg under the table. Tommy again fell under her spell and again changed his mind about what he wanted. He decided that he was the worst decision maker in the world.

The evening was brilliant. It was like a first date and Tommy had so much fun. Louise was the perfect date. She hardly took her eyes off him all evening and the end of the evening was as good as she had promised it would be.

They both woke early the next morning and Louise was still in the same mood of the day before. She took Tommy's hand and led him into the shower. Later they dressed and headed down for breakfast. They agreed that it was one of the best breakfasts either of them had ever had and they were both in a buoyant mood as they left the hotel for a walk along the river.

At lunchtime they found The Weirside, a quiet back street pub and ordered a couple of sandwiches and a drink each. The pub was virtually empty but Louise decided that she liked the 'vibe' and she had seen a poster by the door saying there was a band playing on Friday. She convinced Tommy, not that he needed much convincing, that this where they should spend Friday evening.

Little did either of them know that the evening would turn out to be another turning point in their lives.

CHAPTER 14 - JOHN, 1990

John was having a proper night out with his footballing friends for the first time in ages. Sure he had been to the pub for a quick drink after training but he was always home after one or two pints. Having twins had put a stranglehold on his social life for a long time and he had been happy to stay at home with his wife every evening for the last 5 years.

Mary was a very nervous mother and she had struggled with all aspects of being a mum. She was lucky that John worked from home and she relied on him heavily. She knew that she had put a lot of pressure on John and that she had somewhat stifled him while the children were young. She couldn't help it. She felt helpless when he wasn't around and with no other family to turn to she leaned on him and his positivity and his good nature.

A couple of months ago John had asked if he could start football training again on a Tuesday evening. The children were now five years old and he felt that Mary should now allow him a little freedom. He knew the worries she had and the nervousness she felt whenever he was out of the house but he believed he had been extremely patient for five years.

He also suggested that she could find a hobby or sport and take an evening out, away from the children whenever she needed to although deep down he knew she would not. He was more than happy to stay home when she was out but her anxiety had stretch far beyond the worries about the children and she had reached a stage where any time outside the house, or even inside the house when John wasn't there, was frightening to her.

John loved Mary but her anxiety was frustrating him. He needed some time away from the house and joining the football club was something he really enjoyed. He was not a good player, his fitness levels were not great and his lack of skill was only highlighted by his over enthusiasm but he had been accepted in the club and he had enjoyed the last few weeks of training. A quick pint or two in the pub afterwards was, although by no means compulsory, fun and a great way to get to know his new team mates. Returning home afterwards was not so much fun.

After the first two training sessions he had returned to find Mary in bed, she had obviously been crying and after a quick shower he had joined her in the bed, forgoing his dinner, and comforted her. She had apologised profusely and insisted that she would get used to Tuesday evenings alone with the children.

The third week she was much better and had his dinner ready for him when he returned. Although she had tried to put on a brave face he could tell that she had again been crying but he was happy that there had been some progress.

Things gradually got easier for Mary and when John mentioned that some of the players had planned to go out to see a band the following Friday and had invited him along, Mary had smiled and said she was happy that he was making new friends and that he should go. Deep down she was happy for him but she was also still struggling with being alone after the children were in bed.

So here John was drinking in The Weirside pub with some of his new teammates. He was slightly older than most of them and certainly less boisterous. When the band had come on for their first session he had watched from a seat at the bar as the others stood in front of the small stage singing along and laughing and joking. He was enjoying himself and as he watched around the crowded room he could see that everyone was having fun. He ordered another pint and started to sing along to a tune the band were playing that he recognised.

As with his quick visits to the pub after a training session he could not fully relax as his thoughts would often return to Mary and how she was while he was not there. He needed this evening and he told himself that Mary would be fine. She would be in bed by about 9:30 and he hoped that she would be sleep by the time he got home.

As the band finished their first set the pub quietened a little and his teammates returned to the bar for more drinks. John was trying to pace himself as he was not a big drinker and so he declined the offers of another pint, pointing to the half full glass beside him. He got a tap on the shoulder and turned to see Matt, the team goalkeeper beside him.

"Look at that." Matt said and pointed his elbow towards the couple walking in the door. "She is gorgeous."

She was. John had to admit that he was looking at a real beauty.

He turned back to the bar and thought again about Mary. Mary was beautiful. He had fallen in love with her the first time he had seen her and throughout their marriage he had often marvelled at how she maintained both her beauty and her figure despite having had twins and being close to a nervous breakdown.

Another tap on his shoulder and it was Matt again. This time he wanted to talk music. "What do you think of the band?" He asked. "Not really my kind of music, too many old rock covers for me but they certainly know how to play their instruments."

"They do. I think the drummer is amazing and the two guitarists too. Not so sure about the lead singer though, seems too self obsessed but then most lead singers are, I suppose.

Lawrence, the team captain had caught the last part of John's comment and he turned and nodded.

"Completely agree. The guy loves himself. The drummer is brilliant and can sing a bit too. I love the old covers. Their version of 'Black Dog' was fantastic.

John smiled. He was out having fun and talking music for the first time in years and he loved it.

After being bought another pint, this was his third and he would have to take it slow, the band returned to the stage to rapturous applause. Again John was left on his own at the bar as his mates moved forward to the stage.

He noticed the couple next to him were drinking shots and he wondered how people could go out of their way to get so drunk. He had never been like that and even as a teenager he had started to dread a hangover the following morning long before his forth pint. That was pretty much his limit and he turned towards the stage and watched the band.

CHAPTER 15 - TROUBLE, 1990

Louise and Tommy were late to arrive at the pub having called into another pub on their way. They were both in a happy mood and had been drinking vodka in their hotel room since lunchtime.

After a couple of drinks in the first pub they had moved on to The Weirside and although they had missed the first set from the band they were not concerned.

"Get some shots in while I go to the toilet." Louise told Tommy.

As Louise stumbled and swerved her way across the bar to where the toilets were she noticed a tall man watching her. She smiled at him and headed to the loo. On her way out she noticed that the tall man had gone and she looked around to see where he was. She caught his eye a moment later and smiled again. He smiled back and raised his glass in salute. Louise looked towards the bar and could see Tommy talking to the barman. She decided that she needed a drink and headed towards Tommy.

The band had now started their second set and having downed their shots Louise and Tommy headed towards the group of people near the stage. Louise danced with the rhythm of the music and Tommy could feel his toes tapping along to the beat. He loved live music and was impressed with the band but being pretty drunk he was having trouble staying in time to the drummers beat. He didn't care, it was probably the drummer who was out of time he thought to himself.

Louise was dancing as if she was the only person in the room. Totally unaware that there were many eyes on her. She too loved live music and she was enjoying herself.

The band had saved their best songs for the second set and the place was rocking with the sound and atmosphere of well over 200 people singing along, dancing and laughing together.

Louise stopped, found Tommy and led him towards the bar. Four more shots were ordered and Louise counted down from five and downed the first one. Tommy followed suit and when they picked up the remaining two shots he started the countdown. Five, four, three, two....

"Too slow." Shouted Louise over the noise of the room as she had downed her drink on three. They laughed and ordered some more. Tonight was going to be messy and something in the back of Tommy's mind told him that he should be careful. However, the back of his mind was miles away as he was enjoying himself so much and was far from sober.

As Tommy turned and leaned against the bar he surveyed the room. His sight was bleary and the whole room seemed to be jumping up and down as the band played a Clash song. Even so, Tommy's eyes settled on the tall man standing on the other side of the room. There was something about the way he stared at them and not at the band that unsettled Tommy and he was about to step towards the man when Louise grabbed his arm and shouted that she wanted to dance with him. Tommy immediately forgot the tall man and followed Louise onto the dance floor.

The dance floor was quite big but half of it was taken up by the crowd lining the stage. Space was limited for those wanting to dance but that didn't deter Louise. She grabbed

Tommy and pushed him into the middle of the floor then joined him and started dancing. Tommy was not much of a dancer but Louise didn't care. She was in a world of her own and completely let herself go.

The band changed tack and slowed things down a bit and Louise wrapped her arms around Tommy's neck and relaxed. He was surprised how heavy she had become in that moment. Two minutes earlier he had watched her dancing and she seems to float like a fairy, now she was a dead weight in his arms. He lifted her off her feet and made his way back to the bar. They found a couple of bar stools and Tommy ordered himself a pint of lager and Louise a vodka and tonic. They laughed more than they spoke because of the volume of the band and because they were both completely drunk. Louise leaned over and kissed Tommy hard on the lips.

When the band came to the end of their set they played three encores and then left the stage to load applause. The bar was still very noisy but now it was because of the excited chatter from the crowd extolling the virtues of the band and the clammer for the bar. Last orders had been called as the band finished and everyone wanted one last drink before they had to go home.

Louise and Tommy were still in an embrace when someone shouted out above the noise. The room went quiet and everyone stopped and looked at the woman who had shouted. She was a small chunky woman with short blonde hair, a crop top that showed off roles of fat above her jeans and tattoos on each arm.

No one really heard what the woman said but after seeing the way she staggered across the room towards the door they all turned and carried on their conversations and a tall man took her arm and led her outside.

John had managed to make his third pint last for the rest of the evening despite numerous attempts by his mates to buy him another one.

He was ready to go home but as they were all sharing taxis he was waiting for a couple of the lads to finish their drinks. Eventually, as the bar was emptying out, they were all ready to leave and as they made their way to the door Matt spotted the dark haired young girl he had commented on earlier, in front of him. He turned to John and whispered "I wish I was taking her home tonight."

John smiled. "She's out of your league mate and besides she's completely wasted."

They laughed and continued to made their way to the door.

Outside was busy. Everyone seemed to have stopped on the path in front of the pub and were waiting presumably for taxi, lifts or buses.

Lawrence was pretty organised and had pre-ordered three taxis to arrive at 11:30 to take the teammates home. He looked at his watch and there were still 10 minutes to wait so he led the men over to the car park at the left hand side of the pub to wait. It was slightly quieter here and they could chat without having to shout.

Louise and Tommy had also turned left out of the pub and were about to start walking back to the hotel.

As they passed the car park the small blonde, chunky woman from before appeared from the darkness.

"I saw you eyeing up my husband earlier, bitch." She screamed at Louise. "Come near him and I'll scratch you fuckin' eyes out, you hear me?"

Louise had no idea who this woman was or what she was talking about but she was up for a fight. She leant forward and swung a fist at the woman's head. It missed but a strong pair of arms grabbed the woman at almost the same time as Tommy grabbed Louise.

The two men, each holding onto their respective women stared at each other. There was menace in both sets of eyes and it seemed that the women had just been the starter course for what was to follow.

The tall man threw his wife to the ground and charged towards Tommy. He fired a punch that caught Louise on the cheek and smashed into Tommy's shoulder. Tommy recovered fast and shot out a punch of his own.

John had seen Louise get hit and as she fell to the ground in front of him he had stooped down to pick her up.

"Hit him again Reg." shouted the blonde.

Tommy and Reg engaged again and as the fight continued both made telling punches. Tommy was the stronger of the two by far but the tall man, Reg, was quick and sneaky. He kicked out at Tommy and Tommy only just managed to avoid the kick aimed at a very sensitive place. He grabbed at the leg and spun Reg around and threw him on the ground. He jumped on top and a couple of punches later Reg was finished.

Tommy turned to see John leaning over Louise. He got completely the wrong idea and grabbed John by the back of the collar. He was in a fighting frenzy now and as John hit the floor again Tommy got on top of his man. He would have ended the fight with John the same way he had with Reg had it not been for the three pairs of hands that grabbed him and pulled him away. Matt and Lawrence sat on Tommy and with the rest of the team congregating around, Tommy realised that he was beaten.

Behind this crowd Louise rose and surveyed the scene. She was not aware of what had happened but had seen Tommy sitting on the man moments before he had been grabbed. Now the man was laying next to her and as she rose she kicked him as hard as she could in the head. She kicked and kicked and kicked until someone stopped her.

Reg and his dumpy wife had gone, the group of footballers had picked up John and got into the taxis that had arrived and left. Louise and Tommy were sitting on the grass and about a dozen people were still mulling around outside the pub. It had all happened so fast and Tommy had no idea what it was all about.

Louise was smiling. "Wow, that was fun. You could have killed that man if it hadn't been for his mates. Who was he and why did he start a fight." She asked.

Tommy looked at her. She was actually enjoying herself and obviously hadn't seen the state of the mans face she had kicked or heard her own yelps of excitement as she swung kick after kick into his face. Tommy was sickened by it and slowly got up and walked back to the hotel. His mind was made up, he would leave first thing in the morning and catch a train home. This time he was adamant that he wouldn't change his mind.

CHAPTER 16 - DEATH, 1990

Tommy rose early, saw that Louise was still fast asleep and quickly and quietly dressed and left the hotel. He had no idea where the train station was and as he put his hand into his pocket for his phone he realised that he had left it in the room. He was not going to go back to get it now so he set off down the road.

He had about £8 in his pocket from the money that Louise had been giving him and he had his credit card that he hadn't used since before the funeral. He was happy and relaxed for the first time in a while and the clarity in his mind assured him that he had done the right thing in leaving.

After asking a couple of passing strangers and walking for what seemed like miles he found the station, bought a ticket for the first train leaving for London and made his way to the station cafe for a coffee and a bacon sandwich.

He felt good being alone and with only himself to worry about again and he wondered what Louise would think when she woke up and saw that he had left.

He wasn't really worried about Louise any more, in fact he had been scared by her brutality the night before and how she relished the danger and the violence. She may be beautiful on the outside, he thought but she is ugly on the inside.

He would try to forget about her from now on and he decided that once he got home he would pack up his things and move on. Somewhere new, somewhere quiet and somewhere far away from Louise.

Louise had slept really well and woke excited for what the new day would bring. She looked over to her right and saw that Tommy was not there but she assumed he was out for a walk as he would often do if he woke early. She got up showered and made herself a cup of tea.

An hour later Tommy had not returned and so she tried to call him to tell him that he would miss breakfast unless he got back soon. As she held the phone to her ear she heard Tommy's phone ringing and she looked around to see that it was on the floor beside the bed. She was confused and wondered why he would go for a walk without his phone. Then, she realised that he might not just have gone for a walk but actually left. She checked the wardrobe and saw that his ruck sack and clothes were missing.

She sat on the bed and wondered what to do next. She couldn't contact Tommy as he had left his phone behind and she had no idea where he was. She got up, finished dressing and went for breakfast.

John had woken even earlier than Tommy that morning. He had crept into the house the previous evening and spent 30 minutes in the bathroom tending as quietly as possible to his wounds. He had then got into bed next to Mary and whispered into her ear that he was home. She had reached behind herself for his hand as reassurance and gone back to sleep.

Now awake John realised that he was in a lot of pain and that when Mary saw the state of him she would freak out. He put on a pair of boxer shorts and went down to make himself a coffee and find some pain killers. The twins where still asleep and John realised that they too would be frightened by the wounds he had on his face. As the kettle boiled he looked at his reflection in the stainless steel of the cooker and wished he could save his family from the shock to come.

After drinking his coffee and taking some painkillers he sat on the sofa and tried to relax his muscles. His head was pounding and he closed his eyes.

The next thing he remembered was waking up in hospital. Mary was sitting beside the bed holding his hand and he could hear Richard and Rachel arguing somewhere over a toy. They must be on the floor he though as he couldn't see them. He tried to sit up but for some reason his body wouldn't respond to his brain.

Mary noticed the flicker of John's eyes and immediately started crying. She called for the nurse and tried to talk to John. He could see her lips moving but could not hear what she was saying. He again tried to move but could not. Richard and Rachel were now standing next to their Mum and he could see the concern on all three faces. Three beautiful faces he thought.

The nurse arrived and John's vision was filled with her large round face and the white of her uniform as she leaned over him. He closed his eyes and pictured the three faces he had seen moments earlier. Then he died.

The next 15 minutes were like opening time at a Selfridges sale. There were doctors and nurses rushing in and out and the twins were confused. Mummy was screaming and a young nurse had knelt down between them and put her arms around them then she had taken them to get some sweets from the vending machine.

When it had quietened down and most of the people had left the room, Mary was still crying loudly. She called the children in from the corridor where they were eating chocolate and hugged them tightly.

Rachel was starting to cry when Richard took hold of her hand and whispered "I think daddy is dead."

Mary heard the remark and cried even louder. How was she going to cope without John? How would the children cope without their daddy? Where and to whom could she turn? She had no idea.

After she had found John slumped on the sofa that morning she had called an ambulance. With no one to help out she had dressed the children and when the ambulance had arrived she insisted that all three travel with John. The ambulance men were reluctant but Mary had been adamant that she was going with John and she was not leaving the kids alone. The older of the two men relented after he had examined John and he sent the other one to sit up front with the driver. They were only 5 minutes from the hospital and there didn't seem like much of an alternative.

About the time John died Tommy was looking out of the train window having left Exeter station an hour earlier. He was happy that for once in his life he had been decisive and knew that from now on his life would be much simpler. Back to what it had been like before 'D' day. Was it really less than a month ago that he had met Louise? It seemed like forever.

Also at this time Louise was on a call to Baz. She had been left in Exeter and as she couldn't drive she wanted Baz to send someone to collect the car. She would make her own way to where she was going next. She told Baz that there would be a handsome payment for this service and for his discretion.

We were bought up by a wonderful couple who initially fostered us and then adopted us. We were very lucky. After the not so lucky part of our parents being dead that is. The powers that be had looked favourably on us and decided that we should be kept together.

The first two fostering homes had been very short term and I can remember very little about them but I do remember the day we first set foot inside the house of Mr and Mrs Hamstead.

Grant and Fiona, as they always preferred we called them were and still are perfect parents to me and Rachel. We walked into Highcliffe House as five year old children, tightly holding hands and I remember the smell of the cakes that had been baked that morning. It was a large house and I knew that this would be our home for a long time. Within a couple of hours Rachel and I had made ourselves at home.

Grant and Fiona were very open with us from the beginning. They never pretended to be our real parents and they told us what they knew about our birth parents when we were 12. It turned out they actually knew very little about John and Mary and it wasn't until our 18th birthday that we were handed a sealed envelope giving us some more information.

Enclosed in the envelope was a letter from Mary. I call her Mary now as, despite the early resistance, Rachel and I fell into the habit of calling Grant and Fiona, Mum and Dad.

We knew John and Mary were our real parents but Grant and Fiona have given us love, understanding and support throughout almost all of the lives we can remember.

Let me tell you what the envelope that we received on our 18th birthday contained.

Firstly I should explain that the envelope was trusted to a solicitor who had been given the job of keeping track of us until we turned 18. The solicitor was a Mr J. Norton who had met Mary in January 1991. Mary had handed the envelope and the instructions to him and explained that she had to go away. He had no idea what the envelope contained or where Mary was going. I only found this information out a few months later.

When we received the envelope I had no idea what was in it or who it was from. I knew it was something important and perhaps believed that we were going to receive some long lost inheritance. We immediately told Mum and then we went up to Rachel's bedroom to open it together. Mum and Dad had arranged a party for us on the Saturday after our 18th birthdays but as our birthdays fell on a Wednesday we had had a small birthday breakfast before Dad had driven into town on some business. I had opened the door to Mr J Norton and accepted the envelope. He had confirmed my identity and then made me sign for it. He had then asked that I call Rachel and he asked her to sign too. He then left.

Once in Rachel's bedroom I open the envelope to find a short letter from Mary. I was confused as to why she had written to us before she and John died, she couldn't have predicted their deaths could she? I was keen to read it immediately but Rachel has other ideas.

"A letter from the past? I don't understand. Mary wrote this nearly 13 years ago? This is either very spooky stuff or a stupid hoax. I'm not sure we should read it. There can't be anything in it that affects us now."

"Rach, if we don't read it we will forever wonder what it said. I agree it's strange but I need to read it. What if Mary and John didn't die and are still alive somewhere? What if…?" I was out of ideas.

"OK." Rachel replied.

I put the letter on the bed and picked up the first of the two page.

Here is what it said….

Dear Rachel and Richard,

I hope that you are reading this letter together and that you are both happy and healthy. I have asked that this letter gets handed to you on your 18th birthday and I hope that it is not too upsetting for you.

First of all I want to say sorry. Sorry for leaving you both and sorry for not being strong enough to stay around. Believe me there is nothing I want more than to see you both grow up but I know I will not make a good mother, without your father. He was my rock and I have been lost since he died. I cannot cope with even the basic daily chores and am at my wits end.

I have sent you to school today knowing that I will not be there to pick you up and that the school will act in your best interests once they realise what has happened. I will be joining your father and although I am not a religious person I fully believe that we will be together and that some day, hopefully many, many years from now you will join us.

Having made this decision I am more calm than I have been for weeks. Three months ago your father was murdered. Three months ago I was left to bring you up alone and I am unable to do that. I am so sad that you will face the rest of your lives without us but I also recognise that you are likely to have a much better upbringing without me. I pray this is the case.

Rachel, my angel, even at this young age I can see that you are a strong young girl and you have a very determined and loving nature, I hope this has continued throughout your childhood and into your adult life.

Richard, my darling, you are inquisitive, energetic and impulsive. Please do not change.

You both have so much to offer and I know that you will become much stronger adults than I have managed to be.

Your father was a very strong man who took on all the weight of parenthood that I was unable to bear. He looked after us all and he did it with a smile on his face. I put so much strain on him and I know that my actions today will put a lot of strain on the two of you. Again I am so sorry.

In the three months since your fathers death the police have been unable to trace the people responsible for his murder. Someone, somewhere, is living with the knowledge of who those people are and I hope that by the time you read this they will be rotting in a prison cell. They killed your father, they killed me and they changed your lives forever.

Despite my apologies and rambling I really hope that you will forgive me and understand the sickness that I have. I want the best possible life for you both and that means without me.

I will forever love you and I know your father will too.

Mum.

I admit that there were tears in my eyes and while Rachel finished the second page I thought about the words. Mary had a 'sickness'? John was murdered and the culprit never found. Mary is sorry for leaving us. They died three months apart?

78

All we were ever told was that Mary and John, Mum and Dad, had died when we were five years old. I think I used to have some recollection of that time but now it is lost. Somewhere along the way I think we were told that they died in a car crash or maybe we had just made that up ourselves? Either way, the news in the letter was life changing, at least for me. I awaited Rachel's reaction, she seemed to be taking a long time reading the second page.

Rachel was still staring at the letter and I could see that she too was crying. I put my arm around her and hugged her tightly. We stayed wrapped together for a long time without speaking and I think neither of us wanted to be the one to let go.

Eventually I felt the arms holding me so tightly relax a little and I stepped back as Rachel sat on the bed and looked up at me.

"Mary was so depressed that she felt the only way out was suicide? She didn't die with John, it appears that she took her own life three months after his death. How is it that I can not remember that?"

I had no real answer to that but suggested that we were both very young, traumatised by the events and perhaps blanked out the reality. Feeble explanation I know but it's all I had.

"I think we need to tell Mum about the letter and see what she says. She might know more than she has told us. I will call Dad and ask him to come home early so we can all discuss it before we decide what to do." I suggested.

"Decide what to do? There is nothing we can do but I need Mum and Dad right now so yes ask him to come home.

Although it's sad news, it really doesn't change anything does it." Said Rachel.

I wish I had felt the same way but I felt sadness and anger and had so many questions that I knew Mum and Dad would not be able to answer.

I called Dad and he assured me that he would be home within the hour. In the meantime, Mum had put the kettle on and opened the cake tin. There was and had always been plenty of cakes in the house and you may be forgiven for thinking that we were a fat family but in fact all of us were very slim. I was probably the thinnest, always hyperactive and on the move so I could eat whatever I liked and never put on weight. Rachel ate the cakes but trained incessantly so maintained a healthy weight. Mum and Dad were just naturally thin people, I assume.

When Dad arrived we sat around the dining room table to discuss the letter. We had always discussed any problems we had as a family around the table and we had always solved any problems we encountered. We were a strong group and although we occasionally disagreed we never fell out for more that a few minutes.

This time I had a feeling that things might be different.

It is fair to say that Mum and Dad were as shocked as we were by the letter. At the time we were fostered, and later adopted, they had been told that our parents were dead and they were advised to keep a close eye on us for any signs of trauma although they were assured that that was unlikely. They had inquired at the time about John and Mary's deaths but had been told that they had died in Exeter many months ago and that the circumstances were not on record. They lived in Oxford and they were over the moon about the adoption so did not pursue the matter.

When we were 12, they had told us that they had assumed our parents were involved in an accident but they would do anything we asked of them if we felt the need to trace them or any other possible family. At that time Rachel and I had no such inclinations.

As we sat around the table talking I began to realise that I was the only one who felt the desire to delve deeper into what had happened to Mary and John. I voiced my opinion and Dad said he was 'supportive, if that is what I want.'

Although Rachel sided with Mum and the view that it would be futile to dig up the past now and we should let 'sleeping dogs lie', I knew that I would be able to talk her into helping me if necessary. I had decided that I wanted to find out why John had been killed and by whom. I also wanted to know why Mary was so fragile and could not live without John.

Rachel and I would be going to separate Universities in the autumn and I wanted to resolve all the questions I had before then. That meant we had less than two months. I didn't want to spoil our birthday party so I vowed to myself to start some research the following Monday.

That night, after Mum and Dad had gone to bed, I waited in front of the television for Rachel to return from the Gym. Rachel had missed her usual 8pm class due to our discussions and a late dinner so had left about 9pm for a personal session and said she would be back late. Although the four of us had continued to discuss the letter throughout the day I felt that I needed some private time with Rachel to try to convince her that we had to investigate John's death and our family history.

The thought that John had been killed had played on my mind and I knew that I needed Rachel on board if I were to try and find out the details. Rachel was always far cleverer than me and she always had a logical way of thinking about things. I tended to just act as I saw fit and then deal with the consequences. We did make a great team though and I think that being twins was a bonus as we could almost read each others minds at times.

When I heard the key in the front door, I turned off the TV and waited. Rachel had seen the light on and so came into the living room.

"I knew it would be you still up and I bet I know why you are waiting for me too." She said with a smile. "You want my help to try and find some information about John's death, don't you?"

It was a rhetorical question and I smiled back at her. "Really Rach, are you not just a little interested in our birth parents?"

"Of course I am but I didn't want to upset Mum and Dad, didn't you notice how Mum was taking the news? She needs our support as much as we need hers, you know."

I hadn't really thought of how my eagerness to find out more about John and Mary may have affected Mum and Dad. "Great, so you're in then." I said to Rachel. "We need to find out as much as we can before we go off to University, I'll start researching on Monday assuming I don't have a hangover from the weekend.

With that I got up from the sofa, kissed Rachel on the cheek and went up to bed.

CHAPTER 18 - MARY (deceased), 2003

Of course I couldn't wait until Monday so the following day I started looking at what I could find out. My initial investigations were not easy, especially as I was trying to find out about historical stuff and had no idea how to go about it. I had decided to start with John and Mary's, and of course our, families.

OK, I knew from Mum and Dad that our 'family' name had been Barnes. They had told us that years ago. My first action was to Google John Barnes and Mary Barnes. Obviously the first gave me many returns but I was pretty sure our birth father was not a famous Liverpool and England footballer and was not black. I was also sure that Mary was not an artist born in the 1920s.

I was a novice and had no instructions as to how to find out more information.

Dad came to my rescue a little in that he bought up to me a box of belongings that had been given to him when we were first adopted. It seems that when a family home is emptied following first a murder and then a suicide, most items such as clothing and furniture are either sold or trashed. All personal items and money are handed over to the next of kin. It was these items that were in the box.

Dad had looked in the box when it was first given to him, sorted out the financials such as contents of savings and bank accounts and moved them into an account in mine and Rachels name and left the rest in the garage attic.

Now, looking at the contents of the box, I found pictures, a diary, some jewellery, a passport for John, some birth, death and marriage certificates, some NHS certificates and an almost empty address book.

There were some glaring omissions such as nothing at all from Mary's side of the family, no passport for her and only three items of jewellery and the diary. There were about a hundred or so photos and I could see that most of them were, I assumed, of me and Rachel. There were however about 15 photos of John and Mary's wedding and a similar number of photos of what appeared to be John and his parents.

I had wanted to share these immediately with Rachel but she had left for the gym at 8am this morning and as of 12am she had not yet returned. I decided to open and read the diary alone.

The diary, although dated 1980 was actually a collection of notes written intermittently over the years until Mary's death. They were very personal notes and there were times when a note was written every day for a month and then some periods of weeks and months where nothing was written at all. What they told me was that Mary was a broken woman long before John's death. Even before Rachel and I were born, Mary suffered panic attacks and was scared of meeting people. After our birth she became more and more worried that she couldn't cope with life. She had spoken to John about how she felt and he had been very patient and kind with her but had failed to get her to speak to a doctor or professional about her insecurities.

There were however two entries dated 1983 that were in complete contrast to the rest. First was the day she met John and the second was the day of their wedding. Mary was obviously madly in love with John and had described him as 'the man of my dreams' and said '...we will be together forever...'

I read through the diary quickly and found much of the same comments about Mary's worries and her reliance on John.

At our birth the entries stopped for over three months and then there was a glowing two page entry about how beautiful we both were and how she doted on us. There was also concerns about whether she would be able to cope and her feelings of ineptitude and unrest.

Again there were large gaps in the dates of the entries and apart from a few that echoed the previous concerns there was nothing particularly startling until 1990.

Mary was trying hard to be supportive of John's decisions to leave her alone with us children while he went out but she was obviously in pain. She was hiding her true feelings so that he wouldn't feel guilty and she knew that he deserved to have some fun and be relieved of the constant pressure he had in the house.

Then came the day she found him collapsed on the sofa, his face covered in blood. She actually described the panic she felt, her actions and the time spent at the hospital in detail.

Then after a week of no entries she started a series of daily updates on the police enquiries looking into John's death and how she was coping with me and Rachel. It seems that I was not an easy child to look after at that time and I was often sent to bed without dinner. Rachel at that time had become very quiet and I had become the opposite.

The complete lack of family left Mary with little support and the offers of support from the police and health departments appeared to have been shunned.

I decided that I would read through the latter entries in more detail later and I put the items back in the box and went out. I needed some fresh air and a chance to think both about the box and the party planned for the weekend.

CHAPTER 19 - MUM & DAD, 2003

The party on Saturday night was great. Rachel and I had a lot of school friends plus there were friends of Rachel's from the gym and a few friends I had made while taking WuShu classes at the local college. There were also a few relations from our 'new' family and a few neighbours.

Mum and Dad had gone completely overboard in every respect. A marque tent had been erected in the back garden, a disco and a catering and bar firm were employed and Rachel and I were given the keys to a brand new Vauxhall Corsa each, one in red for Rachel and one in blue for me.

We were toasted by Dad who made a fantastic speech about how we had grown into wonderful children and now into fantastic adults. Mum smiled all evening and I think she hugged me about 100 times. She even dragged me onto the dance floor when unfortunately the DJ played the Cliff Richard song Congratulations. I loved dancing but it was, I think, the first time I had ever seem Mum on a dance floor. I did once catch her and Dad dancing in the living room to a Beatles song when they thought Rachel and I were asleep. They didn't see me so I had crept back up the stairs to bed.

Neither Rachel nor I were big drinkers but on an evening like that there was always someone to top up our glasses and to remind us that it was the first time we were legally allowed to drink alcohol. At 11pm Dad had appeared next to us as we talked with school friends and quietly asked us for the car keys he had given us earlier, which, he told us would be returned the following day if we were sober enough to drive by then.

On the Sunday morning, with the garden and my head still a bit of a mess from the night before, we rose late to a lovely day and Mum telling us that there was another surprise in store for us. We washed, dressed and all left the house while a team of cleaners entered the side gate into the garden to start dismantling the marque and clean up. Dad had already moved the cars around in the drive so that his was nearest the gate and we all got into his big shiny Jaguar and headed out. Rachel and I having no idea where we were going and Mum and Dad said nothing but sat there with huge smiles on their faces.

The surprise we received was amazing and took us both completely by surprise.

Dad drove us all from Oxford into London. We left the car in a car park somewhere near Chiswick and got on the tube. I was desperately trying to guess what the surprise was and kept asking questions but Mum and Dad were staying quiet and Rachel seemed uninterested or at least she was masking any excitement she may have had.

I had finally settled on a guess that we were being taken to a restaurant in the West End followed by a show. As we had left mid morning I knew we would be in central London by lunchtime so I was guessing a matinée performance of some kind. I was only partially correct and the fantastic Sunday Lunch we had at, what had to be the poshest restaurant I had ever been to, was only a prelude to the surprises to come.

While we were finishing our desserts and I was still pestering Dad with questions about the show we were going to see, we were interrupted by a small muscular man in his 50s who introduced himself as Colin Compton and asked if he could join us. To mine and Rachel's surprise Dad stood up, shook the man's hand and indicated a seat at the table. After ordering some drinks and a little small talk, Dad took a deep breath, looked at me and winked. I could tell that something was about to happen.

"Richard, Rachel, I would like to introduce you to Colin. Colin was a finance manager with JBC investments and he looked after some of my portfolio. We have got to know each other pretty well over the years and Colin is a genius with money but he is also a most resourceful man." Dad began.

"The investment skills of Colin were very welcome and very profitable but some of his other skills may be even more useful in the period between now and the end of September, when you both depart for University." Dad took another deep breath.

"After our meeting around the dining room table on Wednesday, I contacted Colin because I knew that he was someone who could help you with finding everything you need to about your natural parents. Fiona took a little convincing but we agreed that we should do whatever we could to help you." Dad paused and Mum gave him a smile and took up the story of the last few days.

"I've never met Colin before but I spent over an hour on the telephone with him on Friday and your Dad is right, he is the right person to help you. I hope you can satisfy your need for answers and …" Mum choked a little and I could see tears in her eyes.

I rose but was beaten by Rachel who moved quickly to put her arms around Mum. The table stayed quiet for a while until Colin started speaking. Colin was very quietly spoken and he said very little.

"Before I became an investment manager and I will save the reason for my career change for another day, I was firstly in the armed forces for 16 years and then a policeman for a further 13 years. I would like to meet with the two of you next week to discuss what I can offer you." He whispered. "If you agree, I will find out what I can. However, as it is Sunday and I have made an exception to my rule of not working at weekends to be here, I need you to provide me with my daily fee of £750 before I speak further."

"What the ....." I started and then I saw the smile on his face and the wink he gave Dad.

Everyone was laughing and I wasn't entirely sure if they were laughing at Colin's joke or at me for my reaction. I laughed too.

Within minutes or introducing himself, Colin was on his feet again and telling us that he would be in touch tomorrow he shook everyone's hands and left.

Everything had happened so fast and I was still trying to form an opinion of Colin when Dad explained a little more. Apparently Colin and Dad had know each other for years and had formed quite a friendship.

"I know this all seems little odd at the moment but I trust Colin and if you are determined to find out about your birth parents and in particular how your father was killed, I thought it best to have someone on side who can not only use his experience and contacts to help but who will also watch over you both in the process." Dad explained.

"But..." I began but couldn't really think of anything further to say.

"Dad, you are a dark horse. Colin seemed like a nice man but how well do you really know him? And how much is he going to cost us for the work that may come to nothing?" Chipped in Rachel, the ever practical and extremely logical Rachel.

Dad laughed. "Rachel my dear, firstly as I have said, I trust Colin. I am only asking him to do a little investigation for a couple of months and he has agreed that he will only accept a fee if he is successful. You do not need to worry about the financial agreement. Secondly, from Mary's letter we already believe that your father was murdered. I do not want either of you..." and Dad looked straight at me and continued "getting into any trouble or involved in anything where you may be at risk."

I found my voice. "This is all crazy. If John was murdered..." I began but Dad put his hand on my arm and stopped me.

"Please keep you voice at a reasonable level and think about what I have said. I know you are confused by everything that has happened over the last few days but I assure you we will all work together to get you the answers you want. Think about everything and we can discuss it all tomorrow. Now we need to get out of here and go see a show."

With that Mum, Dad and Rachel rose from the table. I followed them out of the restaurant and on to the street but walked a few paces behind as they laughed and talked as if today was just another normal day. My mind doesn't work like theirs and I was deep in my thoughts when Mum turned and took hold of my hand. She didn't say anything but strangely I felt more loved in that moment than I had in my entire life and believe me I knew how much Mum and Dad loved us.

CHAPTER 20 - COLIN, 2003

Monday morning and again Mum, Dad, Rachel and myself were sitting around the dining room table. Mum had done what Mum does best and prepared pancakes, waffles, fruit, cream, smoked salmon with a lovely hollandaise sauce plus some freshly made scones and some coffee. There was also a large piece of birthday cake left over from the party. We were not going to go hungry.

I had calmed down since the night before, an evening at the theatre does that to you. We had seen The Buddy Holly story and it was impossible to think about anything else while singing along. I had fallen asleep on the drive back home and we had all gone to bed as soon as we got in. The next morning Rachel went for a run and I spent an hour on my exercise bike. Dad had been around the garden checking on the job done by the cleaners and as you know Mum had been cooking.

It was 10am before we all assembled around the table and we were all hungry and in good spirits. I was waiting for Dad to speak first but he didn't look like he was going to as he tucked into his pancakes and fruit so eventually I decided to start.

"I have so many questions about Mary and John and I really do want to know what happened to them. From the little information we have Mary seems to have been very fragile and John was her rock. I know that they both loved me and Rachel and that what happened to John changed all our lives. I am sure Rachel agrees with me that you will always be our parents and we both love you very much but there is something inside me that say I need to know more."

I paused, to look around the table and received three smiles but no words so I continued. "I know I can be a bit clumsy with my words but we have had an absolutely amazing upbringing and we are the people we are because of you. You have given us everything and taught us our life values as well as being there for us whenever we've needed you. I guess I'm just saying thank you and that I love you both."

I felt I had said too much and could feel the thumping of my heart in my ribs so I reached over, took a scone and started spreading some butter and jam onto it.

Still no one else spoke for what seemed like ages and I was beginning to think that perhaps I had said something wrong when Rachel finally spoke.

"Mum, Dad, I think for once Richard has said exactly how I feel too. I did not want to hurt either of you so feigned apathy towards our birth parents when we got Mary's letter but you have been so great about it and I am so pleased that you have arranged for Colin to help us. I love you both very much."

Mum and Dad looked at each other and I could see that under the table they were holding hands. I could also see a tear in Mum's eyes and as I looked at Dad and Rachel I could see the same in their eyes. That started me off too and before we knew it we were all standing around Mum in one big hug.

We stayed like that for a long time and only parted when there was a knock at the front door. After checking that his eyes were dry, Dad went to see who it was.

I sat down and started on another scone.

Dad returned to the dining room with Colin and announced that we should all finish breakfast and get to know Colin before we start any talk of investigations.

I remember looking at Colin and deciding that he looked like, as Dad had described him 'a very resourceful man'. He would be able to determine in no time at all that I was not the offspring of a famous Liverpool and England footballer.

Colin was like no one I had ever met. I knew that we had had a privileged upbringing in Oxford but I was also very aware that we had not really encountered people who had grown up in less privileged surroundings. I realise that this makes me sound snobbish but it was just the way it was, until Colin entered our lives.

For a start, Colin was not the quietly spoken man he had appeared to be the day before, He swore at every opportunity and in front of everyone. He apologised every time he swore in front of Mum or Rachel but then just carried on doing so. He was quite 'common', there I've said it. His laugh was raucous and he spoke loudly and seemed to be an expert on everything. He was the opposite to what he had appeared to be when we had met on the Sunday. Obviously he had been on his best behaviour then or he had decided to put on a show for us 'toffs."

He was, as I mentioned before, a small muscular man with a short crop of grey hair that was balding at the front. He was calm and confident and I guessed that came from him having spent 29 years combined service in the forces. It turned out to be the navy and then the police.

I liked him immediately and I knew Dad did too but I could see that Mum and Rachel were less endeared to him.

Colin asked for copies of everything we had on Mary and John including the photos, diary and the letter and said that he would start looking into things immediately. I was keen to point out that I wanted to be included in the investigation as much as possible and did not just want Colin to take over. As the others did not seem as interested as me, we agreed that Colin and I would keep in constant contact and update each other when any new information arose.

"We'll make a fuckin' great team, you and me, providing you do as you're told." He told me and then burst out laughing. "Can't do much more until I get the copies so do you fancy a pint in the boozer?"

I realised that he was definitely playing up to his 'common' persona around the family of 'snobs' but I was happy to join him and Dad for a couple of pints in the Green Man up the road.

When we left the pub, Colin got in a taxi to the station, Dad promised to send him the copies he needed and then me and Dad walked home.

CHAPTER 21 - LOUISE, 1990

A lot had happened in Louise's life since the day she left Exeter and all of it had happened under Louise's strict control.

She too had caught a train to London on the same day but a few hours later than the one Tommy was on. She had made up her mind to forget Tommy and she had already started thinking about her future and what she would do with her life.

She needed a drink and when she got off the train at Paddington she immediately sought a pub. After a few drinks and a lot of thought she had the outlines of a plan. Tommy was not part of it, he was now the past.

That plan changed within days when the following Wednesday she received a call from her friendly gangster, Baz. What he told her meant that for the second time in just over a month her life would be turned upside down by a death.

Baz was one of those people who could put two and two together and always make four. He had his ear to the ground and somehow knew things that he had no business knowing. He had found out about John's death and who knows how he had realised that there was a connection to Louise. Perhaps it was the description of the people involved in the fight outside the pub the previous Friday, he knew Louise was in the vicinity as he had dispatched Vince to get the car from the hotel.

Actually he had been keeping an eye on Louise, via his network of associates since the day he had handed over the car and he had been concerned by the reports he had received.

Louise and Baz arranged to meet in a small restaurant in Finsbury Park the next day. It was far enough away from their daily lives so they would not be recognised and it was quiet enough on a Thursday evening to allow them to discuss the many things they needed to.

Baz had told Louise about John's death, explained that the police were looking for a couple matching her and Tommy's descriptions and that there was every possibility that she would be arrested. He exaggerated the police investigations and failed to mention to her that they in fact had very little to go on. He wanted to protect her but he also saw an opportunity to make a lot of money and he knew she would become more dependant on him if she was scared of being arrested.

Louise hardly thought twice about the fact that she may have killed a man. She remembered the frenzy she had got into and the hands that had pulled her away from the man on the floor but she could not recall the man at all. She knew that what she had done was wrong but that the thrill had taken over and although she hadn't done it on purposes she just put it down to the man being in the wrong place at the wrong time.

Together with Baz she would devise a plan that would give her a new life. Baz believed that it would give him complete control over Louise and her future.

Baz was a little infatuated with Louise but that would not get in the way of him taking her for as much as he could. He knew she was very clever and also that she could be dangerous to both him and his business but he also knew that he too was very clever and ruthless and he was sure he would make a lot of money from helping Louise.

First he would help her all he could. He had the contacts and he had the knowhow. He also believed that he had Louise's trust.

His first action was to convince the young girl that she was in a lot of trouble. He offered to help her but stressed that his help would not come cheap. He was after all putting his own neck on the line, perverting the course of justice and helping a killer.

Baz let Louise come up with her own plan. Mildly steering her in the direction that best suited him. She wanted a new identity and Baz could provide that, it was not something he hadn't done before and he was sure it wouldn't be the last time. She wanted to access all of her savings and her inheritance and then disappear forever. Baz toyed with the idea that the best way for her to disappear forever, after he had gained access to her small fortune was to kill her but he wasn't sure he could do that to her.

Instead he would charge a hefty fee for sorting out all her finances and a new identity and then he would send her far away.

Within a year he would be a million pounds or so better off and she would be living a new life as someone else far away. Only he would know who and where she was and that gave him a future leverage if ever it was required.

Louise on the other hand didn't trust Baz as far as she could throw him but she needed him and was happy to play the scared little girl until she got what she needed.

Louise was smart and she only told Baz half of her plan. On the day she had found out that she had killed a man and that Baz would help her, she went into survival mode. Before she met him at the restaurant she visited first her bank, then her family home, then her bank again.

She moved all the money she could to new 'secret' bank accounts, she raided her father's safe and removed everything she could that would lead to any financial gain and she took all the expensive jewellery that her parents owned. She knew that she would inherit everything anyway but she would be relying on Baz for a number of things and she did not want him to know everything about her wealth. She knew that if the police were after her she had to work fast and ensure that even if she was never able to claim her inheritance in full she would have enough to help her disappear.

Using her father's study she planned everything she could and as she sat in her father's chair she remembered how he had sat there, whiskey in hand as he told her how much she meant to him. A tear rolled down her cheek and she roughly wiped it away with the back of her hand. She had no time now for sentiment. She controlled her feelings well until she entered her parents bedroom. She had been in the room thousands of times and could even remember when she was young, creeping into the room and getting into bed with her parents during the night. Mum had always rolled over and cuddled her, then lifted her into the middle of the bed and gone back to sleep. Dad knew nothing about the intrusion until the alarm went off and he saw her laying beside him. He would cuddle up to her and say "Gerry, can you put the kettle on while I give this little monster a cuddle and tell her the rules about sleeping in her own bed again."

Louise laid on the bed and hugged a pillow. She knew that all the grieving she had done following their deaths was during the period where she had not been herself. Now she could grieve quietly, genuinely and with calm.

She slept a little on the bed and when she woke she felt better than she had for a long time. Her mind was clear and she knew that leaving her old life behind and embarking on a new one was not only what she had to do but what she wanted to do.

She rose from the bed, collected all the things she had come for, called a taxi and returned to the bank where she deposited as much as she could. She then returned to the taxi which had waited for her and directed the driver to Battersea where she paid the drive and hailed another taxi to take her to where she was staying. She hoped that this deception would help if the police were to find out who she was.

She had three large suitcases with her and as she left the second taxi in a road around the corner from where she was staying, another precaution she decided to adopt, she realised that she would have trouble moving all three on her own. She looked around her and saw an old man walking his dog on the other side of the road.

"Excuse me sir," she called in her politest voice and with her biggest smile, "please would you help me with my luggage, I only live around the corner."

She knew that she still possessed the charm she had always had and the man was more that happy to help her. Once she had thanked the man, offered him a tenner, which he rejected, and wheeled the suitcases into her room, she sat down on the old sofa and relaxed. She still had a lot of work to do but she now felt prepared and in control.

She knew that the mind games between herself and Baz had only just begun and she intended to ensure that he saw and believed that she was at her most vulnerable.

Over the course of the next few months Louise put her plans into action. She initially asked Baz to arrange for a solicitor to engage an estate agent to sell the family home. The solicitor dealt with all the probate issues too and determined that Louise was the sole heir to the inheritance and the house. When the house was sold and all the finances, including the proceeds of the life assurance policy, were concluded, Baz was paid a full 10% of the proceeds which didn't quite meet his aim of £1m but was close.

Next she asked Baz to introduce her to someone who could arrange a completely new identity for her. Baz charged a flat fee of £20,000 pounds for the introduction and also asked his contact, Remi, to inform him of Louise's new identity. Louise had anticipated this and brokered a new agreement with Remi who would provide her with two new and untraceable identities, one of which he would not share with Baz.

All in all, Louise was happy that she had covered all eventualities and it had not gone unnoticed to her that the police had been nowhere near her. She could see that Baz was far from 'fully behind her' as he had claimed.

Louise was now a wealthy woman with a new identity. She was aware that there were chinks in her armour and made a list of problems that she could potentially face in the future. This list included Baz, Remi, the police, the financial trail of her fortune and a few other people and problems that had cropped up over the months since her parents had died.

Louise had grown up quickly and had adapted well to the world in which she now lived. She had developed a hard shell and a ruthlessness that perhaps she had always had but that was now being redirected towards protecting herself.

Deep down she was still a young girl, a gifted student and a loving daughter however she had developed a taste for violence and the satisfaction and release that that gave her.

Her mind was now filled with thoughts of fake identities, illegal financial transactions and protection for her future.

From the list of potential problems she had identified she also determined a plan to counter any issues that could arise.

The world had not seen the end of Louise Whitwell even though she would no longer be know by that name.

CHAPTER 22 - RACHEL, 2003

Rachel had been very quiet since Colin had been introduced into our lives and I had not really had a chance to talk to her in any detail about our investigation. I was aware that we would both be going off to separate Universities in the next few weeks and I didn't want to fall out with her or cause her any concern.

I decided that in order to talk to her at length and in private, I would take her out for a meal, get her away from the house and delve deeper into her thoughts.

We sat down at Gorge and Fernando's Mexican Grill and discussed preparations for University, Rachel's friend who was getting married in a couple of weeks and general stuff like last nights TV programmes while we waited for drinks and food to be served. It was a Thursday evening and the place was quiet. In fact it was always quiet here, I knew, mainly because it was too far away from civilisation in the heart of Oxfordshire and also because the food was not brilliant. I had booked it because of this quietness, so that we could talk at length.

Although the food was not particularly good, the service was great and before long we were tucking into our meal. Mexican music was playing in the background and a couple of waiters were hovering near the front door but we were not likely to be disturbed. I asked Rachel what she really thought of Colin.

She finished what was in her mouth, sipped her Mexican beer and looked up at me.

"He seems like a nice enough chap, although he does swear a bit too much especially when Mum is around, she hates swearing but is too polite to say so. I thought Dad would have stepped in and said something though. How good he is as a private detective remains to be seen. I'm glad that you have been saddled with keeping in contact with him and not me. You will keep me up to date though won't you?"

I nodded. "Of course I will."

She continued. "I am doing a little digging of my own and want to see what I can come up with. I already have Mary and John's old address, the hospital where he died, the name of his employer and a few other interesting things. I was going to tell you once I had a little more but it's a start."

"Bloody hell, Rachel, you're a genius, how did you do that?"

We discussed what Rachel had been doing and I embarrassingly explained my feeble attempts that had amounted to nothing.

We laughed a lot, mostly at my expense and after the meal we drove home to leave the car and then walked to the Green Man for a couple of drinks and to continue our chat.

It had been a while since Rachel and I had been out together, just the two of us and we quickly picked up our old 'twin habits' of knowing what the other was thinking and not needing to complete every sentence. Anyone who overheard us would probably have been very confused if they tried to decipher our conversation. I must say that I liked Rachel's company but as we had got older we had spent less time together than when we were children and I really enjoyed it when there was just the two of us having a drink, a chat and some laughs.

By the end of the evening I realised that Rachel was indeed as keen as me to find out as much as we could about our birth parents and as we strolled home, arm in arm, she said "If John really was murdered and the killer was never found, we will find them and bring them to justice, however long it takes won't we?"

I nodded to her, smiled to myself and was happy that once again Rachel and I were back on the same page. I knew that together we were a great team and with Colin hopefully giving us some of his experience and knowhow we would eventually get to the truth and get some justice. At that time I was not aware of just how long that would take or what obstacles and problems we would face along the way.

CHAPTER 23 - COLIN, 2003

Colin decided that he liked the Hamstead family and although he found them a little posh he admired the down to earth and 'all for one' way the family gathered together to solve their problems. He had not been so lucky in his life although whilst in the Navy he had found the family he had lacked as a child.

Joining the police after leaving the Navy, he knew, was subconsciously his way of searching for a new family to belong to but he had only found in-fighting, inherent bigotry, lawlessness and snobbery among his colleagues. He was not proud of the police force and he had left under a cloud of accusations against him merely because he had the audacity to stand up and say what he believed was wrong with them. None of the accusations had become charges but he had been made to realise that he had to move on.

As he sat at his computer searching for some answers to the many questions he had listed about the death of John Barnes he took a moment to think about his current situation. He looked around the room he was sitting in and reflected on the lack of any input into the room other than his own. Sure it was a nice room in a nice house but it lacked the touches of another person. He knew that deep down he was lonely but that he was strong enough, most of the time anyway, to push these thoughts aside and to focus on the task in hand. He had become very adept at not worrying about what was missing in his life and he had become an expert at covering up his feelings and insecurities with a boisterous and exaggerated show of confidence. He knew that the image he was projecting for the Hamstead family was not the real him and he hoped that if they found out they would not be offended by his duplicity.

Enough of that he thought and refocused his mind on the computer screen. He had found some old press releases from Exeter in which John's death had been reported and he had contacted Exeter police for some information about their investigation but he knew that even if they were prepared to help him it would be some time before they got around to it.

He was now, sitting at the screen trying to formulate an email to an old friend, Charles, who was still in the police force, albeit now in Sheffield, who could perhaps pull some strings for him. He was struggling to word the email correctly and so decided to start with a list of what he needed. He would add the personal stuff later.

Satisfied that he had included full details of his requirements he rose from the computer and went into the kitchen to make some coffee. The thoughts from earlier returned and he looked around his stylish, clean and functional kitchen and wished he had someone to share it with. Why were all these thoughts arising now?

Of course he knew the answer to that question and he thought about the time he and Charles had lived together and the secret relationship they had developed. In the police force at that time such 'friendships' had to be kept secret and that had put a lot of pressure and strain on their relationship. Eventually Charles had moved to a different part of the country to further his career and the relationship had come to an end. Colin had left the force and although he had had a few brief encounters since none had matched his expectations and the feelings he had had for Charles.

Finishing his coffee, Colin carefully washed and dried the cup and tea spoon and returned to the living room. Beside the computer was his notebook and as he looked through his notes he saw his reference to Mary's diary. Grant had been true to his promise and had sent him copies of everything he had in the box of possessions that had been provided when he and Fiona had adopted the twins.

Looking up at the clock on the wall Colin realised that it was getting late and he immediately regretted having a coffee after 8pm. He would find it difficult to sleep tonight. He decided that he would go to bed early and read the diary.

He found the diary very boring and awoke at 6am the following day realising that he had only read about half of it before falling asleep. The copied diary pages were still laying on the bedside cabinet at the page he had stopped reading. He picked them up and decided on another hour of reading before he got up.

Bingo! The first page he started reading was the account of Mary finding John on the sofa, calling the ambulance and going to the hospital. This was more interesting to him and he sat up in bed and continued. After 10 minutes of reading he decided that he had to start making some notes and that mundane stuff like washing, dressing and breakfast would have to wait. He rose, put on his dressing gown and went down to his computer desk in the living room.

An hour later he had written a page of notes, revised his requirements list in the email to Charles, showered and was sitting having a coffee and toast. He was happy that Mary's notes about the police investigation at the time had proved useful and also that she had named a couple of John's friends who had been at the pub with him that night. He would have eventually got this information from the police but now he had it without the delay.

Matthew Brading and Lawrence Chale. He knew that it was some 13 years after John's death and that a couple of his mates, who would have been interviewed by the police at the time, would probably not have much to tell him now, even if they could remember but it was worth a try. He had already decided that he would have to visit Exeter and now he had a couple of leads to talk to.

He would not bother the Hamstead family until he actually had some news for them, he decided, even if Richard had already called him twice for updates.

After a few phone calls and a bit of internet research Colin packed a small overnight bag and left for the station. The email to Charles would have to wait. He knew that he was just putting it off but he had an excuse to do so now and any excuse however small was sufficient for him.

Arriving in Exeter Colin sought out a cheap hotel and booked in for one night. He took a quick shower after the long train journey and then set out to find the first of his 'targets', Matthew Brading. He had found Matthew, or Matt as he seemed to prefer, on Social Media and this told him where Matt worked and a little about what Matt was like. He would get to Gaston Motors about lunch time and hope that Matt was free to talk over a coffee or a pint.

Colin had also investigated Lawrence Chale through Social Media but unfortunately he had found that Lawrence had emigrated to Australia in 1997 although he was still in touch with Matt so there was a possibility to speak to him via Matt later.

Colin approached the garage office and asked to speak to Matt.

"Who wants him?" Came a brusque reply from the petite secretary who failed to even look up from her desk.

"A friend." Said Colin, equally curt.

The girl looked up and smiled. "I don't recognise you, what's your name?"

"My name is Colin but I need to talk to Matt. What time does he break for lunch?"

"In about 15 minutes but he's offered to take me to the burger place on Bude Street, so you'd best talk to him before lunch. Matt, some fella here to see you." The last sentence was screamed at about 100 decibels and took Colin by surprise.

A minute later Matt poked his head around the door and Colin immediately recognised him from his online posts. "Can I help you sir?" Matt asked.

Colin took the three steps to the door and whispered quietly so that the secretary couldn't hear. "I need an hour of your time and what I need to say is far more important than a burger with little miss Rude here, believe me."

Matt looked confused but had sensed the underlying threat in Colin's voice. He started to answer and then saw the look on Colin's face and stopped. "Sorry June," he said, "Me and Mr err, we have an important issue to discuss, we'll have to reschedule our lunch for tomorrow."

June was not best pleased and said so loudly but Matt had read the situation right and meekly led Colin out of the office and into the adjoining parking area.

"Are you police?" Matt asked once they were outside. "I haven't been in any trouble for years now honest."

"No Matt, I'm not police and I'm sorry if I scared you a little in there but I am only in Exeter for a couple of days and need to ask you some questions. Nothing for you to worry about, you're not in trouble although you might be if Anabel finds out about you and June."

This was a gamble by Colin but he was practiced at reading people and knew from Matt's social media that he was married with a couple of young kids. He had also seen the look from June that told him there was something going on there.

"How do you....? OK give me a few minutes too clean up and I'll be all yours for the next hour, OK?" Matt answered.

They walked the short distance to a small cafe, ordered a sandwich and a coffee each and Colin started his questions. Matt was happy to answer everything and even gave a few of his own thoughts about who the couple in the pub that night might have been, although 'Russian Spies' seemed very unlikely to Colin. Matt was at pains to talk about how beautiful the girl had been and even said that he still thinks of her from time to time, all these years later.

Colin left Matt sitting at the cafe table. Matt had told him the name of the venue where John had been "kicked to death" that night and Colin wanted to see it for himself. He hailed a taxi and asked to be taken to the Weirside Pub.

As the Taxi weaved its way west towards the river Colin opened his notebook and added a few notes based on what Matt had told him. The description Matt had given him of the couple who had fought outside the pub that night was interesting. The guy: tall, muscular, dark. Nothing more. The girl: tall, athletic, beautiful, green eyes, blonde hair, sexy, like a model, etc etc. Matt had obviously focused more on the girl. He had however also mentioned that he was pretty drunk that night as were the couple.

When the taxi stopped Colin peered out of the window and looked at the run down mess of a pub. He paid the driver, got out, and entered the pub.

It was as rundown on the inside as the outside had suggested and Colin assumed that there had been a conscious decision to restrict the light in the bar. A small dingy bar to the left and an even smaller one to the right. Then Colin saw the door with the sign above saying 'Bar and Stage This Way'. He pushed the door open and saw that indeed there was a large room with a stage at the far end.

"Can I help you?" The voice came from a man behind him.

"Ah, yes please, I'll have a pint of whatever bitter you have and could you tell me if you were working here 13 years ago?"

It turned out that the pub had changed managers many times over the years and the staff even more so. So this was a dead end. Colin drunk his pint and left. He called another taxi and hoped in.

The taxi driver was an old man who wanted to chat and this irked Colin until he decided to ask the driver about the recent history of the pub. Within minutes they were discussing the fateful night when a fight broke out and someone ended up dying in hospital the next day. "I heard they were Londoners involved. A couple from the Sowton area were involved in the fighting but apparently it was the 'London girl' who completely lost it and kicked the poor man almost to unconsciousness."

"Do you know the name of the local couple, I would like to speak to them?" Asked Colin hopefully.

"What, are you a reporter? No, never knew who it was but chances are they drink in one of the Sowton pubs or else someone who does will know of them. There's two pubs, The Moors and The Beehive, I'd try the Moors its more of a local's pub."

Colin recorded the drivers words in his notebook and asked the driver to take him to The Moors Pub, where he paid the driver, gave him a £5 tip and said goodbye.

As Colin entered the pub he was aware that there were many eyes upon him, like many 'locals', their inhabitants are wary of strangers. He ordered a pint of bitter at the bar and looked around. It was another dark bar and Colin wondered why this seemed to be a theme in Exeter although in truth he realised his observation was based on just two examples. Perhaps all the other Exeter pubs were brightly lit, clean and full of life but he doubted it.

There were only ten people in the bar and Colin determined that the old man sitting alone at a table in the corner would be his best bet for information about an incident over 12 years ago. Having paid for his pint he picked it up and wandered over to the man.

"Would you mind if I ask you a few questions please sir." He asked.

"Who you calling 'sir' and yes I do mind. Piss off." Came the reply.

Colin was a little taken aback but was not going to give up easily. "So you won't be wanting another pint then?" He responded.

He immediately saw the slight glimmer of desire in the man's eyes and knew he would get a chance to ask his questions. After a lengthy tirade about the cost of a pint, the price of a packet of cigarettes and the small state pension, the man, Harry he introduced himself as, asked about the questions Colin had for him.

Colin opened with the obvious one. " How long have you been drinking here Harry?" It turned out that Harry was indeed the correct person to be speaking to.

"I have lived just up the road for nearly 40 years and have been coming in here nearly every day since my wife died over 20 years ago, why?" Harry asked.

Colin explained what he was looking for and Harry was more than happy to help. After buying Harry a couple more pints and confirming that he was not a policeman or a drug dealer he got some of the answers he wanted.

The man he was looking for was Reg. Reg and his wife had indeed inhabited the Moors and Harry had heard of the night in question, heard how Reg had fought with the Londoner and how Reg had bragged about beating the man and pouring a pint of beer over his head. However, when Reg was beaten up by Priestley and his gang of thugs a few years ago and was hospitalised he stopped going out much and he was now apparently pretty much a recluse. Priestley was a big time drug dealer in the city and rumour had it that Reg was taking too big a share of the profits that were due to be passed up the chain to Priestley. Reg had had minor beatings before but the last time had been serious and had left him in hospital for over three weeks. Since then Harry had not seen Reg around.

All this information had taken Harry a couple of hours to divulge and Colin was really no further to knowing anything other that the name of a man who had got into a fight over 12 years ago.

Harry finally finished with a warning. "You're a stranger around here and if you go round asking too many questions you could get yourself hurt. Priestley has eyes and ears everywhere and if he finds out you're asking about Reg he will come after you!"

Colin smiled. He knew from his police days that local gangsters liked to spread fright among their communities and show how tough they were. He also knew that he needed more than just a name.

"Just a couple of last questions and then I'll be on my way." Colin started. "Do you know where Reg lives and do you know his surname?"

It was Harry's turn to smile. "We don't use surnames in these parts and as for his address, I am told that he moves house every few months so that Priesley can't find him. If Priesley can't find him then you've got no chance."

Colin sat for another 15 minutes making notes of the conversation he had just had then he got up, thanked Harry and left. He would be on the train back to London tomorrow but he had one more place he wanted to visit first. This could wait until tomorrow morning so Colin made his way back to his hotel.

CHAPTER 24 - CHRISTMAS, 1992

Louise Luccombe (nee Whitwell) was sitting alone in her small rented apartment in North London surrounded by paper. She had made up her mind that 1993 would be a turning point for her and she would finally get her life back on track. The last two years had been a period of organisation, mourning, stagnation and boredom. On more than one occasion she had been tempted to contact Tommy but she was strong and she had only known him for a matter of weeks so forgetting him was actually easier that forgetting most of the people in her life before her parents deaths. She had to forge a new future for herself. She had maintained her habit of making daily notes in her diary and when reading them back she was often disturbed by her entries. She was lonely and scared and yet she was also strong and determined. "I can cope with anything and anyone." She told herself.

Initially Louise had been scared. Scared that somehow she would be identified as a murderer but as the weeks and months passed she knew that this was unlikely. She was also scared of Baz. Him knowing her new identity was a problem and she was sure that at some stage he would try to blackmail her but again as time passed this did not seem to be his plan. In fact, Baz had been very helpful to her and asked for nothing in return since her initial huge payments. She had not told Baz her address and all communication was by phone but she was not naive enough to believe that he was not capable of finding her whenever he wished to do so. Although she was happy with his help she was still very wary of both his motivation and his capabilities. Finally she was scared that her new identity was not foolproof enough and that she would be found out to be a fake.

Over two years on and most of her fears were behind her and she could now start to look forward with confidence. She still had her moments where she needed to curl up in bed, cry a little and remember her parents but the regrets that she had of not grieving properly during the weeks after their death had subsided and she was now at peace with herself.

As she scanned the papers spread out on the floor around her, her eyes landed on the pile of Estate Agent literature. She had decided that it was time to use some of her wealth and buy a property. The properties she had got brochures for, where all small village properties and were dotted around the country. She had not yet decided where she wanted to live but knew it would be far away from London.

The TV, on in the background, caught her eye and she watched as a famous actress cum presenter, climbed a steep hill all the while talking to camera and telling the viewers what magnificent scenery could be found in this part of Wales. That's an idea Louise thought, why not Wales. She made a mental note to add that to her list of possibilities.

Tomorrow was Christmas Day and Louise knew that for the third year in a row she would be spending it alone. This didn't bother her too much but she promised herself that next year she would not be alone.

Louise's eyes returned to the piles of papers, bank statements, bills, insurances, investments, car paperwork, etc and started gathering them up to file back away in the cupboard beside her bed.

As part of the necessities Louise had needed to get to this stage of her life unaided she had set up multiple investments, passed her driving test and not least learned how to cook. As she filed the paperwork into the cupboard a single sheet of paper slipped onto the floor and she picked it up and read what was written on it. It was a list she had made a couple of years earlier of all the potential problems she had or may encounter. She smiled as she read the entries, happy that she still had everything very much under control.

As she walked back into the living room she decided that although she would be spending Christmas Day alone, she did not have to be alone tonight. She had been very careful not to make any new friends since she changed her name but she knew that if she went out, like she often did at weekends, she would easily find people, mostly men, to chat to. She always declined their advances but never their drinks and often returned home with the same amount of money she had left with. It had become a game she played with herself. Could she get someone else to buy all her drinks?

Tonight though she had one of those rare moments where she wanted to spend and spend big. She decided that she would get dressed up and go a bar in Knightsbridge that she had been to a couple of times before where, it seemed, everyone had plenty of money.

She called and booked a taxi to pick her up from the corner of her street at 8pm then picked up a bottle of vodka and headed into the bathroom to get ready.

By 11pm Louise was very drunk and had a posse of young men around her who, she guessed, would all get pretty pissed off when she left the club alone. As she looked at the three men standing over her while she sat, half listening to another man next to her at the table she realised how boring her life had become. Even getting dressed up and heading out to a posh nightclub on Christmas Eve left her thinking that she needed more excitement in her life. She looked at the man talking to her and decided that things had to change.

"Gareth has asked me to go home with him tonight but you seem much more interesting although he would be so upset if I said I was going with you, Mark," she chided, "will you tell him please?"

Mark looked astonished and rose from his seat. He hadn't expected to be leaving with the most beautiful girl in the room and he would do anything to do that. He took Gareth to one side and whispered into his ear.

Louise watched intently. She could see that the two men were arguing but as yet it was still convivial. She stood up, approached them and joined the conversation.

Within minutes Gareth was seething and he threw out a punch at Mark. A fight broke out but within 60 seconds the bouncers had intervened and Louise was left disappointed as both men were removed from the club. She had felt her body tighten with excitement as the fight began only to be let down by the final outcome. She knew that she needed to see some violence.

She picked up her bag, retrieved her coat and left the club.

So many nights over the last couple of years or so had ended like this or with a more violent ending. She knew that she thrived on causing trouble and that tonight she would cause more before she got home.

Louise was aware that there was something wrong with her and that her need for physical violence was not normal. She had tried on a number of occasions to act responsibly and politely but something inside her always pushed her to cause trouble. She may have been drunk or nearly out of control on countless evening but she was also very careful to ensure that she was not seen as the instigator or of leaving any clues to what she was up to.

Outside the club the cold air raced into her lungs and she wrapped her coat tighter around her and hailed a taxi. She asked to be dropped off in Finchley High Road, deciding that she would walk home from there. There were still a few people wandering home along the high street and as she turned into Dollis Park she saw a woman sitting alone on the wall ahead of her. As she walked passed she swung her handbag hard against the woman's head. The woman collapsed on the floor and showed no sign of getting up. Louise felt her heart thumping in her chest and she leant over and punched the woman in the head.

A car was turning into the road behind her and Louise was suddenly aware of what she had done. She rose quickly and walked off up the road. The car passed apparently having not noticed the woman on the ground and Louise let out a huge sigh of relief and kept walking. She was both excited by the attack and concerned that she had nearly been seen. She had to start getting herself under control although she knew that the excitement she had felt was like a drug to her.

Colin was sitting at breakfast thinking about the day ahead of him and how he hoped to be home before lunchtime. He knew that there was a train at 11:05 leaving Exeter Station and if he managed to catch that he would be home no later than 1:30. He also knew that once home he would have to complete the email to Charles and he was already starting to get nervous about that.

But first he had to visit Exwick cemetery. Mary had mentioned in her diary that this was where John had been buried and Colin wanted to see the grave for himself. He didn't know why, perhaps just his desire to be professional and cover all the bases or because he felt that he owed it to John to 'check in' with him and let him know that he was investigating his death. Something in his mind had told Colin that it would be the right thing to do.

It was only a 15 minute walk to the cemetery according to Google maps and Colin fancied some fresh air so after checking out of his hotel he made his way by foot. On arriving at the cemetery he realised that he had no way of knowing where John had been buried and searched for someone to ask. The main office was closed and as Colin looked around he began to wish he had called ahead and asked where the grave was.

As luck would have it, an old woman in a bright yellow winter coat and holding a pine walking stick walked up to him and asked, "Are you lost Sir? You look like you don't know which way to go."

Colin explained what he was looking for and the woman gave him some directions. "All the post 1987 graves start in the section marked 'G' just down this road here and on your left after about 100 yards. By 1990 they would have been about 25 rows further back and if your friend died in November he would likely be towards the end of the row over there near that tree." She said pointing towards a huge oak standing in the distance.

"Thank you very much." Colin said and turned towards the road the woman had indicated. About 30 seconds later Colin stopped. "Did I really tell her that John died in November?" He wondered to himself. He turned to look at the woman he had spoken to but she was nowhere to be seen. Strange, he thought. Very strange!

Slightly distracted by these thoughts Colin continued on his way and after a couple more minutes he found himself next to a fairly overgrown grave. Indeed it was in row G25 and was right next to the Oak tree. Again Colin looked around for the woman in the bright yellow coat but there was no sight of her. A shiver ran down his spine and although he was far from religious, he crossed himself and mumbled a few words to a God.

After a few minutes he had gathered his thoughts and crouched down at the graveside. The cemetery staff obviously looked after the cemetery well and the grass between the graves had been cut fairly recently but the grave itself was a mess. There was however a bunch of chrysanthemums, still in their cellophane wrapping in the flower pot beside the headstone and this drew Colin's curiosity. The headstone read 'John Barnes beloved husband and father, died 3 November 1990'.

Colin picked up the flowers and looked for a card. There was nothing. The flowers were perhaps a couple of weeks old and the cellophane wrapping had faded a little but he was still able to make out the writing on it, 'Belle Blossoms, 17 Ennerdale Way, Exeter'. He had walked passed the shop on his way this morning and had noticed the fresh flowers outside. He would visit them on his way back.

Before he left the cemetery Colin returned to the main office. It was still closed and as there was no-one around he was unable to ask about the woman he had spoken to. He wanted to know who she was and how she had known exactly where John's grave was. He still had a feeling that he had not mentioned the month of John's death to her and as he headed towards the flower shop he crossed himself again.

The young girl in the flower shop was as bright and colourful as the blooms around her and gave Colin a huge smile as he entered. "Good morning Sir, how may I help you? A lovely bouquet for a special occasion or perhaps just some roses for the one you love?"

"I think I will buy some of your lovely flowers but I would like to ask you a few questions first please." Colin said with an equally large smile. It seemed that smiling really was infectious and Colin immediately thought of the Spike Millican poem he loved.

"I'm more that happy to answer your questions but you should know that the more you ask, the more flowers you have to buy," The young girl replied, followed immediately by "only joking LOL".

Colin laughed. He liked the girl and decided he would buy flowers and leave the girl a nice tip if she gave him the information he wanted.

"OK, firstly, I have just come from Exwick cemetery....".

"Oh, I'm so sorry Sir I didn't want to come across as flippant I should know better than to assume everyone is buying flowers for a happy occasion." The girl cut in.

"No, no, that's alright. My question is, do you know a woman who wears a bright yellow winter coat and uses a walking stick from around here? I spoke with her at the cemetery and then she disappeared."

"Disappeared? What as in like magic?" The girl laughed. "Sorry, me being flippant again, I really must learn to think before I speak, that's what my mum always says. No, sorry I don't know anyone fitting that description."

"That's OK. It did seem rather like magic though. My next question is about flowers purchased from here probably within the last two weeks. Chrysanthemums, yellow and white. I know it's a long shot but do you know who purchased them? That's all the information I have I'm afraid."

The girl smiled at Colin and asked, "Is this in relation to the cemetery? The reason I ask is that we have a long standing order for flowers to be delivered to a particular grave every few months and I am told that this has been going on for well over 10 years and oh it's so romantic don't you think?"

"Er, well, yes, I suppose." Colin replied. "Can you tell me who sends the flowers and who pays for them?"

"I don't think I am allowed to tell you that but I will ask Mavis when she gets in and ask her to ring you, or you could pop back this afternoon if you prefer. Mavis is the shop owner by the way."

Colin thought about raising the stakes by saying that he was a private detective and that it was important to have the information immediately but he dismissed the idea and left his number with the girl. Even though she had failed to answer either of his questions she had made him smile and so he purchased a bunch of roses and when he received his change he handed over a £5 tip to the girl and thanked her for her time. Reminding her that she was to ask Mavis to call him.

Colin left the shop with his bag in one hand and the roses in the other. He decided that he would give the flowers to the very next person he saw and he headed towards the station. The mum with a small child in her pushchair was very happy to be given the roses by a complete stranger, although quite suspicious of Colin's intent until he hurried off towards the station, waving goodbye.

CHAPTER 26 - LOUISE, 1993 - 1995

The thought of what she had done on Christmas Eve played on Louise's mind a lot over the next few months. If she thought about it during the day she was disturbed and concerned by what she had done and what the consequences could have been. However, if she dreamed about it during the night she invariably awoke with a sense of excitement. This contradiction was causing her problems and she knew that there was an element of her mind that she had no control over.

Her partial solution to this problem was to fill her mind with things to do, to keep busy, spend more time on her diary and not to linger on her thoughts of violence. They were still there, especially at night but they could be subdued by concentrating on other things.

The most important 'other things', became the search for a house and a job.

Although Louise was, by most 21 year olds standards, pretty wealthy, she knew that at some stage she would have to get a job and wherever that job was she would need to live nearby. She had remained cautious about making friends or having any attachments to others and she had never had a job before, so had no idea what she could or wanted to do. She had dropped out of school before finishing her 'A' levels and had no idea what affect that would have on her finding a job.

By August 1993 she had solved both these issues. The job had come first. She had visited a job centre, scanned newspapers and searched online and had settled on a job in the finance sector. A job in a large company where she could hopefully stay relatively anonymous appealed to her and her first ever interview for a Call Centre for a major Life Assurance company had gone extremely well. The job was to be based in Norwich however, the interviewer had mentioned that a new Call Centre was being opened in South Wales and there were also openings there for new staff.

Remembering the TV program she had watched on Christmas Eve Louise saw it as an omen and was delighted. She agreed that she would await the opening of the Wales Call Centre and start looking for a house. The job offer dropped onto her doormat a few days later and as she had requested, her start date was to be the first Monday in September.

Finding a house was also pretty easy and after spending a couple of weeks staying at a rented cottage in Swansea, where the new call centre would be opening she had found a lovely two bedroomed detached and secluded cottage on the outskirts of the city.

With a new house came the need for furniture and Louise spent many hours furnishing her new home. She was a little underwhelmed by the salary that she was to receive but she was also happily surprised by the cost of the house. She spent a great deal on the furnishings and decided that a new start meant a new car and new clothes too. She was careful not to go too crazy as she believed that someone somewhere might be watching and so she spread her spending around and paid cash wherever she could.

By the end of the year she was settled and had even made a few friends at work despite her desire for remaining in the shadows. She had been busy but now that things had started to become a little more settled in her life, the violent dreams returned.

Louise was aware that her craving for violence was more than something that could be satisfied by watching boxing on the television or even by seeing a fight outside a pub. She needed to be part of it and that had only happened when she was drunk. Between Christmas 1992 and her move to Wales she had kept her drinking under control and although she was far from tea-total she had done most of her drinking at home, alone.

Now in a job in a new city and with friends from work she was being invited out most weekends. She had forgotten what it was like to have people who cared about her, wanted her company and wanted her to enjoy herself and she craved a night out where she could dance and drink.

The first invitation she accepted was to a small club in the centre of Swansea where her colleagues and their friends were going to celebrate a win for the welsh rugby team against the mighty All Blacks, they hoped. She knew nothing about rugby and had very little interest but she had been convinced by her colleague, Pauline, that there would be plenty of dancing and that she would have a great time. Pauline had been responsible for Louise's training and they had got on really well and as this was about the fifth time Pauline had invited her out Louise decided that she would go.

Louise declined the many offers of a lift and instead arranged for a taxi. She decided that she could not go out as early as many of her colleagues as she had no interest in watching the rugby but that she would join them later on. She arrived at the club at 7:30 and found that Wales had indeed won the game and that most people were already quite drunk having started drinking over four hours earlier. Over the course of the next few hours pretty much everyone she knew from work had bought her at least one drink and she had forked out for a couple of rounds too. She was drunk but not excessively so and had successfully fended off a few advances from the young lads in the club. She had danced for hours and really enjoyed the company of her fellow workers. At 1am she left the club in a taxi and by 1:45 she was tucked up in bed with a large glass of water beside her on the bedside drawers.

That first night had gone off without a hitch and when Louise woke up on the Sunday morning she smiled to herself and decided that she would be happy to do the same thing most weekends.

Louise's life in Wales was good most of the time and she was grateful for the fact that for the first time in years she was beginning to feel 'normal' again.

After a few nights out where she controlled her drinking and got a taxi home alone she started to think that she had got herself under control. The dreams were the worst of her need for violence and she controlled the desire well. Working during the week and partying at weekends became her life and as a young woman alone in a new country she began to relax and enjoy her youth again.

Unfortunately, things took a decisive change when a short, broad-shouldered man in his early 20s decided that Louise's 'No' didn't really mean No and was waiting for her when she left the nightclub. Louise was unaware of his presence as she got into a taxi and headed home. She was drinking some water in the dark at the kitchen sink when her doorbell rang and as she had had exactly zero callers in the six months since she moved in and it was past 1am, she decided to ignore it. She stood frozen at the sink hoping that the doorbell would not ring again. After a couple of minutes and no further ring she relaxed and headed up to bed.

Roger had followed the taxi to Louise's house and watched as she paid the driver and headed inside. After a couple of minutes he walked up to the door and rang the bell. No reply., so he decided that Louise must have gone straight up to bed and he was unsure if she lived alone or was now snuggled up to a husband or boyfriend. He decided that he would not want to get into a fight and he left.

Over the course of the next month of so, Roger saw Louise a couple more times in the clubs and bars in Swansea and decided that if she was married or had a boyfriend she couldn't be that happy with them as she was always out with a group of friends and always appeared to be unattached. He had watched her closely on the occasions he had seen her and he marvelled at how relaxed and unaware she was. He would, he decided have to try to talk to her again.

Louise was far from unaware of the attention she was getting from the short stocky man and hoped that he would not try to chat to her again. She was enjoying her evenings out and along with Pauline and a couple of other colleagues she would dance for hours and actually drink far less that she was used to, on a Saturday night.

Two weeks before Easter 1994 as she left a pub in Swansea high street alone, she was grabbed by the arm. She turned around to see Roger standing close to her in the shadows and fearing that she was about to be attacked she pulled her arm away and moved quickly towards the awaiting taxi.

"I only want to talk," he started, "and I know where you live." He slurred.

That was enough for Louise to get genuinely scared. She jumped into the taxi and asked the driver to get her home quickly. Once at home she checked all the doors and windows were securely locked before she began to calm down a bit. Roger had done very little wrong other than grab her arm but his last sentence had worried her. Did he really know where she lived and was he threatening her? She knew that he was drunk but that was no excuse. She decided that she would have to deal with him when she next saw him and that he would have to be made very aware that he should not pester her again.

It was Easter weekend when she next saw Roger watching her at a club. She was nervous and spent less time on the dance floor than normal and more time drinking. By midnight she was drunk and angry. Seeing Roger at the back of the room, she headed over and asked him for a dance.

When he smiled and agreed she grabbed his hand and led him onto the dance floor. She had picked her time well and as they arrived at the dance floor the DJ played a slow track and the floor filled up with couples. Roger put his arms around her waist and as he leaned forward Louise whispered into his ear.

"This is just a warning but believe me when I say that if I ever catch you watching me again I will ensure that you never dance again. Understand?"

Louise had practised this line and in her head it had sounded much more threatening than now having been spoken aloud. She decided that she would bolster the threat with a little action and she bought her knee up between Rogers legs hard and fast. He stumbled backwards a little but Louise had hold of him and pulled him back towards her. She was enjoying this now and whispered in his ear again.

"Understand? And if I ever see you anywhere near my house you will wish that I hadn't. Now piss off you ****!"

This time Roger stumbled backwards because Louise had pushed him. He turned and walked away, then turned again and starred at Louise. She would not get away with this he thought to himself.

The next day was Easter Sunday and Roger arrived at Louise's house early. Louise would still be in bed and he would sit in his car until he saw some movement in the house before taking action. Both his pride and his testicles had been hurt and although he was unsure what he was going to do, he knew that he had to catch her by surprise. It was 10am before he saw Louise's shadow pass by an upstairs window and he got out of his car, looked around, then jumped over the the garden fence and made his way to the back of the cottage.

He noted that there was already washing on the clothes line and realised that Louise must have been up longer than he knew. He was about to try the back door handle when it opened. He stepped back quickly and fell backwards over a rose bush. Louise found him sitting on the floor and although shocked she acted quickly. She grabbed the spade that was leaning against the cottage wall and smashed it down on Roger's knee. Her breathing shortened and there was a glint in her eye as she smashed the spade down again on the same knee. Roger screamed and tried to scuffle backwards but his leg was broken, he was sure and he was in too much pain.

"Don't, don't." He pleaded as he saw Louise raise the spade again.

That was the last thing Roger remembered until he woke up in a dark room. He tried to move but was hampered by two things. Firstly there was the pounding in his head, he had obviously been hit on the head and there was dried blood that had run down the side of his face. Secondly both his hands and feet were tied to each other and to the legs of what he perceived to be a workbench. It was too dark to see much but he could smell oil and he knew that he must be in a shed or a garage.

In fact, Roger was in a small outbuilding at the end of Louise's garden.

Since she had moved in she had only been in the outbuilding twice herself. Initially to see what was in there and then to have a bit of a tidy up as the previous owner had left a lot of junk behind. It had been used for gardening tools, a lawn mower and some other bits and pieces that Louise did not recognise. Probably parts of an old car she had decided.

At the time Roger woke up, Louise was inside the house drinking a tea and trying to decide what to do about the man tied up in her outhouse. She sat at the kitchen table with two old men, one on each shoulder. The guy on the left shoulder had whispered in her ear that she needed to call the police and have the creep put in jail for harassment. The guy on the right shoulder was not so logical and suggested that she should kill the intruder and bury him in the field at the back of her garden. Having listened to both arguments Louise remained calm and thoughtful for a long time. Eventually, she decided that Roger was a concern in her life that would not go away unless she did something drastic. Not something as drastic as killing him but certainly not as soft as informing the police who would more than likely give him a slap on the wrist and tell him to behave.

Louise had no qualms about killing Roger but she saw the problems that this could cause her. Presumably Roger had driven to her house and she had no idea what his car looked like. It was likely that someone at the pub the night before had seen then dancing together so if he went missing she would become a suspect or at least a 'person of interest' to the police. She decided that the best course of action would be to convince Roger that she was more powerful than him and that he was out of his depth when it came to a battle of the minds. In order to do this she needed to, or wanted to, crush the fight out of him and that would involve physical violence.

As she rose from the kitchen table to put the teacup in the sink she was beginning to formulate a plan. She put her jacket on and made her way to the outbuilding, only stopping to pick up the spade as she went.

It was a bright and breezy day in April and as she opened the heavy wooden outbuilding door a ray of midday sunlight filled the room beyond. Roger was where she had left him but was now awake and had contorted his body into a strange tangle whilst trying to extract himself from the ropes. She left the door open and approached the man on the floor. She searched his pockets and found his wallet, his phone and a piece of string with three keys attached.

Roger hadn't said a word since she walked in but his eyes were clearly focused on her and she sensed the anger behind them. Good, she thought. It will be easier to do what must be done if he is awake and angry. She sat down on an upturned plastic bin opposite the mans head and spoke quietly.

"I can see from the driving licence in your wallet that your name is Roger Davies. I can also see that you are 24 years old and I can see where you live. Now, Roger I am going to ask you a few questions and I expect you to tell me the truth in a calm and polite manner. If you do not, I will have no problem in hurting you. In fact, I am quite hoping that you make this difficult so that I can prove to you that I mean business.

Question number one, why have you been stalking me, watching me and threatening me?"

There was a long silence and Louise took this as Roger being obstructive. She raised the spade and hit him hard on the same knee she had hit earlier. This time his scream was significantly louder and his eyes began to water. He started to talk but his words came out in a jumble and she could not understand him.

"Ssshhh, calm down a bit." Louise said quietly. "I know that must have hurt but I told you what would happen. Now, I need to be assured that you will not be a threat to me in the future and I can only think of two ways to make that happen. Either you answer my questions and then we discuss some form of oath that you can swear to me or I kill you. What's it to be?"

This time Roger answered quickly. "I didn't want to do you any harm, I just wanted to spend some time with you and when you rejected me I suppose I wanted to make you suffer a bit but nothing violent I promise. I also promise that I will not come near you again. I have learned my lesson."

"Well that's better Roger isn't it. I am not sure there is any sincerity in what you said and it certainly doesn't fill me with confidence that I will be safe from you in future because....."

"I am being...."

"No Roger, you do not interrupt me, just tell me how we can come to an agreement that you will stay away from me and how you can reassure me of that."

" I, I, I promise I will never come near you again but I have no idea how to give you any reassurance." Roger stuttered and his mind raced to think of what else he could say. He realised that he had wet himself and he saw that Louise had also seen the wet patch on the front of his jeans.

Louise smiled "OK Roger, I am pleased with your promise but that is not enough. I have an idea that will keep you to your promise. How good are you at acting?"

Roger had no idea what she meant or what to say. He just nodded his head and started to cry. Louise rose from her seat and left, leaving Roger once again in the dark, this time laying in a puddle of his own wee.

As Louise walked up the path towards the house she was thinking about how to direct the play she had devised. She needed some form of collateral that would deter Roger from any future actions against her and she had decided that she would get him to denounce himself on video. Now all she needed to do was write a script, get him to learn it, it would have to be short as Roger didn't seem to be the brightest of lads and then film him. She hoped for his sake that he was a good actor. All this needed to be done quickly as she did not want to keep Roger in the outhouse over night.

The script she devised was really just a list of three statements but she wanted them to sound natural and unforced. She set up a chair in her living room and then remembering the state of Rogers jeans she covered it with a bin bag. Then she set up a place for her to sit her video camera so that the chair was centre screen.

Happy that everything was set she took a small knife from the kitchen drawer, the spade would be no use now, and retrieved Roger.

Roger had no fight in him and as Louise had shown him the knife before untying him he did exactly as he was told. He limped slowly into the house with Louise close behind him. On Louise's instruction he washed his face and hands in the toilet sink and then moved into the living room.

He read the scripted statements and again began to cry.

"If you don't think you are up to this I can revert to my other plan. Believe me, I will ensure that you die in pain and your body is never found." Louise lied. She had no intention of killing him but she didn't want him to know that.

After cleaning his face again and having a few practices at saying the three sentences on the paper Roger believed he was ready. Louise too had been happy with his last reading and was now ready to record.

'I broke into the house with the intention of raping and possibly killing the young lady. I had been watching her for a few weeks and had become obsessed with her. The idea of rape gets me very excited and knowing that I have full power over a woman is like an aphrodisiac to me.'

Well, Louise thought, not my best writing but it will suffice. Roger is not clever enough to realise that these statements are worthless or that I have no intention of ever using them. All that matters is that Roger thinks I might.

After four takes, when Louise finally said she was happy with the recording, she gave Roger a couple of painkillers, a glass of milk and his phone, keys and wallet back. She made sure that Roger saw her take a picture of the driving licence with his address on it and then led him back into the back garden.

"I assume you can manage to drive home?" She asked.

Roger nodded. He wasn't sure at all but he needed to get away from the crazy woman.

"I will be sending the video to a friend of mine for security. Now piss off and just hope that you never see me again."

Louise never did see Roger again although throughout the remainder of 1994 and well into 1995 she always watched out for him. She eventually assumed he must have left Swansea.

CHAPTER 27 - COLIN, 2003

Colin didn't have long to wait for the phone call from Mavis. Her initial response was as Colin had expected, that she felt obliged to not divulge the name of the person who was paying for the regular monthly flowers delivered to the grave of Mr John Barnes. She did tell him that she actually delivered the flowers herself, despite her dodgy hip and that she received a quarterly payment by direct debit. The request had come about 3 or 4 months after Mr Barnes death and she had only ever spoken to the person twice since then. She confirmed that the choice of flowers was left entirely to her and she took pride in her choices.

Colin needed more information and decided to charm as much information out of Mavis as he could. He chatted with her for over 45 minutes and she seemed happy to tell him about her shop and how she had grown up in Exeter. She had mentioned that her husband had died a few years earlier and Colin sensed that she was lonely and enjoyed having someone, anyone to talk to.

Eventually she let slip that the purchaser of the flowers was male and Colin pounced on this information.

"I bet it's Matt." He said. "Him and John were best mates back then. I saw Matt a few days ago, he's still living in Exeter. I bet the old softie is the one sending the flowers."

"Oh no, I remember the man telling me he didn't know Mr Barnes or where he was buried, I had to find that information out for him. He was a Londoner and just said that he had his own personal reasons for the flowers." Mavis replied.

"Well it's been nice speaking to you Mavis, thank you for calling me. I need to go now. Stay well and look after that hip of yours. Bye." With that Colin hung up and reached for his notebook.

A male from London. Not much to go on but it was a start. Of course the flowers may have nothing to do with how John died but his intuition told Colin that they did.

Colin really needed more details than Mavis would give him but he knew that there was no way he would get details of the direct debit payments out of her. He would have to try something different. He was pleased that again the information he was collecting hinted at a London connection. He needed the information from the original Exeter police investigation and realised that he had to contact Charles in order to speed things up.

As Colin sat in front of his computer trying to word his email to Charles, his mobile rang. He saw that it was Grant and answered immediately.

"Good morning Grant, what can I do for you today?" He said brightly. Maybe too brightly he thought, he was just trying to cover up how he felt.

"Morning Colin you sound in full fettle today. I was just calling to invite you to the send off party for the kids on Saturday. Richard has been hustling me to call you for an update on your investigations and I thought we could combine the two and have a few drinks together. What do you think?"

Colin accepted the invitation and after a little general chat he promised to be at Grant's house by 8pm the following Saturday, then he said goodbye and returned to staring at his computer screen.

Finally, Colin finished the email and looked up at the clock in the corner of the screen. It had taken him nearly three hours to write a one page email. It had exhausted him, he felt both physically and mentally drained and decided that he would take a long relaxing bath after lunch. Lunch consisted of a quickly made tuna sandwich and a fresh orange juice but Colin hardly noticed the taste. His mind was torn between his thoughts about Charles, his list of information he needed and what he was going to tell the Hamstead family on Saturday.

As Colin ascended the stairs he decided that when he met with Richard and Rachel on Saturday he wouldn't exaggerate the little progress he had made and would instead play down the chances of solving the mystery quickly. He didn't want to raise expectations and he certainly didn't want Richard getting too excited. He needed to devise a plan.

Grant had offered to pay him for his work so far but he had declined as he declared "I haven't solved a bloody thing yet and we agreed on payment for results."

Having retired from his Investment job a year or so ago with a fairly sizeable bonus and with generous pensions from both the Navy and the Police, Colin was by no means hard up. In fact, his outgoings were so small that he was earning more that enough income from his pensions and personal investments to live the way he wanted. He did not need any extra income, what he needed was something to fill his time and occupy his mind.

CHAPTER 28 - UNIVERSITY, 2003-2006

By the time Rachel and I left for University, Colin had devised a plan for tracing the 'Londoners' and he promised us that he would continue his investigations, albeit in his own time and at his own expense while he were away. Colin had partially updated us about his time in Exeter but had not mentioned what he had done the morning before he returned to London.

Rachel had listened carefully to Colin's update and realised that the investigations into John's death could be a very slow process. She determined that she would put it to one side while she was at Uni as Mum and Dad had suggested, after all it was not something that was as urgent as her education.

I was frustrated. I thought things would have moved quicker and now, having to go away without a resolution, I felt anger and annoyance. I decided that I would keep in regular monthly contact with Colin and ensure that things did not stall. I was grateful that Colin was not taking a payment but in some ways wished he would so that I could put more pressure on him to succeed.

Grant and Fiona had encouraged both of us to enjoy the University experience, to work hard and to put all our efforts into our respective degree courses. They were not too worried about Rachel as she was a very controlled, determined and bright student. Me, on the other hand, although very good academically, always had a tendency to get distracted and they were concerned that my busy, inquisitive mind would distract me from my studies.

As it was things did not turn out as Mum and Dad expected. The years between 2003 and 2006 threw up a few surprises for our family.

First of the surprises was that I met Hannah during the first weeks at Manchester University and all thoughts of the investigation into my fathers death left me. Hannah was on the same Finance course as me and we became friends immediately. By Christmas 2003 we had become almost inseparable and when we started back at Uni at the start of October 2004 we decided to share a flat together.

I called Rachel often and was always full of apologies for not having kept in touch with Colin, for putting fathers death to the back of my mind and for spending most of our calls extolling the beauty and intelligence of Hannah. Nearly every call ended with my apology followed by Rachel telling me how happy she was for me.

Rachel was in Cambridge initially studying Geography but at the end of the 2004 summer term, having discussed both with her tutors and our parents, she switched courses. It would mean an extra year of study but she had been unable to relate to her Geography course and instead switched to Human, Social and Political Sciences.

Rachel knew that the reasons for her change were two-fold. Firstly, unlike me she had not been distracted by love and although she socialised and made new friends she remained concentrated on our fathers murder. In fact, having started her own investigation she had become obsessed with killers and their motivations. She was good at Geography and her tutors had tried to talk her out of switching courses but she was very strong willed and knew what she wanted to do. The new course included Criminology and would allow her to focus on the criminal mind which had become something she really wanted to make a large part of her future study. She had also taken up where I had stalled and started keeping in touch with Colin. So much for her promise to our parents that she would put it all to one side while she studied.

Grant and Fiona, as always supported both Rachel and I in our decisions. After long discussions with Rachel they understood her need to find answers and they felt that the switch in course would actually lead her to greater things. An extremely bright girl with a passion for her subject should not be underestimated.

Rachel had indeed found her passion and I knew that she was destined for great things, not just at University but beyond. She was the most intelligent, organised and determined person I knew and I had no doubt that she could do anything she put her mind to.

We spoke regularly throughout our years apart and she was always busy and juggling millions of things at once. She maintained that her social life was interesting, although during our calls I would often tease her about it.

"Rach, you need to get out more, being a member of a running club and going to the gym a couple of times a week with friends is not really socialising. You need to get out to a pub or club occasionally and let you hair down. Get yourself a boyfriend, enjoy life." I would chide.

"Oh you don't need to worry about my social life, you'd be surprised what we get up to after our gym sessions." She would always answer, although she never went into any detail.

CHAPTER 29 - COLIN, 2004

Three months after the twins had left for their respective universities, Colin had not received a reply from Charles. He was disappointed but not surprised. He had also not received anything from the Exeter police follow his request for information and again was not very surprised. Initially he spent much of his time transferring his notes onto his computer and preparing himself a 'Crime Board' in which he included everyone from his investigation plus any scraps of information he had managed to uncover. They really were scraps and Colin was running out of ideas.

What had he really achieved in the time he had been investigating? The killer or killers might be Londoners or Russian spies. They had got into a fight with a local low level drug dealer who had gone into hiding over something totally unconnected. Someone was still leaving flowers on John's grave some 13 years after his death. The police were not going to provide him with any help. Charles did not want anything to do with him and Mavis had a dodgy hip.

Colin couldn't help but laugh to himself at how badly the investigation had progressed.

Colin was getting bored with the lack of results and had taken up learning to play keyboards, just to fill his time. He needed something to occupy his mind and quell his boredom. It was while he was sat in front of the keyboard that he had bought on a bit of a whim, struggling to get his fingers on the right keys, that he had a brainwave.

It was not a huge brainwave but something he could actually work with. He would look into couples leaving Exeter for London in the days after John died. Obviously if they had travelled by car he was going to be out of luck but he could look into train and coach passengers and he could look at a few hotels in the area of the pub to see if they had records of clients for the days surrounding the day of the fight. It would not be easy but what else did he have to do? He also decided that, just to be thorough, he would contact Lawrence Chale via his social media pages and try to arrange a telephone call to see if he had anything useful to add.

It was towards the end of December 2004 before anything useful came to light and during that month three things happened that changed the course of Colin's investigations and his life. They stopped him from going mad. He had hit so many dead ends in his search for hotel clients and couples travelling to London in 1990, he had spoken to Lawrence who could remember nothing useful and he had realised that his fingers were far too clumsy to master the keyboards. Boredom had set in again and Colin was depressed. He was not just depressed, he was lonely. Somehow his life had turned a corner and his thoughts were getting darker and darker by the day. He had questioned who he was, who he had in his life and what his purpose was. He had even considered ending his life on Christmas Day but had felt that he didn't even have the strength of mind to follow that through.

The first and definitely the most important thing that changed Colin's life in December 2004 was that he received a phone call from Charles. Not a single reply to his email over a year earlier and then out of the blue a phone call. It was an emotional call and they spoke for over two hours. Charles said that he would be visiting London in a couple of weeks and would like to see Colin again. He had apologised for not getting in touch earlier and explained that he had been going through a tough few years since he had split with Colin. The call ended with both men in tears and looking forward to meeting up although both were careful not to read too much into what might result from their meeting.

In the days after the call despite his determination not to get too excited, Colin's mood definitely changed and the world became a brighter place to live. He woke early each day, put some music on his headphones and headed out for a run. He was unfit and subconsciously wanted to get in better shape before he met Charles.

One day, about a week later, he returned home from his run to find a letter on his doormat from his contacts at Exeter train station. He had received a few letters from them over the last year but they had all led to absolutely nothing. And he had assumed they had given up. This one showed a glimmer of promise. Among the data provided he spotted that a lone traveller on the day John died had bought a ticket from Exeter to London and had paid by credit card. His name was Thomas Appley and although there was nothing to connect him to John's death, Colin felt a little flutter in his stomach and again his intuition kicked in. Perhaps the fact that he was now in a happier place in his mind made him decide that he would follow this up

That very same day Colin received a phone call from Rachel. This call too was out of the blue. Until November 2003 Colin had been speaking regularly with Richard who pestered him almost weekly about his progress only to be annoyed and even angry by the lack of any. After November he had only spoken to anyone from the Hamstead family a few times and each of those times had been with Grant who had called to wish him a Merry Christmas or a Happy Birthday or just to chat about investment opportunities or the lack of progress on the investigation and although Colin had promised not to give up, they both agreed that it was looking unlikely that they would get to the bottom of John's death.

Now Rachel phoned to explain that she too had been investigating John's death and wanted to meet up with him to compare notes.

CHAPTER 30 - COLIN & TOMMY 2005

In 2005 Tommy was not the man he had been 15 years earlier. He was living in Southend and working as a mobile phone shop manager. He was married to Zoe and together they had a four year old daughter, Tanya. He had moved to Southend in late 1990 to start anew and had met Zoe a couple of years later when he had made a delivery to her house. Zoe would say that it was love at first sight and that Tommy had been delivered from the stars. Tommy had to agree that there had been an instant attraction but the 'delivered from the stars' was just a play on the fact that the delivery he made was from the Comet superstore. In 1999 after being together for what Zoe described as being far too long without a proposal, Tommy got down on one knee and the following year they were married. Tanya arrived as planned 10 months after the wedding.

Tommy was happy, very happy. He had the family that he had always wanted. Zoe's family had become his family and when Tanya arrived Tommy knew that she and Zoe were the best things to have ever happened to him.

But then one day Colin walked into his shop.

"You want to speak to me about where I was over 14 years ago? That's a strange request from a complete stranger. I don't think you have any right to come in here and bring up my past. I have never been in any trouble if that's what you're asking." Tommy replied after Colin had introduced himself and asked his first question.

As soon as Colin had asked "Is there somewhere we can talk in private." Tommy had known what Colin was going to get around to asking him about and he sure as hell didn't want to have that conversation in the shop.

As they settled in the small office at the back of the shop Colin asked Tommy if he had been in Exeter on 1 November 1990 and returned by train the following day. Exactly what Tommy was expecting. He was just surprised that it had taken over 14 years for someone to ask him.

"What makes you think that?" He asked defiantly.

"Well, I have it on good authority that you purchased a ticket from Exeter station using your credit card on 3 November 1990 and I have spent the last few days tracking you down. I see that you left your London address that same day and moved here to Southend. Can you explain why you did that?"

"I was on that train but I do not have to tell you anything. You said you were not police so why should I answer any of your questions."

"Oh, would you rather I get the police involved then?" Colin challenged.

"And how would you do that? I have nothing to hide but I do not have to answer to you, what are you some sort of private detective?"

" Actually, Mr Appley, I am acting on behalf of two people who lost their father on 3 November 1990 and I have been charged with finding out who killed him. You are quite right, you do not have to answer any of my questions but I would like to establish if you were in any way involved." And then, on a whim he added "I also believe that you have been sending flowers to the grave of the aforementioned man for the last 14 years. Of course I can verify that because you pay for the flowers by Direct Debit to the flower shop."

Tommy broke down inside but tried to maintain a tough exterior.

"Look, I was there when the man was beaten up but I did not kill him. I found out later that he had died and I, I don't know, I just felt I had to do something. Every year I think about cancelling the flowers. For sure, I could do without the expense but I haven't been able to bring myself to actually do it."

"Mr Appley, I understan … " Colin started.

"Please, call me Tommy, I have thought about that night a lot and the weeks that led up to it. I never thought about the man's life before that night but I do remember reading that he had a wife and children. I didn't go to the police at the time because I thought it was just a drunken brawl that got out of hand on a Friday night. It was only much later that I found out that he had died."

"I think we have a lot to talk about, Tommy. Just so you know, the evidence I have so far points to you being with a young girl and that it was her who attacked John while he was on the floor. It is likely that it was her kicks to his head that led to the brain haemorrhage and subsequent death. Please can we arrange to meet again so that I can record your story of what took place that night?"

"I think I did knock him over but I'm sure that's all. Yes, I think it is now time to tell the whole story and hopefully give his wife and children some closure."

Tommy took a deep breath and realised that for the last 14 years he has been waiting to get this weight off his chest. It was time to move on and he would cooperate fully with the man in front of him.

They arranged to meet the following Sunday morning back at the shop, as it would be closed and they could talk, in private, all day if necessary.

When Colin left, Tommy asked his assistant manager to take charge and to close the shop at the usual time and take the keys with him. He then called Zoe to say that he was coming home early because of a headache.

After the first meeting with Tommy, Colin had returned home. He had driven back to his house in a mood that he could only describe as 'buzzing'. His life had always been full of ups and downs but the last two weeks had been the biggest 'up' he had ever had. In two days he would be meeting with Tommy again and then the following weekend he would be meeting Charles. Things were starting to happen for him and his previous thoughts about not getting carried away had deserted him.

As he sat updating his 'Crime Board' and making notes of his conversation with Tommy he really felt that the end of the investigation was in sight. He was looking forward to meeting up with Rachel too, especially as he hoped to have virtually sewn up the investigation by then. They had arranged to meet during the last week of February and that left him just a few weeks to solve the mystery of John's murder. He assumed that Tommy would give him the name of the girl he was with that night and he would then track her down and confront her. What happened after that would be up to Richard and Rachel under the guidance of Grant and Fiona. His work will have been done.

How wrong he was.

Firstly the meeting with Tommy went extremely well. Tommy explained in detail the period he had spent with Louise from their meeting in Sizzles right through to his journey home from Exeter. He was able to provide the names of Louise Whitwell, Elizabeth Whitwell, Doctor Brook and someone called Baz. He also detailed the decline of Louise following her parents death, the 'mood' swings (he wasn't sure how else to explain them) and the change following the funeral. However what he focussed on most was the attitude and desire that Louise seemed to have for violence. He explained that she seemed to thrive on it and that that was why he had left her in Exeter the morning after the pub fight.

Colin recorded the whole discussion and when Tommy had finally finished speaking Colin asked a few further questions.

"Wow, that is some story. It seems to me, from what you have said, that Louise was very disturbed and vulnerable following her parent's death. It can't be easy for an 18 year old to lose both parents at once like that."

"Do you have an address for Louise now?"

"Did you ever have any contact with her after that night?"

"You mentioned that Louise didn't drive. Do you have any idea how she would have got home from Exeter and where the car you were using is?"

"Was Louise on any medication?"

"How did you find out about John's death?"

"Does your wife know about any of this?"

Colin knew that there were probably many more questions that he should be asking but as Tommy was unable to answer most of the ones he had asked, he decided to stop there. Tommy had already agreed to give him his phone number in case any further questions needed to be asked. All of Colin's extra questions had been answered with a straight "No." Except for the penultimate one.

Tommy had learned about John dying, purely by accident. About three month after he returned from Exeter he was living in Southend and had met a woman in a pub one Saturday night. They had a couple of drinks together and she informed him that she was a nurse. For some unknown reason the woman mentioned that a friend of hers, also a nurse, in Exeter, had had the horrible task of looking after two young children while their father died in the room next door. Tommy was not sure how the conversation had got to that stage and was confused as to why this woman would tell him this but something about her story made him want to find out more.

"It was like one of those 'out of body experiences' that you read about in the newspapers, you know?" Tommy said. "Somehow I just knew that I was connected to the story. I managed to get hold of an Exeter newspaper that covered the story of the man's death and realised that it was the man from the fight we had outside the pub. I put the whole thing down to coincidence but I had a strange feeling about it and tried to find the nurse who told me the story but no one seemed to know or remember her, even when I described her bright yellow coat. To this day I ...."

Colin interrupted. "Wait, you say a bright yellow coat? Can you rememb......."

Now it was Tommy's turn to interrupt. "From all that, you focus on the colour of the coat."

Colin apologised and said that he thought the story was strange but that stranger things have been known to happen. He rose from his seat and before he left he promised to send Tommy a copy of his notes from the meeting once he had typed them up so that Tommy could add, subtract or change anything Colin may have misunderstood.

Tommy was surprised that the meeting was seemingly coming to an abrupt end but shook Colin's hand and said goodbye.

This time when Colin returned from Southend his mood was somewhat different to the previous time. The information that he had received from Tommy was more than he could have expected and he should have been happy that the investigation now appeared to be gathering pace and entering its end phase. What had stopped Colin in his tracks had been the mention of the nurse who appeared out of the blue in Tommy's pub, wearing a bright yellow coat and who then disappeared without trace. Was the similarity with his encounter at the grave yard just a coincidence?

CHAPTER 31 - COLIN & CHARLES, 2005

A week later, Colin was dressed as smartly as he could and was waiting in a bar in central London for Charles. He was surprised at how nervous he was feeling and although he had only been waiting a few minutes he was already on his second whisky.

In the two weeks since their original conversation Charles had only contacted Colin once and that was a quick call to arrange this meeting that Colin was now so nervous about. Colin had wanted to pick the phone up and call Charles a number of times but had refrained from doing so.

As Colin watched the door and then the clock behind the bar and then the door again he began to worry that Charles wouldn't show. The clock was showing 2:05 and they had arranged to meet at 2. Colin turned to order a third whisky and as he spoke to the barman he felt a tap on his shoulder. He spun around and stood staring at Charles. Neither said anything for what seemed like hours but was merely a few seconds and then Charles moved in for a hug.

Colin ordered Charles a drink and they found a table by the window.

"I though you weren't coming, you were always so punctual, what have they done to you up in Sheffield? Colin chided.

"I am perfectly on time." Charles responded smiling. "You really need to start wearing that watch I bought you and stop relying on clocks. That one behind the bar is running at least 5 minutes fast!"

They both laughed and after ordering some more drinks and a couple of sandwiches, they started chatting about what

Charles had been up to since they last saw each other. Charles explained how hard he had found it in Sheffield to start with and how much he had missed Colin but as they had split on fairly acrimonious terms, he didn't want to contact Colin.

Colin remembered the arguments that they had about Charles moving away and how he had reacted. He had sworn a lot and told Charles to 'piss off up north then'. Charles had responded with words of a similar nature.

Charles said that he had often wanted to call but as time passed he felt that he had missed the opportunity. He put all his energy into his career and tried to forget Colin.

Colin said pretty much the same and then said that they should forget the past nine years and focus on the future. Both had endured years of being alone and now that they were back in conversation they could decide if there was any chance of a future together.

Although they were in agreement that life had been much better when they were together, Charles pointed out that nine years was a long time and that they should take things slowly. They were different people back then compared to what they were now and he wasn't sure that getting back together would be a good or an easy thing to do. He then turned the conversation to why Colin had written to him in the first place.

"I have done a bit of digging and called in a few favours but there is not a lot of information that is of any use I'm afraid. The Exeter investigation at the time of John's death seems to have focused on a street fight that went too far. Little work appears to have been done on finding the people involved and I saw one comment from the then Chief Inspector asking for the case to be closed quickly as there were far more urgent cases to be investigated. It was even suggested that the death was the result of football hooliganism as Exeter had been at home to Portsmouth on that Saturday, although there is nothing I can see that supports that theory."

Colin wasn't surprised. He told Charles of the more recent developments regarding Thomas Appley and asked if it would be possible for Charles to check to see if there was a criminal record in that name. Charles promised that he would.

It was dark by the time they eventually left the pub and they decided that after nearly six hours of talking they needed to separate, digest what they had discussed and talk again the following day.

Charles was booked into a Hotel in West London and as Colin's house was east of the bar, they parted ways and Charles ordered a taxi. They had a brief hug before he got into the taxi and then Colin was alone on the pavement. He walked towards the nearest tube station and headed home. He was happy with the way the afternoon had gone but wasn't sure about what Charles wanted or indeed what he wanted.

After a restless night Colin woke and descended the stairs in search of coffee. He usually treated himself to a cooked breakfast on a Sunday but he was not in the mood to eat. He had thought about what Charles had said and had to admit that they were very different people now. Physically, Charles had aged quite significantly. He was only two years older than Colin but where Colin had maintained his weight and fitness, it appeared that Charles had let himself go at bit. Not that that was as much of a concern as how they had matured in personality.

They had laughed and got on very well yesterday, without touching on anything intimate and now Colin was trying to determine if his thoughts about Charles were those of love or not. He had definitely had strong feelings for Charles all those years ago and the split had been painful for both of them. Now, he wasn't sure if he could rekindle those feelings.

Surprisingly though, Colin's dreams had not been about Charles but about the information Tommy had given him. Was this a sign that his life had moved on and that Charles was not a part of his future?

At 10am Colin called Charles and arranged to meet up again, this time for a good old Sunday roast at a pub they used to frequent when they lived together. The pub was in Camden and they agreed to meet at noon, with Charles promising to be on time providing the pub clock was correct.

Charles had obviously done some soul searching since the day before too and the lunch started off quite subdued while they ate and made small talk before getting down to the more serious conversation that was required.

When they finished what they both agreed was a fantastic roast beef dinner, they moved into the bar and found a table before deciding that actually despite the cold they would, instead of drinking, go for a walk along the canal.

They walked and talked all the way to Kings Cross and then turned around and retraced their steps. Neither of them had come to the conclusion overnight that they should get back into a relationship but neither had they decided that a future relationship was out of the question. They talked mainly about the practicalities of such a relationship, what with Charles living in Sheffield and it was only when they were approaching Camden High Street that the talk turned to their feelings.

" I have really missed you Colin. I have been pretty lonely for so many years and since I retired two years ago I have been thinking about the future and the need for the sort of relationship and companionship that we had when we were together. I am sure that with a little work we could rekindle the feelings we had for each other. I know you have been lonely too. What do you think we should do?"

Colin thought for a while. He remembered the feeling he felt for Charles when they were together and had they not split up when they did he was sure that those feeling would have endured. However, they did split and although they had got on well this weekend Colin had noticed a few things about Charles that seemed new.

The talk of companionship in retirement, the frequent stops they had to make on their walk along the canal for Charles to regain his breath, the apparent increase in age gap between then in terms of thoughts and energy. All these things and more convinced Colin that a future with Charles would not work.

"I think, Charles, that our time has passed. We had a great time together all those years ago but we are different people now. Our lives have changed and as much as I was hoping that we could pick up where we left off I really don't think that is possible. I'm sorry Charles. We should remain in touch and I hope that we can at least regenerate our friendship but anything more is unlikely."

"I was afraid you might say that." Charles said. "Deep down I think I feel the same way but I was hoping things would be different. Yes, we should keep in touch. We may not be in love but there is no need for us to be lonely. You are more than welcome to come up to Sheffield anytime you want."

When they said goodbye Charles hugged Colin and for a while Colin thought he may never let him go. Eventually, they parted and agreed that they would speak on the phone together at regular intervals.

When Colin returned to his house he actually felt better than he expected. They had cleared the air, forgiven each other for past demeanours and decided that they should move on with their lives whilst still remaining friends. Not exactly the perfect ending but one that helped Colin see a future and cleared out all his negative reflections on the past.

CHAPTER 32 - LOUISE, 1995 - 2003

Just a couple of months after the 'Roger incident' Louise was in trouble again. This time she had got very drunk after work with Pauline. Pauline had split up with her latest boyfriend and needed someone to commiserate with, so they had left work at five and by 10 they were completely hammered. Louise bundled Pauline into a taxi, gave the driver Pauline's address and waved as they left. She had then looked around to see that there was not another taxi immediately available. She sat on the wall waiting and a group of girls joined her, she assumed also waiting for a taxi.....

"You can't sit 'ere darlin' this is where we sit." Said the biggest of the four girls. The others sniggered and looked towards their leader to see what would happen next. Nothing happened. Louise ignored the comment and remained seated.

"Did you hear me? This is where we sit." The girl asked, now standing directly in front of Louise. Louise stood up and in one quick move she landed a heavy punch on the girls nose. Still saying nothing she turned and looked at the other three girls. She could see that none of them had any real fighting spirit and were reliant on the big girl to get their bullying kicks. She turned back to the leader who had staggered back into the road following the punch. Blood was dripping from the girl's nose but she wasn't finished just yet.

"You bloody bitch, you're going to regret that." And she charged at Louise who calmly sidestepped the charge and flicked out her leg to catch the girl with a sound kick to the knee. The girl went down. Before she could get up again Louise was on top of her raining blow to her face.

The next thing Louise knew was that she was being pulled away by a very strong pair of hands. She fought hard but the hands would not let go.

"Calm down now or I'll have to get rough with you." Said a deep voice. " She has suffered enough now and if I was you I'd be getting out of here before the police arrive. An ambulance has already been called for your sparing partner here."

Louise ceased he struggling and looked around. The bully was lying on ground and covered in blood. Her three friends were standing over her. A tall, broad man in his 40s was holding Louise's shoulders in an iron grip.

"I saw it all, she started on you but she has three witnesses which I guess will be saying something different so go on, get out of here." With that the grip was released from her shoulders and when she looked around again the man was walking up the street.

Louise didn't need telling twice and she quickly headed down the street towards the centre where she knew she would be able to get a taxi home. She was buzzing from the fighting and her adrenaline was pumping. She looked down at her hands and saw that they were covered in blood but not hers. He stopped at the next pub she saw, went to the toilets to clean herself up and then ordered herself a double vodka at the bar. Having drunk it down quickly she made her way back onto the street and was lucky enough to see a taxi waiting on the other side of the road. As the taxi took her home they passed the wall where the fight had occurred and Louise saw the ambulance men carrying the girl into the ambulance.

"Always some trouble or other around here. Why can't youngsters these days just go out and have fun?" Said the taxi driver but Louise didn't reply.

Louise knew that her actions that night were not her fault. She didn't start the fight but she sure as hell wasn't going to back down to a bully. The following morning there were two things worrying her as she sat down with a coffee and a couple of slices of toast. Firstly that she had lost track of what she was doing, during the fight. She remembered sitting on the girl and punching her but then nothing until she was being pulled off. Judging by the amount of blood on her hands she must have punched her a good few times. Secondly, she could remember the elation she felt as she walked off in search of a taxi. She knew that her dark side had once again shown itself.

The months and then years that followed threw up the same situations time and time again until in late 2002 when things took an even eerier turn.

At the age of 29 Louise had cut back on her drinking and taken up a couple of hobbies. She had joined a running club and was running three or four times a week. She had also started to go to the gym with a few friends from work.

In her youth, pre D-day she had been a promising athlete and she longed to be back to the fitness levels she had reached then but years of heavy drinking and a secluded and somewhat lazy lifestyle meant that she was now having to work extremely hard just to match her colleagues.

During 2002 she started to feel like her old self again. And by April she was able to run with the elite group of runners from her club and was beginning to achieve some very good times. A half marathon in May that year gave her the opportunity to test herself and she managed a very respectable 1 hour ,19 minutes, 13 seconds for the race.

In the gym, she was beginning to outgrow most of her female friends and trained mainly alone or with a couple of young men she had met there. She had regained her desire to be the best and when she went to bed each evening she felt satisfied with the way her life was turning out. The only two clouds on the horizon, as far as she was concerned, were the anger and darkness she knew was within her and the lack of a partner. She felt that she had very little control over the first and far too much control over the second.

Her lack of control over her eagerness to fight and the darkness that descended upon her in those moments had plagued her life and when she was sober and sensible enough to think about it she knew that at some stage she was going to do something terrible, again. She realised that her daily diary entries were getting darker and writing was focusing on her thoughts about violence rather than the positive things in her life. She vowed to herself that she would focus on the way her life had generally turned out and not just on her dark side.

Her tight control over her relationships with men was something she had been proud of. She had not been completely celibate in the last 12 years but she had been careful not to let anyone get too close to her. Now as she was getting older she often thought about how nice it would be to have someone to share her life with.

Men had always been attracted to Louise but she rarely felt attracted to them for more than a few days. She was scared of exposing herself and so never got too close. Things changed when she met Cliff. Cliff was a guy she had seen in the gym a few times and although she realised that he was probably ten or more years her senior, she had admired him from afar. They had said hello or nodded at each other a few times but nothing more until one day Louise was sitting on the exercise mats stretching and facing the large wall mirrors. She saw Cliff approaching and hoped that he would sit down next to her.

Cliff did indeed sit next to her and they started chatting. He came across as a charming, confident man. He introduced himself and joked about seeing Louise but not having the courage to approach her because he assumed she had a husband or boyfriend.

"Not that that would stop me," he said with a smile, "but your friend, the one with the streak of red hair told me you are unattached."

Thanks Pauline.

"Perhaps we could go out for a drink or a meal sometime. What do you think?"

"Well it just so happens that I have an opening in my very busy social calendar tonight if you want to take me out." Louise said giving him her best smile.

The smile left Cliff's face. "Oh I'm sorry, I'm busy tonight but I am free tomorrow night. I can pick you up and take you to a favourite restaurant of mine in Oxwich. They do really good sea food. You do like fish don't you?

Louise felt a little silly for being so obviously keen but covered it well with "I love fish and I just so happen to be free tomorrow too. I have a gym session booked for 5:30 but perhaps you could pick me up from here afterwards if that's ok?"

"That sounds like a plan then, Louise. I will be here to pick you up at 7:30." They chatted a little more and then Cliff got up and left.

By the time Louise finished her stretching, showered and got home it was 8:15. She put some of the previous days leftover dinner in the microwave and sat down waiting for the the ping. She was smiling to herself and decided that perhaps things could work out for her and Cliff. She also decided that she was prepared to let her guard down a little for the first time in many many years.

The following day was a Friday and Louise spent some time before work deciding what she would wear that evening. She wanted to look smart and glamorous but without appearing to be dressing smart and glamorous. A conundrum encountered by most women at some time in their lives.

Having decided what she would wear she packed her evening clothes into a bag, packed her gym bag and set off for work. Working for eight hours seemed like 80 hours and Louise was delighted when it was over. She hadn't felt so excited or nervous for a long time and her workout was not as focused as usual. By 7:30 she was sitting in the gym cafe with a sparkling water. By 7:45 she was starting to get anxious and by 8:00 she was getting angry. Where was Cliff? At 8:15 she decided that even if he turned up now she would ignore him and go home. She had felt silly sitting there dressed up but with no where to go and decided that Cliff had missed his chance.

As she left the building a car pulled up in front of her and Cliff jumped out. "I'm really, really sorry. I don't have your phone number so couldn't contact you to let you know that I had been held up. I can see you're upset but please let me made it up to you. Come on get in the car and we can go for a nice meal."

"I'm not upset, I'm just disappointed. You are 45 minutes late and you might not have my number but you do know the gym number and could have called them!"

"Again Louise I'm so sorry, I didn't think of that. You look absolutely beautiful by the way. I'll definitely make it up to you, if you'll let me."

Louise relented and got in the car. It took over 30 minutes to get to the restaurant and throughout the whole journey Cliff apologised profusely explaining the reasons for his tardiness and how his work sometimes infuriated him. Louise remained fairly silent, letting him know that although she had got in the car, he still had work to do to make things better.

By the time they arrived it was nearly nine and Louise was starving but Cliff had spoken the truth and the food was wonderful. Good food, a couple of glasses of wine and Cliffs good company were what she needed. Cliff was a charmer and apart from arriving late he had been the perfect gentleman. They joked, laughed and smiled together and when they eventually left the restaurant and got in the car Louise leaned over and kissed Cliff. It was a good kiss, she decided and a good start to what she hoped would be a good relationship.

After so many years of being careful, not getting too involved and to be honest not meeting anyone who she wanted to be with for more that a few days, this felt right. She had high hopes but she would play things slowly and when Cliff asked where she lived so that he could drive her home she politely explained that her car was at the gym and that he should drop her there.

She could see that he was disappointed but their time would come. She just needed to be strong willed tonight and set the right impression. She did not want him to think that she was too easy or just a short term fling.

"Does your busy social calendar have a gap tomorrow evening, by any chance?" He asked as they pulled into the gym car park. "I know quite a few other good restaurants in the area and I really enjoyed your company tonight."

"I am sure I could move a few things around and make myself available but only on one condition. Tomorrow, you let me pay for the meal, although I will leave it to you to decide where."

Cliff parked the car and got out. Louise could see that his intention was to walk round and open her door for her, a true gentleman but she got out quickly depriving him of that action. After all she was a modern woman who could open a door herself, still she appreciated the thought. They stood talking for another 45 minutes and when Louise said she though she should be getting home, Cliff took her in his arms and kissed her. She kissed him back and was enjoying the whole experience when eventually Cliff stepped away.

"I am going to need your address if I am to pick you up tomorrow. I'm happy to drive so that you can have a drink or three and I'll choose a good restaurant, what type of food do you fancy?

"I think I quite fancy an Indian, are there any good ones around? I have heard good things about the one in the High Street but I'll leave it up to you." Louise gave him her address and they agreed on him picking her up at 7:30 again. This time Cliff promised that he would not be late. After another kiss they parted ways and both headed out of the car park and on their respective ways.

Louise headed home in a similar mood to that of yesterday. She had forgiven him for being late and had enjoyed a lovely evening. As she lay in bed she began to think about her future in a completely different way to what she had done for the last 12 years. She was approaching her 30s and had a desire to live a 'normal' life. She had good feelings about Cliff and hoped that he would be the one to give her the future she longed for.

Saturday was a busy day, first Louise went clothes shopping then she was home again to clean the house. If things went well tonight she would have no real reason not to invite Cliff in for a coffee and she knew where that might lead. By the time she had finished the house was spotless, her bed had been changed and the dirty sheets were already washed and out to dry. There was a bottle of wine and a few bottles of beer in the fridge along with the ingredients for a good English breakfast should Cliff stay the night.

At 5:30 Louise was soaking in a warm bath and by 7:20 she was clean, dressed and ready to go.

As promised Cliff was on time. "Wow, you look absolutely amazing." He said as she walked down the path to the car. He continued to flatter her as they drove to the restaurant. They did not turn towards the town centre though and instead headed out of town and east.

"Where are we going?" she asked but all Cliff would say was that it would be worth the wait.

Only a 20 minute drive and they entered Port Talbot. After driving around for another 10 minutes they found the Indian restaurant Cliff was looking for. It looked pretty rundown and nowhere near as nice as the one on Swansea High Street but Louise didn't say anything. By the end of the meal Louise wished she had chosen the restaurant. As before Cliff had been good company and she had enjoyed his sense of humour and his confidence but she had not enjoyed the food.

"Not the best curry I've ever had." She said as the left they restaurant.

"No, it was not as good as usual." Cliff explained "Sorry, I've had a couple of lovely meals here before but next time we'll try somewhere different.

It was still only 10:15 and Louise wanted to head back to Swansea for a couple more drinks but Cliff was not interested. "Let's go back to yours and we can have a drink there, I can pop into an off licence and get some drinks."

Louise was disappointed but agreed with Cliff and they headed home.

The rest of the evening made up for the disappointing meal and when Louise woke the following morning she looked over at Cliff who was still asleep beside her. She crept out of bed and headed for the shower. When she returned, Cliff was sitting up in bed. He smiled at her and she felt, for the first time in 12 years that she knew exactly what she wanted. She took off the towel that was covering her body and threw it at him. He reached out and grabbed her wrist and pulled her towards him. They were both laughing until their lips met.

An hour later Louise was back in the shower.

When they were both showered and eventually made it down the stairs Louise put the kettle on and offered Cliff a cooked breakfast. He accepted and it was nearly mid day before they were ready to leave the house. They had decided that they would spend the day together but first Cliff had explained that he had to head home to feed his dog and change. When Louise said she would come with him he had explained that the dog was quite old and very nervous of strangers. Instead he suggested they meet at Swansea beach in one hour.

When Louise arrived at the agreed meeting place, Cliff was already there and they spent the rest of the day walking along the beach holding hands. At six Cliff said that he needed to head home as he needed to prepare for a meeting he had the following morning and they said their goodbyes, agreeing to see each other in the gym on the Tuesday.

The next three months were wonderful, although due to Cliff's work commitments and terribly timed meetings that he had to attend in New York on 24th and another on 29th December, leaving her to spend another Christmas and New year alone were not ideal. When he returned he bought her a huge bunch of roses and the obligatory 'My boyfriend went to New Your and all be bought me was this lousy t-shirt' t-shirt and he was forgiven. She saw Cliff most weekends and occasionally during the week. Although she was not entirely sure what job Cliff had, she became aware that it kept him very busy and that occasionally he had to work late or over the weekend. He had described his job as Service Management but mentioned to her that he was fed up with both his job and Swansea and wanted to leave but had never got round to it. When they went out they always headed out of town and Oxwich became their favourite destination.

One Sunday morning she woke early. Cliff was laying next to her in bed and he was snoring lightly. She watched him and felt a little pang of sorrow that he would not be there that night. It had become a regular thing for him to stay over on Friday and Saturday nights but the rest of the week he insisted on going home. Although he frequently went home to tend to the dog she was yet to see his house. She suspected that he was ashamed of where he lived or that he was a pig

172

when it came to house cleaning. Either way she wanted their relationship to grow and she wanted more than a couple of nights a week plus an occasional evening during the week.

They had tentatively discussed a future together but there were no real plans made. Deep down she felt that Cliff was happy with the arrangements as they were as she easily fitted around his work and other commitments. Still, she hoped for more.

To describe Cliff as confident was somewhat of an understatement. He was very charismatic and never short of something to say although he confessed that he was very shy around strangers and apart from that one conversation with Pauline in the gym he was yet to meet any of the friends she had made at work.

Louise had worked very hard at hiding what she now referred to as her dark side. She occasionally ended up with scratches or bruises following a mid week drinking session which had increasingly become something she did alone. She would finish work, go home get changed and head by taxi to a pub. A different one each night if she could. She was beginning to look forward to these solo drinking session almost as much as seeing Cliff and they would often end with her getting involved in a fight with some overbearing man or mouthy woman.

The fighting was her release and she loved it. She always told Cliff that the injuries were as a result of her clumsiness at the gym or while out running. On many occasion she had had to be pulled off someone as her darkness took over.

There were a number of people in and around the Swansea area who bore the scars dished out by Louise and who had needed hospital treatment merely as a result of being in the wrong place at the wrong time. The fact that

Louise could become a target herself by the people she had hurt did not bother her, in fact she enjoyed the pain and the peril, but she did gradually find that she had to travel further afield in order to find new prey.

The two sides of Louise's life appeared to contradict each other with Cliff being her saviour for a few days a week.

As she always did, she rolled carefully out of the bed and left Cliff sleeping while she went downstairs to prepare breakfast. As she opened a tin of tomatoes she heard the ringing of a mobile telephone and then Cliff's whispering voice. She had never seen the need for a mobile phone herself but knew that Cliff had one and assumed that as before someone from work was asking for his assistance.

Within minutes Cliff was by her side, unwashed but already dressed. He was in a panic and explained that he had to leave immediately, they would have to cancel the plans they had made for the day. He kissed for on the cheek and left, ignoring her questions about what was so important and promising to call her later to explain everything.

Louis was left with the tin opener still in her hand as everything had happened so fast. She would be tied to the house too as she needed to wait for Cliff's call. She put the utensil down and made herself a cup of coffee.

As she sat drinking and staring out of the window into the back garden she started to think about a few 'strange' things relating to their relationship. Cliff only stayed at weekends, he never wanted to visit pubs or restaurants in Swansea, he kept the location of his house a secret, merely saying it was across town in a pretty rundown area and he wasn't keen to meet any of her friends. And then there was this mornings exit.

It suddenly dawned on her that she was being taken for a fool. How could she have been so blinded by what now appeared to be so obvious. Cliff was a fraud, he had another woman! Or other women!

Although Louise was annoyed with Cliff, she was far more annoyed with herself. Why was she so easily taken in by this man, was she just too eager for a normal life, did she deliberately ignore the warning signs, what would she do now? So many questions but the one question she didn't ask herself was if she was being premature or overdramatic and was reading too much into a few harmless facts. She knew that she was right.

She called Pauline who all but confirmed her suspicions with one comment.

"I met him in Tescos a couple of months ago with a woman and two small boys and he smiled and greeted me but didn't introduce them which I thought was strange at the time. However, he caught up with me in the car park and explained that it was his sister and his two nephews. He was completely convincing so I never thought any more about it." She said apologising. Two children! That complicated things. After a few minutes chat about what bastards men were and whether Louise needed a shoulder to cry on, which she declined, they said their goodbyes and hung up.

Louise reached for the vodka bottle. It was before 11am but she needed a drink.

An hour later Cliff called.

"Sorry about this morning darling," he began, " there has been a takeover bid for the Company and as the Service Manager I have been asked to assess the impact. All pretty boring stuff but it needs immediate attention. I might be very busy for a couple of weeks but hopefully things will settle down again soon. I hope you're not too disappointed that we had to cancel our plans."

Louise did her very best to act normal, to tell Cliff she missed him and to reassure him that she understood and would see him soon. She hoped that he wouldn't suspect anything by the tone of her voice and finished with a comment about how much she loved him.

Now, having finished the call she had some plans to make. She decided that because of the extent to which she wanted to punish Cliff her plans would need to be big plans, dramatic plans, life changing plans. It was now Sunday afternoon so any plans she made would have to commence implementation tomorrow. She opened her computer and started typing.

1. Find out as much as possible about Cliffs 'other' life/lives.

2. Determine what revenge should look like.

3. Sell the cottage and move away.

4. Find another job.

5. Forget Swansea.

The last one was going to be sad. Not because she loved Swansea but because she had made a good friend in Pauline, the first real friend she had had in many years. Under each of the five items on her plan she went into as much detail as she could. It was time for her to start all over again and it would be hard but nothing she hadn't done before.

Her anger boiled over twice the following week as she drank heavily and took it out on those around her. She had called Pauline on the Monday morning and explained that she was not well and would need a few days off work. Pauline was happy to approve this. On both Tuesday and Wednesday she had got very drunk and started fights. Tuesdays affair was pretty mild as everyone in the pub just backed off until the landlord called her a taxi and sent her on her way.

Wednesday was much worse. She spotted a couple of, what she deemed to be, 'ugly cunts' in the corner of the bar and sent over a couple of drinks for them. Soon they were chatting and Louise knew that by the end of the evening they would be fighting. The anticipation was building in her and she was buying the two men drinks almost faster than they could drink them. Her plan looked like it was going to fail when one of them said they had to go home as they had work the following day and his mate agreed. But then they invited Louise to go with them.

As soon as they were outside the pub Louise attacked. She hit the first man over the head with her heavy bag and as he went down she kicked out and caught him between the legs. By the time the second very drunk man realised what had happened he too was on the floor. Louise was quick and lethal. She punched, kicked and scratched until she was completely exhausted. The two men had been taken by surprise and now lay on the ground not moving in front of the standing Louise. She picked up her bag and walked away.

She was pumped full of adrenaline and as she walked around the corner she nearly bumped into an old man walking his dog. Without thinking she lashed out at him and caught him with a right hand punch to the throat. He immediately fell to the floor coughing and spluttering. Louise smiled and walked on. Five minutes later she had found a taxi and was heading home.

On Thursday she again called Pauline and said she would not be back until the following week. Pauline sympathised and offered to visit her but Louise said she needed to be alone. Now she started to put her plans into action.

She went to the gym Thursday morning but rather than work out she spoke to the young boy on the front desk. It was not their policy to give out personal information on their clients but Louise was able to convince him otherwise. She leaned over the counter and kissed the boy on the cheek. He blushed profusely, gave her Cliff's address and then promised that he would keep it secret until the day he died.

Louise had been extremely impressed with the work Remi had done on her new identity back in 1990 and she had no concerns that the second identity that he had provided her with would prove just as efficient. Now, after what she had planned for Cliff, she decided that it was time to change her identity again and as soon as she completed her list she would become someone new in another part of the country. She would sever all ties with everyone she knew and even Baz would not be able to find her. There was just one problem so she added a 6th action to her list.

6. Kill Remi.

CHAPTER 33 - COLIN & RACHEL, 2005

A few weeks after his last meeting with Charles, Colin was standing at another bar in another pub waiting for another meeting. This time the bar was in a pub in Cambridge and Rachel was the one not on time.

When she eventually arrived Colin was on his third pint and beginning to appreciate the fact that he had decided to take the train rather than drive. He had received a couple of messages from Rachel explaining that she would be late so he had settled in. He was listening to a group of young men at the far end of the bar showing off about what they had planned for the summer holidays and where they would travel too.

Rachel tapped him on the shoulder and he jumped before turning round and seeing her. She smiled, took off her coat and asked for a glass of dry white. He assumed she meant wine and asked the barman. Once served they moved to a table and although feeling a little awkward as he'd not really got to know Rachel, he asked her about how she was getting on.

Rachel was obviously happy and really enjoying her time in Cambridge. He knew from one of his conversations with Grant that she had changed course after the first year and she was very enthusiastic about the new course.

After Rachel had asked Colin about how he was, to which he said very little other than 'good', they moved on to the reason for the meeting.

Colin gave a long summary of what he had found out. He told her about his visit to the Exeter cemetery, his contacts at Exeter railway station and his meeting with Tommy and how helpful he had been. He said that he had a number of leads and would be chasing each one up and that he had first started with trying to find Louise Whitwell but without any luck so far but he stressed that he had only commenced initial enquiries in the last week or so.

Rachel was excited by the revelations and asked many questions. Colin was impressed with her understanding and speed of thought and was happy to expand on his own thoughts as the conversation went on. Eventually Rachel turned to her own investigations. She had not had a great deal of time but had taken a slightly different approach to Colin. She had focused on the life (and deaths) of John and Mary and she had also visited the Exwick cemetery. She had found John's grave and had also searched for Mary's grave but without any luck, initially.

"I sat at John's grave for over an hour and perhaps would have stayed longer had I not been interrupted. The grass was wet and a young lady advised me not to sit on the floor for too long so I stood up and started looking around for Mary's grave. I assumed it would be nearby as they died just 3 months apart but I couldn't find it. I found a bench to sit on and made a few notes about the wording on John's headstone and the fact that there were flowers there. It never occurred to me that I could trace who or where the flowers were from."

Rachel smiled again at Colin, paused for a breath and then continued.

"When I looked up, the lady I had spoken to earlier about sitting on the grass was standing about 30 yards away and waving. I looked around to see who she was waving to but there was no one else there. When I looked back she was gone. For some reason I walked over towards where she had been standing and that's when I found Mary's grave."

"Was the woman wearing a bright yellow coat?" Colin asked tentatively.

"Oh, is she a colleague of yours? I wondered where she came from and where she disappeared to but I had no idea you knew her. Did you already know that I had been there then?" Rachel replied, accusingly.

Colin looked at Rachel and asked again. "What colour was her coat?"

"Yes, it was bright yellow but…."

Colin raised his hand and Rachel stopped talking.

"You've got it wrong, she is not a colleague of mine but yes I have met her. Now you might find this hard to believe, I certainly do, but I think we have something very strange going on." He then went on to tell Rachel of his communication with the old lady in the bright yellow coat and of Tommy's mention of meeting a lady in a bright yellow coat in 1990.

Rachel laughed nervously. "It can't be the same person. The lady I met was only 25 or so and you described her as an old woman. It's just a coincidence isn't it?"

Colin agreed that it was nonsense and obviously just a coincidence although he shivered as he said so.

Before they concluded the meeting Rachel handed over a memory stick which she explained held all her notes and asked if Colin would send her everything he had. She wanted to work closely with Colin but she still had her degree to obtain so she set out that they could do their own thing but that they should talk at least once a week or more often if any advances were made.

Colin agreed. He would send Rachel all of his notes and he would put together a plan and update her regularly, on a Sunday afternoon, as she had requested.

Rachel leaned over, kissed Colin on the cheek and said goodbye. She then picked up her handbag and left. Colin ordered another pint and sat back down. Bright yellow coats are quite common I suppose, he thought. He vowed to count the number of women he saw wearing a bright yellow coat on his way home later.

After what had potentially been a few mentally straining weeks beginning at the end of December with the call from Charles and ending with the meeting with Rachel, Colin was feeling much more relaxed than he had been for a long time. He was sitting at this computer, reading all the notes Rachel had made over the last couple of years when he realised that his meeting with Charles had actually given him some closure on his past and that he was in fact quite content now. Sure he wasn't overly enthralled with having to read so many pages of notes that would eventually lead to nothing but perhaps that was why his mind had wandered.

"My new life will start today." He declared out loud even though he was the only one in the house.

After the meeting with Rachel he had sent her all his notes. He had bundled them together as best he could and saved them on the memory stick, after copying Rachel's notes to his computer, and posted the stick to her. Now reading Rachel's notes he realised how disorganised and messy his own notes were. He was however pleased that at least his investigations had given them some leads.

The obvious first lead was Baz. From what Tommy had told him, Baz had been implicit in their escape following the funeral of Louise's parents. Tommy had warned him that Baz did not look like the kind of guy you should mess with and Colin was happy to heed that warning. When the time came to approach Baz he would ensure that he had the upper hand. Firstly though he needed to trace him and as the last known address for Baz was "probably somewhere in West London" and over 14 years ago, it might not be easy.

Perhaps easier to trace would be Aunt Elizabeth or Dr Brook.

Before he started any further investigations though, Colin needed to go for a run. What had started out as a subconscious need to look trimmer for Charles had turned into a daily habit and every morning, Colin donned his tracksuit and headed out. Today he had decided that he would try to extend his run to 12 or 15km. When he was younger he would often do longer runs but after years of inactivity he had had to start somewhere near the beginning again. He had got back into it pretty quickly and now after a few weeks he was beginning to get back into his stride and living in Bethnal Green gave him plenty of options for running routes. The route he had planned for today was along the Hertford Union Canal and then left up the River Lea. Once he was on the river he would decide how fit he was feeling and then decide from there where to go.

As he trotted along the road towards the canal his phone rang and two minutes later it pinged indicating a message but he was not going to interrupt his run now and vowed to look at it only once he was home again. Ninety minutes later he was home again and in the shower. Having completed 15km in 87 minutes he was pretty pleased with himself and after making a coffee and a bacon sandwich he settled down in his computer chair and looked at his phone. There was a missed call and a text message, both from a number he didn't recognise. He opened the text.

"Colin, I am not sure if you remember me but we did meet once many years ago. I am Charlie's little sister, Maddie. I tried to call you but there was no answer so I am hoping that you could give me a ring please on this number."

That can't be good, thought Colin. He put the phone down and walked into the kitchen, then walked back to the desk again, picked up the phone and dialled the number.

"Hello, is that you Colin. Thank you for calling back. Charlie only gave me your number a couple of weeks ago but he was insistent that you should be one of the first people to know about his death. I ......"

Colin didn't hear any more of the speech from Maddie and dropped the phone on the desk. How could it be that after not seeing Charles for so many years and then meeting up with him just a few weeks ago that he was now dead? After a few minutes Colin regained his composure and picked up the phone again. The line had been cut and he redialled.

"I'm so sorry Colin, I'm not very good with words and rather sprang it on you. I didn't mean to spurt it out like that."

"No, no, you are not to blame, I was just stunned a little. How are you, it must have come as such a shock? What was the cause of his death?"

"No Colin, it was not a shock. I have had the last 18 months or so to get used to the idea. In September 2003 he was diagnosed with a tumour and was told he only had about a year to live. He told me that Christmas and also told me about your email to him. It was only last Christmas that he told me he hadn't contacted you and I insisted that he should. Obviously Charlie didn't tell you, I think he was afraid to."

"He never mentioned it." Colin mumbled into the phone. "I'm in shock a bit, it's such sad news. When did he die? I would really like to be at the funeral?"

"He died in the early hours of yesterday morning, in his sleep. I found him when I went over to make his lunch. I have been living in Sheffield for a while now so that I could keep an eye on him. I haven't got round to organising a date for the funeral yet but will let you know, when I know. He would be happy to know that you are there, I'm sure."

"Of course I'll be there. And Maddie, if there is anything I can do to help please let me know."

After a few quick words they hung up and Colin moved into the living room and sat in an armchair. He wasn't thinking of anything in particular but needed to close his eyes and take a few minutes for the information to sink in. All investigations would have to be put on hold until after the funeral, he decided. He would call Rachel later to tell her of the delay.

CHAPTER 34 - LOUISE, 2003

Before Louise picked up the ringing phone she looked at herself in the hall mirror, took a couple of deep breaths and smiled. She knew it was Cliff calling and she wanted to sound upbeat and loving when in actual fact she was seething inside.

She picked up the phone, "Good morning. Who is this?" She laughed falsely. "Which one of my many boyfriends could be calling today I wonder?"

"Very funny. I'm really sorry for not calling yesterday but I've been so busy. Still lots to do but I was hoping we could meet up on Friday, perhaps go out for a meal."

"Friday, but that's still four days away, can't we meet up sooner. I miss you." Louise said in a pleading, girly voice. She hoped that she was not overdoing things.

"You really wouldn't believe what I have to do this week. I'm already knackered and don't expect to get too much sleep until the weekend. I might even have to go to New York again. This is not a good time to get needy, please understand." Cliff replied.

Normally Louise would have bristled at the term 'needy' but she let it go. It just added to her anger. She agreed to meeting him on Friday and when she hung up she started planning her revenge. She had visited Cliff's address the day before and had watched the house for a while noting that far from a being a run down area, it was actually quite an affluent part of the town. Cliff had left the house at 7:45 and about 30 minutes later a woman and a young boy left, presumably heading to school. Louise followed them.

Sure enough they stopped at a school five minutes later and once the boy was safely in the school, the woman returned to her car and headed into the centre of town. Again Louise followed.

It became apparent that the woman worked in a cafe on the corner of the main street and after parking the car Louise made her way there and ordered a coffee. Cliff's woman, she wasn't sure if it was his wife just yet, served the coffee and when Louise also ordered a bacon sandwich she promised to bring it over to the table. The place was fairly empty and Louise found a table where she hoped she might be able to strike up a conversation with the woman.

It was actually much easier that she could have hoped as the woman was a 'talker'. She confirmed all of Louise's worse thoughts. As they got talking Louise found out that the woman was indeed married. The woman also told Louise what a lousy week she was having. Her eldest son had fallen from a tree on Sunday morning whilst at her parents house and was rushed to hospital. She told Louise that her and the children spent most weekends with her parents as her husband, Cliff, often had to work weekends.

The woman spoke in glowing terms about her husband and how he and the kids meant the world to her. She said that once her son was out of the hospital they would be going to Disney World in Paris and that Cliff had asked her if they could try for another child, hoping for a girl.

The woman was very outgoing and obviously enjoyed talking about herself, she had even sat down at the table as there were no other customers coming in. She was a petite woman in her late 30s with stylish short black hair and immaculate make up. She asked Louise about her life and Louise made up a pack of lies.

Eventually the woman said, "I'm sorry, I've been telling you about all my problems when you probably just want a quiet breakfast, I'll leave you alone now."

"No don't apologise, as I mentioned I'm new to Swansea so it's nice to talk to someone other than myself." Louise laughed and the woman followed suit.

The meeting with Cliff's wife had been very fruitful.

Now, following the call with Cliff, Louise determined her course of action. She had liked the woman, who had introduced herself as Amy, and she felt a slight pang of guilt for what she was about to do to her and her children but Cliff needed to be dealt with.

Plans were already taking shape and she had instructed an Estate Agent to sell her house as soon as possible. She planned to hand her notice in over the phone and just disappear. Years ago she had transferred much of her wealth into untraceable accounts and what was traceable would be the proceeds from the sale of her house and the bank account that her wages were paid into. She would clear out this account and move the money to her 'hidden' accounts, via a few transactions that both Baz and her accountant had told her about.

She had decide that she would move back towards London but far enough away so as not to ever cross paths with Baz. She decided on North Hertfordshire and instructed another Estate Agent in a town called Buntingford to search for a secluded cottage in the surrounding villages.

Both the selling of her cottage and the purchase of a new one would take some time but Louise had already made her mind up to move out of Wales as soon as Cliff had been dealt with.

Her plan was to ensure that he would never again be in a position to cheat on his wife. She knew what she was going to do and she knew how she was going to do it but she doubted that she had the nerve. Sure, she had been extremely brutal at times and although she wasn't 100% sure she had a pretty good idea that her dark side had killed someone and probably put quite a few in hospital. None of that, perhaps apart from the incident with Roger, had been premeditated though and this time it was.

Cliff arrived at her house at 8pm on Friday evening and Louise was ready for him. She had cooked a nice meal, opened a good bottle of red wine and was wearing a fairly suggestive dress.

Cliff grabbed her as he entered the house and kissed her hard. "Oh I've missed you darling." He whispered in her ear as he kissed her neck and reached for her breasts.

Louise stepped back and moved into the kitchen. "We've got plenty of time for that, dinner is ready so get your coat off and wash your hands and we can start. I bought a bottle of your favourite wine."

By 9pm Cliff was fast asleep at the dining room table and Louise was clearing the table and stacking everything in the dishwasher. The drugs had worked exactly as planned and she knew that she would have a few hours before Cliff woke up again. She had prepared everything and even though she had only had one glass of wine she was savouring what was about to happen. She closed the dishwasher, removed the table cloth and pushed the table into the corner of the room. As she moved the table Cliff fell forward off his chair and landed on the hard stone floor. Blood was now pouring down the side of his head from the cut above his eye but Louise wasn't concerned about that.

This was new to Louise, at least she thought so. She had a dark side, she knew that but now she was sober and calm, yet she knew that what she was about to do was terrible, horrific and brutal. And she was licking her lips in anticipation.

When Cliff opened his eyes he was completely confused by his surroundings. It was quite dark but there was a small light somewhere above him. He looked around at the small space and determined that it was some sort of barn or shed. His head was pounding and when he tried to wipe his eyes he realised that his hands were tied together. When he tried to get up he found his feet were tied together too and that they were tied to a huge concrete roller. He tried to remember what had happened but the last thing he could remember was sitting opposite Louise laughing and drinking wine.

"Oh my God!" He thought. "Is Louise OK?"

That question was answered 20 minutes later when Louise unlocked the door and entered the room. She was smiling and Cliff realised that he had never seen her looking so beautiful.

"What the fuck is going on? I've got one hell of a headache and I'm trussed up like a pig. This is not funny, untie me."

"You have been a right bastard and now you are going to pay. I met Amy a few days ago." Was all Louise said before closing the door behind her and going back to the house. Let him stew on that for a bit, she thought.

When she returned an hour later Cliff was still in the same position on the floor and she could see that he was scared. He was a big man and it had taken all of Louise's strength to get him to the outhouse but now, laying on the cold concrete he looked so small and vulnerable.

"I'm sorry Louise I should have told you. Amy and I are an old story now, we still live together but we drifted apart years ago and only stay together for the children. It's you that I love Louise, I really do. Please untie me and we can go… where are we?… somewhere and discuss things."

Louise knew this was not the truth, she raised her phone and took a number of photos before she replied.

"I've just sent these photos to Amy, let's see what she thinks of them. They are a sort of 'before' set. She won't recognise you in the 'after' set" This was not true as she did not have any contact details for Amy but she knew that Cliff would believe her. "Now, how many times did we sleep together while you were married to Amy? I recon it must have been what, say, 25 times? Perhaps 30? I am going to cut you 30 times and you can scream as much as you like but no one will hear you and I will not stop until I have finished. I will then take you to the hospital, the same one your son is in, and leave you there. Before I start, and I should warn you I am going to start with your dick, is there anything else you want to say?"

"You won't do that, you'll end up in prison for years and I'll be waiting for you when you get out and …"

Louise kneeled down, unzipped Cliff's Jeans and with a quick swipe of her knife she drew blood. Cliff fainted. An hour later she had completed all 30 cuts, none fatal, she hoped but all would be painful for a long time. Cliff had woken up a couple of times during her attack but each time had passed out again.

To paraphrase the Cat Stevens song, the first cut was the deepest and it would definitely need hospital treatment. Louise looked down at her handiwork and after taking a couple of deep breathes she started shaking. The thrill of the attack was subduing and she realised that she still had a lot of work to do. Nerves were beginning to set in and she started to panic.

Cliff was still unconscious on the floor and somehow she had to get him up, carry him to his car, drive to the hospital, dump him at the entrance and walk away unnoticed. She realised that she had to act quickly, firstly because Cliff could bleed to death and secondly because she knew that she could only achieve what she wanted while her adrenaline was still pumping.

Two hour later she was walking briskly away from the hospital towards the taxi rank. At home her car had already been packed with all her most valued belongings and clothes. Now was the time to disappear.

The funeral was held in a small church in Sheffield that Charles had been going to for the last year. Prior to that he had no religious inclinations but the news of his tumour had changed his perspective on life.

As promised Maddie had called and told Colin the date, time and location. She had then suggested that, as Colin would be travelling up from London, he should stay at her house before travelling back the next day. Although he didn't want to intrude, Maddie had been insistent and so he had relented.

There were only two hours between getting off the train and the start of the funeral and Colin had to get to Maddie's house and get changed. He hailed a taxi and hoped that he would be there in plenty of time. He had intended to catch an earlier train but upon his arrival at St Pancras station he had seen that there had been some disruption to the train services due to the weather. He had called Maddie and then sat in a cafe waiting for the next train to Sheffield.

Since their first telephone conversation over a week ago they had spoken a few times and Colin was impressed with how well Maddie was coping and organising things. He couldn't remember what she looked like but he did remember her laugh and he remembered that when they had met many years ago he had liked her. Even despite the reasons for their conversations now, Maddie seemed to have a 'smile' in her voice and some of the things she said immediately reminded him of Charles as he had been when they were together.

By the time Colin arrived at Maddie's house there was just 75 minutes until the funeral and Maddie informed him that she wanted to be at the church at least 30 minutes before the start so that she could greet the guests. They would need to leave in 35 minutes. She showed him to his room and left him to shower and change. There was no time to chat and Colin got in the shower only to find that the water was cold. He had let the water run while he was getting undressed but it was still cold. Never mind it wouldn't be the first time he had to endure a cold shower. He was dressed and downstairs with five minutes to spare.

They got in Maddie's car and headed to the church.

The funeral was a quiet affair with only nine people present and as Maddie had not arranged a follow up drink or food, those present dispersed quickly. By 2:30 only Maddie and Colin were left and as they made their way back to Maddie's house she turned to him and told him how sad she was. She had not shown it at the funeral nor had she mentioned it in their telephone conversations but now Colin could see her pain. It was as if a brake had been released on her emotions and she had to pullover as the tears began to flow.

Colin wasn't really sure what to do but took hold of her hand and held it tightly until the tears dried up. He then persuaded Maddie to switch seats and he drove back.

As they sat drinking tea in the living room Maddie told Colin how close her and her brother had been throughout their lives but particularly over the last year. She was a widow, having buried her husband nearly 20 years ago and not having any children she had been happy to move to Sheffield when Charles had told her of his illness. She had seen Charles at least four times per week since then and they had become even closer as the clocked ticked down.

"He thought the world of you, you know, when you were together but he held a long grudge after the way you split up. He blamed himself but was too stubborn to admit it. Over the last few months he told me about the arguments you had about his move to Sheffield and he realised that he was just being selfish and should have put your relationship first."

"Oh, I think we were both pretty selfish back then. I am certainly as much to blame for the split as Charles was." Colin lamented.

"I didn't want to mention it before the funeral but he decided to leave you some money in his Will. He was pretty comfortable and had put quite a bit of his earnings away over the years. He only changed his Will a couple of weeks ago, it's as if he knew that he wouldn't be here for much longer." Maddie finished the sentence and then rose from her seat. "Where are my manners, I bet you're starving, I'll get some dinner on and then we can get out a bottle of his favourite whisky and toast him properly. I made a beef stew yesterday and it just needs heating up. Come through to the kitchen and we can continue our conversation."

By midnight they had toasted Charles excessively and the conversation had turned to happier subjects. Maddie had always wanted to travel around Europe and she had decided that with the money Charles had left her she would start with a month in France. She had been there before but it was a long time ago and she had always wanted to return. Colin gave her a brief outline of the investigation he was carrying out and the progress or lack of it he had made.

The following morning at breakfast, Maddie asked if Colin would return for the reading of the Will which she expected to be before the end of March.

"I don't think it is absolutely necessary as we are the only two beneficiaries and there will be no challenges but it would be nice not to have to go alone." She asked.

Colin promised not only that he would go with her but that he would arrive with plenty of time to spare unlike his arrival for the funeral.

"I realised this morning that I hadn't put on the Emersion heater yesterday my mind was on other things. Was your shower cold?"

They both laughed.

"I will make sure it's on for next time." She said.

When Maddie dropped Colin off at the station they hugged and promised each other that they would stay in touch at least until the reading of the Will.

By the time Colin got home he was exhausted and although it was only early evening he made himself a drink and went up to bed. As he sat in the bed he decided to call Maddie to inform her that he was home and to thank her for her hospitality. They had got on well and Colin needed some friends in his life.

The next two years proved to be a busy and fairly productive time for Colin.

As expected he had easily managed to track down both Elizabeth Whitwell and Dr Alan Brook. He had visited them both and although he did not tell them the full reason for the visits he did explain that he was trying to trace Louise but was not finding any record of her. Neither of them had any information about her whereabouts but both gave some extra information about her health and actions before her parents funeral.

Elizabeth, although helpful, was slightly confused and at first said that Louise was her sister and that she was in the garden. She then seemed to find her senses and described the period she spent with Louise and Tommy in detail. She had not seen or heard of either of them since the funeral.

The visit to Dr Brook was on the same day as he now also lived in Oxford. Dr Brook's wife had died five years earlier and he had moved. He had kept in contact with Elizabeth and occasionally popped in to see her. He was able to give Colin an unofficial view of her condition and explained that she sometimes lost her train of thought or got confused about her past. She had been diagnosed with Alzheimers but it was in it's early stages and she could function quite happily on her own. He had no further information to add to that provided by Tommy and Elizabeth but did stress that Louise was very intelligent and that if she didn't want to be found Colin would have his work cut out. He mentioned Sergeant Shorwell's involvement in 1990 but admitted that he had not spoken to her or heard any more since early 1991. Again he confirmed that there had been no information on Louise since the day of her parents funeral.

The visits did not progress Colin's search for Louise but he was beginning to build up a picture of her and her complete change of personality during the weeks between her parents death and John's death. Elizabeth had provided him with a picture of Louise. It had been sent to her by her brother when Louise had attended a school trip to the Lake District in 1988. It showed a young girl sitting in a canoe with the paddle held above her head. She looked happy and carefree and was laughing at the camera. Colin would scan the photo and add it to his Crime Board when he got home but first he decided that, as he was in Oxford, he would take the opportunity to pop in and see Grant and give an update on the latest information.

Colin's focus now was to find Baz but with so little to go on he was struggling. He maintained a regular communication with Rachel and it was her who, in September 2005 came up with a comment that Colin latched onto and enabled him to eventually find a trace of Baz. During a chat with Rachel she had suggested that, based on the notes Colin made after his second meeting with Tommy, Baz was obviously a criminal and if he was able to provide Louise with a car he was probably quite accomplished.

"Most criminals start off as drug dealers." She had said. "If Louise knew him well enough to arrange his help he was probably local to where she lived." Colin agreed with her comments but he only had the name 'Baz' to go on and no-one he had spoken with including many of the people who had once known Louise, knew who Baz was.

"Perhaps Baz is just a nickname given to him by Louise. Perhaps his name is actually something different." She had said.

"Yes, I have been looking for Baz when in fact I should be looking for a local drug dealer under any name. I will speak again to some of Louise's school friends." Replied Colin enthusiastically.

"Be careful Colin, it doesn't sound like Baz was or is just some small time dealer. He might be very dangerous."

This was the second time someone had said that to him and he was fully aware of the risks involved.

He received his third warning from Maddie. Since the funeral and the follow up meeting at a solicitors later in March, Colin had kept in contact with Maddie and even met up with her a few times. She had become a sounding board for him and he had shared much of his investigation with her. When he had mentioned Baz and described what image he had of him, Maddie had told him to take no chances.

Three messages to be careful were not going to go unheeded but Colin needed to revisit Northwood in order to find some link between Louise and Baz.

When he arrived in Northwood he headed for Green Lane and the centre of the suburb. In a previous visit as part of his investigation he had spoken to a couple of Louise's old school friends and they had mentioned a pub called the White Hart but when he had visited the pub no-one had heard of anyone called Baz. This time he was just looking for a 1980s drug dealer and he again started with the pub. He ordered a pint and settled down to watch the clientele.

It was over an hour before someone walked in that Colin considered worth approaching. The description Tommy had given him of Baz was his main focus and Colin believed he was looking for someone who was probably in their late 60s now, with an old 'rocker' type image and an evil stare. The man who walked in fitted that description in part. He was the correct age, he was the correct demographic and he looked like an older version of what Tommy had described, albeit he was much taller and slimmer and his stare seemed pretty normal. It was a start.

Colin watched for a while and then walked over to the bar and ordered another pint. Now he was only a few meters await from his target and he listened in to the conversation the man had struck up with a couple of other younger men at the bar. They were discussing football and then later they started on politics. Nothing to helped Colin's cause until the old man lowered his voice and laid his hand on the bar. Immediately one of the younger men laid his hand alongside the old mans and although Colin's view was partially blocked he was sure that drugs and money had been exchanged. What Colin didn't know was who had sold and who had purchased but he decided that he had to question the old man.

About 20 minutes later the old man finished his pint and left the pub. Colin followed. In the pub car park the man headed for a smart looking silver BMW at the back and as he climbed into the drivers seat Colin pounced. He moved quickly and trapped the man's right leg in the car door. He rose to his maximum height of 5' 10" and put on his most menacing face. The old man didn't respond. He looked completely drained and just sat there looking up at the stranger who was attacking him.

"What do you want?" He asked wearily.

"I just need ten minutes of your time." Colin replied.

"You a cop?"

"No."

"Ok, let my leg go and I'll get out."

"No. I'll come round and get in. Don't try anything."

With that Colin let the car door go, walked around and got in the passenger side, all the time watching the old man.

"I need to find a drug dealer who was active in this area around 1990. What can you tell me?"

"What? Are you joking? I can't remember who I spoke to last week, let alone 15 bloody years ago. You've got the wrong man mate, I know nothing about drug dealers." The old man laughed and looked Colin in the eye. "If you're not a cop what are you?"

Colin decided to chance his arm and he guessed that the man sitting next to him was no dealer so that made him a buyer.

"So if I was to search you I wouldn't find any drugs then, right."

"Look, I'm in no mood to get into a fight with someone probably 20 years younger than me, so let's just get to the point. I'm too old for this stuff. Yes I've got some drugs but they're just for personal use. You're not interested in that." Who exactly are you looking for?"

Although Colin was pleased to look younger than he was he had no time to dwell on it. He described who he was looking for based on Tommy's recollection without mentioning a name.

"Yea, I remember him. Used to be a bit of a lad in the 70s and 80s but I've not seen or heard of him in a long time. I bought some drugs from his gang a few times in the early 80s but I believe he moved into much higher level criminality and gained quite a reputation for violence. Had a fantastic old BSA Gold Flash and used to drive passed my office at about 100 miles an hour, you could get away with that in those days."

"Very interesting but I'm interested in a name." Colin stressed urgently. The longer he sat here in the pub car park, the more likely he was to be viewed as suspicious.

"A name, well everyone knew him as Spider due to his tattoos but I think his name was Mark or Pete Newtown. There were two brothers and I think the one you are looking for was the elder of the two. Probably Pete but I can't be sure."

Colin, thanked the man, got out of the car and left. On his way home he tried to call Rachel but there was no answer so he called Maddie to tell her the good news. In fact he had very little good news, just a name but he liked talking to Maddie anyway, so any excuse.

Colin had to plan how he was going to approach Mr Newtown and after finding lots of information on line about the drug dealer/criminal boss/violent maniac and confirming that it was indeed Peter who was of interest to him, he decided that a direct approach would not be his best bet.

He knew, based on past experience that he would not get any help from the police as his previous requests for data had been either lost or ignored, not that he really wanted any. All he really wanted to know was if Mr Peter Newtown (Baz) knew where Louise was but he could not ask that without bringing up their past and that could cause problems. What he needed was a bit of private surveillance and after a lot of research and planning. He was ready for some action.

Colin's plan was simple. He had found out that Baz was still alive, aged 71, married and living in Bournemouth. He, together with one of his old Navy friends, would watch the house for a few of days and if all was clear they would just walk up and knock on the front door, preferably while the wife was out.

He called Jack.

Jack was one of the very few people Colin could describe as a friend and although they hadn't seen a great deal of each other in recent years, they had met a few times at concerts or for a drink and a catch up. When in the Navy, Colin and Jack had formed a friendship based on their mutual like of rock music and Colin liked Jack's eagerness and willingness to listen to different bands. He also like the way Jack deliberately avoided anything that would tie him down. He was a free spirit and spent much of his time surfing or walking long distances, discovering new footpaths and new adventures. After leaving the Navy, Jack had bought a flat in Brighton and an old camper van. He had never had a 'proper' job and instead made a little money working ad hoc on various 'projects' to support his lifestyle which actually didn't require much.

When Colin called, Jack was immediately ready for action and was excited for his next adventure. For Jack everything was an adventure.

They arrived in Bournemouth in late October and set up down the street from Baz's house. They had arrived in Jack's camper van as they had deemed it more comfortable for a long stay but when they arrived they realised that an old camper van would look out of place on such an up market road. So after a couple of hours and some dirty looks from the neighbours, they parked the van in a carpark in town and

Colin hired a white Ford transit van. They would park the van in the street and take it in turns to walk back to the Camper van for some sleep.

After three days it became obvious that Baz and his wife were alone in the house most of the time. They had spotted both of them leaving the house at various times and although the long hair had gone, Colin was sure that the occupant was their man. Each morning about 10am the wife had left the house and returned some two or three hours later. That, they decided was to be their window of opportunity. So, on the forth day they knocked on the front door ten minutes after the wife had left.

Once the door was opened, Jack stuck his boot inside and Colin forced his way in. Between the two of them they quickly overpowered the now old Baz and although he put up something of a fight it didn't last long before he collapsed in a fit of coughing. They moved him to the kitchen table and sat him down, sitting either side of him.

"Do you know who I am? You two are dead men walking, believe me."

"Now, don't be like that Baz. We just want some information." Colin watched Baz's eyes as he used the name and saw a slight reaction that Baz tried to hide.

"You've got the wrong man, my name is Peter. Now fuck off out of here."

"Oh, we know who you are and we know what help you gave Louise Whitwell all those years ago. Now we need to hear it from you." Colin said quietly. Why did everyone always say "you've got the wrong man" when it was obvious that they knew what they were doing, he wondered.

"I saw your reaction when I called you Baz. What was it a pet name? You knew immediately what this was going to be about."

"Are you two police? You don't look like police but I ain't tellin' you nuffin'."

Colin laughed, another standard response to anyone asking questions or could they smell that he used to be police, he knew better. Small criminal mind syndrome.

"Well, if you're not going to tell us anything we'll be on our way. Sorry to have bothered you Mr Newtown." Colin rose and gestured to Jack to do the same.

Baz looked confused and stuttered, "Ok, I'll tell you what you need to know. Remember it was a long time ago now and I've moved on with my life."

For the next two hours Baz was happy to boast about his past. The nickname Baz had come about simply because he had once told Louise that he played the bass guitar and she had pronounced it Baz Guitar. He told them about the help he gave Louise in 1990 but to Colin's surprise he then went on to tell them about the help he provided later that year and into the next year. Colin was recording what was being said and was glad of that when all the details about the change of name, finances etc were divulged. Having made a fortune out of the young girl Baz had pretty much retired and then when he met his now wife had moved to the south coast.

Colin was aware of the fact that the wife would be back soon and when he felt he had all the information he could from Baz he signalled to Jack to go out and move the van to the next road as they had planned. With Jack gone Colin leaned over Baz and sarcastically congratulated him on his loyalty.

Now it was Baz's turn to laugh. "Loyalty, bollocks."

Colin left the house and trotted down the road and round the corner into the next street where Jack was waiting in the van. Happy that he was not followed he jumped in the van and they headed back to the hire company.

An hour later they were on their way back to Jack's house, where Colin would pick up his car and head home.

It was dark when Colin finally opened his front door and he was knackered but he was also buzzing from the thought that they were zoning in on Louise Whitwell. He now had her new name and felt that they were approaching the end of the investigation. Although having said that he had felt the same before.

Over the next couple of weeks Colin and Rachel worked together, although separately, on finding everything they could about Louise Whitwell under her new name of Luccombe. Rachel had much less time to dedicate to investigations but she was quick and reviewed everything Colin found. By early November, just over 15 years after John's death, Rachel and Colin were sat in the same pub that they had sat in nine months earlier.

Rachel was excited because she had new news for Colin. Just an hour before the meeting she had traced Louise to a job in Swansea. She told Colin even before he had taken a sip of his pint and then she read his face and realised that he too had found out this information. They sat together for a couple of hours and discussing their findings and planning what to do next. They had spoken often over the last couple of weeks and compared their investigations. Obviously they were working along the same lines and just before he had left home he found Louise's new name on an employment list for a company in Swansea. Unfortunately Colin had realised that the list was a couple of years out of date and that she had not appeared on last years list, but they had narrowed the search to the Swansea area.

Neither of them had found anything on record since they started looking at the start of the year and Colin said that he would call the Swansea company the next day to see when Louise had left them. He also planned to travel to Swansea as he believed there was nothing like being in situ. If she was still there he would find her, he promised.

Having made that decision Colin told Rachel about his friend Charles who had died at the start of the year and the friendship that had now developed with his sister. Rachel knew nothing about Colin's private life and had never asked. They had become quite friendly since they started communicating on the investigation but Rachel saw it more as a business partnership and was surprised by Colin's openness. She was not sure how to respond other than to say that she was happy for him and hoped that the relationship developed as he wished. Colin suggested that he was developing feelings for Maddie but was confused by this and wasn't sure what to do.

"Colin, I don't really know you well enough to have a say and as I'm only 20 I think you have far more experience in these things than me, I certainly don't feel that I can give any advice."

"I'm sorry, Rachel, I don't really have anyone I can talk to about this and I just needed to say it out loud. I'm embarrassed now. Please pretend I never said anything."

"Don't be embarrassed. It's lovely that you have found someone you like. I just haven't really experienced that yet so I am not sure how to respond. Call Richard, he fell head over heels in love with Hannah within weeks of meeting her. He might help. Or speak to Dad if you feel more comfortable to do that." Rachel said, now embarrassed that she had made Colin feel embarrassed.

"I really don't want to talk to anyone but I am out of my previous comfort zone if you know what I mean. I have never had these feelings for a woman before."

Rachel had no idea what Colin meant until she realised that he had stressed the word 'woman' and then she did. She was even more lost for words now. Eventually she gained her composure and looked Colin in the eye.

"I am happy to listen to your concerns if you have no one else to talk to. Whether I can offer any insights or guidance is another matter. I believe that deep down in your heart you will know if you love someone, certainly I have never had that feeling myself."

When Colin left the pub an hour or so after Rachel had left he felt much better and on his way back to the station he called Maddie and told her how he felt. He was nearly in tears when she said that she too had feelings for him but because she knew he was gay she was conflicted. They arranged to meet up the week after and talk everything through.

Any trips to Swansea would have to wait. Rachel understood that and promised Colin that she was happy to delay things while he sorted out his private life.

A month later, Rachel was planning to return home for the Christmas holidays. She had spoken to Colin and suggested that she would asked Mum and Dad if they would invite Colin and Maddie for Christmas Day. Colin had spoken to Maddie about it and they had agreed that if the offer arrived they would go but that they understood that Grant and Fiona might have other plans.

Nothing had been planned. An invitation for a two day stay was sent and accepted.

Christmas Day 2005 would be another turning point in Colin's life and he planned to announce that there was an even bigger event to be planned for 2006.

After Colin's call, Maddie made herself a cup of tea and sat down at the kitchen table. She had not thought about a relationship since her husband had died and was quite happy on her own although there were times when she felt lonely. Looking after Charlie had kept her busy and after he was gone she had quickly struck up a friendship with Colin. Now she had found out that Colin had developed feeling for her. She laughed that the term 'had feelings'. In her younger days she would have said she fancied him but at their age that sounded strange. There had been a couple of times when she thought Colin was going to kiss her but he backed off each time. Obviously he was confused about his sexuality and she too wondered where a relationship would lead.

When Colin knocked on her door at 8am on the Saturday following that call she was still in her nighty. He had called the night before to say he was coming up but she had assumed it would be mid morning before he arrived and she was surprised when she opened the door to find Colin clutching a huge bunch of flowers. When she took the flowers and laid them on the draining board Colin took hold of her shoulders, looked into her eyes and kissed her. It was a kiss to remember but the most astonishing thing to her was that she could feel Colin's excitement through her nighty.

Colin realised that his reaction had been detected and took a step back ready to apologise but Maddie held on tight and kissed him again. They spent the weekend and beyond together and by Wednesday morning, when Colin had to leave, they had decided that Maddie would come to London the following Sunday and stay with Colin. The length of the stay was undetermined and as Colin walked down the garden path to his car, Maddie was already missing him.

By Christmas Day as they made their way to Oxford, Maddie calculated that they had spent 35 of the last 40 days and nights together. They had decided that they would spend the rest of their lives together and that as soon as Colin had completed the investigation into John's death they would both sell their respective houses and buy somewhere together. Agreement had not yet been reached on where that would be.

Seven people sat down to Christmas dinner and Colin was a little overwhelmed by the happiness and love in the room. Grant was in charge of drinks and since their arrival a couple of hours earlier had topped up their glasses on numerous occasions. Colin had seen little of Fiona as she was working her magic in the kitchen with the help of Rachel and he had sat with his drink marvelling at the obvious love between Richard and Hannah, which he decided matched that of his and Maddie's.

The dining room table had been extended, not because they couldn't get seven people around it in it's non-extended state but because they couldn't get all the food on it. Colin had never seen such feast and it was over four hours later before they finished.

Colin and Maddie had tried to insist that they should do the washing up but Fiona would have none of it. Grant pointed out that they had two dishwashers, one in the kitchen and another in the large utility room and that he and

Richard were expert 'stackers'. They cleared the table, filled the dishwashers and were back to join the others, now relaxing in the living room, within 45 minutes.

Rachel had left the house to visit a couple of old school friends, promising to be back by the time Grant and Richard had finished but she had not returned yet. Grant got out a bottle of brandy and after everyone had protested about the amount of alcohol they had been drinking and tried to say no, they all sat back with a glass in their hands. Grant was very persuasive. The talk turned to Richard and Hannah's final year at Manchester University and their plans to get married after they graduated the following summer. Then Grant put his arm around Fiona's shoulder, wink at her and turned the subject to what Colin had planned for 2006.

Colin had seen the wink and knew that he was being set up to divulge more about his relationship with Maddie. He didn't know that at the dinner table Maddie had whispered into Grant's ear to suggest that Colin may want to announce something special. After Colin had taken a few deep breaths he looked around the room at the other five faces. Grant and Fiona had been married for over 20 years and were obviously very much in love. Richard and Hannah were besotted with each other and planned to marry the following year. Maddie was glowing from both the level of alcohol she had consumed and the love in her eyes.

"I think that it is fair to say that this is one of the happiest moments in my life." Colin started. "Happy because the people in this room have all become good friends and happy because each one of us is filled with love. Maddie and I plan to buy a house and move in together next year or the year after. We have even discussed getting married. I never thought I would be saying that but life is full of surprises. I suggest we all raise our glasses and drink a toast to love and happiness and to thank whoever we believe in for the lucky position we all find ourselves in."

"To love and happiness." They all repeated as they sipped their brandies.

"Didn't you wait for me, I only caught the end of that speech and I haven't got a glass." Said a smiling Rachel as she walked into the room. Grant quickly gave her a glass and poured in some brandy. "I also have something to toast with you all. I have been struggling to keep it to myself this last week but before I left Cambridge on Thursday I was told that I was in the England athletics team for the Indoor Internationals being held in Stockholm in January."

"Well 2006 looks like it will be a pretty exciting time for all of us." Announced Grant.

CHAPTER 37 - LOUISE, 2003 - 2006

Louise got out of the taxi and walked the last mile to her house. A precaution that she had become accustomed to taking. She put the house keys through the letter box, having already given a set to the Estate Agent, got in her car and drove to England. During the previous week she had made sure the house was in a position to be left at a moments notice. While Cliff had laid bleeding on the outbuilding floor she had calmly washed up and tidied the kitchen. After moving Cliff into his car she had hosed the outbuilding floor. She was not too worried about the stone floor itself but knew that a blood stained floor might put some buyers off.

"England here I come". She screamed above the radio as she headed towards the Severn Bridge.

Six months later as she sat in her new cottage, with a new car on the driveway, she was cursing her stupidity. It was not her first time at disappearing and arranging her finances to disappear too but whereas the first time she had had help, this time she had not only done it alone but also in a hurry. Adapting to a new name, easy. Disappearing from her old life, easy. Moving her savings again and again as she had been shown before, easy. But selling a house under one name and arranging for the proceeds to be transferred to another name without leaving a trail, beyond her skill set.

She had thought about hiring someone to help her but she was terrified about leaving any trail that would lead anyone to her. She did not know if Cliff was dead or alive but if he had survived he might want revenge. No, no trail could be left.

The Swansea Estate Agent had told her that he needed a contact number for her and an email address but she had declined. She only called him from a public call box and when he had told her that they had a buyer for her cottage she began to think of the problems that would follow. She decided that she couldn't get the money and so she just stopped calling him.

Disappear. Just leave everything behind. She had lost a substantial sum of money but just had to put it down to her own lack of forethought. It wasn't as if she didn't have more than enough in her savings to live a very comfortable life but she still berated herself.

Not everything had been completely disappointing though. During her first couple of months she had worked hard to find Remi. In her mind he was the one person who had information about her latest incarnation and he had to be dealt with. She was relieved to find out that he had moved to Australia in 1997 and had died five years later.

On the night she finally accepted that she had lost the value of the Swansea cottage for good, Louise Culver (nee Whitwell, nee Luccombe) went out for a drink. She had lived a very quiet existence during the first few months she had been in Buntingford. When she had first arrived in Hertfordshire from Wales she had rented a small flat until she found the secluded property she was after. She had deliberately suppressed her desire to go out and her fear of being noticed by anyone had overridden her need for excitement. She knew, following the thrill she got on her final day in Wales that excitement for her meant violence. She also knew that she didn't have a 'dark side' anymore, she was dark on every side.

That first night out in Buntingford was a disappointment. The village was so quiet and boring that she had drunk alone for most of it, only getting noticed and chatting to a couple of lads about an hour before closing. She had goaded them a little hoping to provoke a reaction but they were pretty sober compared to her and they disappeared while she was in the Ladies. When she returned and realised that they had gone she stumbled to the bar, ordered another vodka and sat alone again. She thought about the effects she had always had on men and how easy it had been to get her own way. She thought about the fact that she was now over 30 and that perhaps her looks were fading. Then the hard truth hit her. She was still physically beautiful, she knew that really, but she was no longer beautiful on the inside, perhaps she never had been.

Over the next couple of years Louise wallowed in self doubt and only really enjoyed herself when she managed to convince someone to react to her provocations. She had taken to driving to a few of the larger towns in the area and in the pubs and night clubs she found what she was looking for. Saturday nights in particular had become her nights where the self doubt would disappear for a few hours after she had downed a few drinks and she could be herself. She drank, danced and let herself go. Occasionally she would go back to the hotel room she had booked alone but that usually meant that she had succeeded in antagonising someone enough to cause a fight. More often than not she would take a man back to the room with her. Even her sexual desires had become violent and when she returned home on a Sunday she was likely to be covered in bruises and knowing that whoever she had been with would be in a worse condition.

Louise was perfectly aware that her behaviour since 'the Cliff incident' was on a downward trajectory and that before long she would encounter someone who would seriously hurt her. She maintained an alertness and carefulness with everything she did, apart from when she went out drinking.

She had not bothered to get a job and was eating into her savings.

One day the postman put a pile of junk mail through her letter box and out of boredom she read each leaflet. One leaflet stood out from the others. It was a leaflet about loneliness and how to overcome it.

"Everyone, at sometime in their life is affected by loneliness and having friends or family that you can rely on is very important. If you find yourself alone there are a number of things and people that can help." Said the leaflet. It then provided a list of such things and places. Louise read the list and realised that the leaflet was very much aimed at the elderly although so much of what it said applied to her. Here she was in her mid thirties being told by a leaflet that she was similar to many people over twice her age.

Louise slid off the sofa onto the floor and cried.

The next day as she sat writing in her diary about her sadness, loneliness and upset, she determined that she would go to visit her Aunt Elizabeth. She had no idea if her aunt was still alive or if she was still living in her Oxford home but she needed to get out of the house and this was a good reason to do so.

She had never been particularly close to her aunt but she was the only family she had and Louise remembered something about her being very helpful after her parents had died although she couldn't remember the details. A drive to Oxford would do her good even if it was only to find out that her aunt was no longer there.

The journey would take a couple of hours each way so Louise had her breakfast and headed out.

When she arrived and got out of the car she could tell immediately that Aunt Elizabeth was still there. She remembered the old wooden bench that she could see over the garden fence and the games she used to play being chased round and round the garden by her aunt. She recognised the pair of old green wellington boots beside the back door. Had her aunt really had those for over 20 years?

Quite unexpectedly she became nervous and wasn't sure whether she should knock on the door or get back in her car and drive away. Had she not driven for two hours without a toilet break and in need for one now she might have taken the latter option but she walked up the short path and knocked on the door. After a long delay an old woman answered the door. It took Louise a few seconds to recognise her aunt and then she flung her arms around her and started to cry.

"That's enough dear, you're suffocating me, whatever has come over you. Come on in I've just made a pot of tea."

Louise was confused by the response to her knocking on the door after 17 long years and followed her aunt into the house.

"Can I use your toilet before we have tea, please." She asked politely.

"Of course you can, you know where it is, you don't need to ask and make sure you wash your hands well, I've got some fruit cake on the table."

Strange. It's as if I had visited only last week, she thought.

When she came out of the toilet and entered the kitchen Aunt Elizabeth was already sat at the table pouring the tea.

"I lose track of the days of the week sometimes but this morning I knew it was Thursday and was looking forward to your visit. How are you?"

"Erm, I'm fine." replied Louise, still completely confused. "How are you?"

"Oh dear, I am very well considering. I did manage to lose my glasses this morning and I found them in the fridge alongside the butter. What am I like. Will Micheal be picking you up later? I think we should make sure we don't eat all the cake or he won't be happy. You can eat as much as you like now that you're eating for two though can't you?"

Wow this is getting really weird now, though Louise. Is she referring to my Dad or another Micheal? She seems very confused. "Aunty, I'm Louise, I haven't seen you for about 17 years. Are you getting me mixed up with someone else?"

There was a long pause and Elizabeth closed her eyes. Louise thought for a minute that perhaps her aunt had fallen asleep but then she opened her eyes again and looked blankly at the table.

"Geraldine, will you pass the butter please. Can't have a piece of fruit cake without some butter. Now, what time did you say Micheal will be here?"

Louise rose from the table, looked around and decided that her trip had been a waste, obviously her aunt had some form of dementia and didn't know who she was. She was about to leave when a car pulled up in the driveway behind her car. Watching from the kitchen window she could see an old man get out and head towards the front door.

"Shit." She mumbled under her breath. Thinking quickly she decided that she had to open the door and pretend everything was normal so that she could make her escape as soon as possible without a fuss.

As she opened the door to the man walking down the garden path she saw who it was and froze.

"Louise, is that you Louise?" Asked Dr Brook. "My how you've changed but I would recognise you anywhere."

"Dr Brook, how nice to see you." Louise replied with a smile. "We were just having tea and cake, you will join us won't you? I have to be on my way in about 10 minutes but not before we've had a cup of tea together. What are you doing in Oxford?"

Dr Brook was stunned. He never thought he would ever see Louise again and he thought back to the man who had been asking questions about her a few years ago. He sat down at the table and explained to Louise about his wife dying and his move to Oxford. Louise sympathised about his wife and then asked about the trip he and his wife had been on. She was full of questions and didn't give Dr Brook time to ask any questions of his own until suddenly she stood up and insisted that she had to go and asked if Dr Brook would mind moving his car. She kissed her aunt on the cheek gathered up her coat and headed for the door.

"Louise, I have so many questions. The last time I saw you was at your parents funeral. No one seems to have heard from you since then. How are you? Where have you been? What …?"

"Dr Brook," Louise interrupted, "I will be back next week but I really have to go now, I'm later already for my appointment." She lied.

Dr Brook reversed his car out of the drive and within a minute Louise was on her way. He sat for a while watching her drive down the road and then turned back into the drive and made his was back to the house.

It was not until Colin and Maddie got back to Colin's house the day after Boxing Day that they could even begin to make any plans. The day before, Colin and Rachel discussed where they were with the investigation and decided that a five or six week break would do it no harm. Both of them had other things on their mind.

Maddie also had things on her mind. A whirlwind romance was fine and she had certainly been swept up in it but now the reality was setting in and the practicalities needed to be taken care of. Her house in Sheffield was full of her belongings and was a warm and welcoming place whereas Colin's house in North London was bland and sterile. She would have to move more that just her clothes south until they finalised their living arrangements.

They had made the decision that they should only sell one of their houses at a time and Maddie, knowing that Colin didn't want to live in Sheffield, had volunteered to sell hers and move in with Colin on a temporary basis. They would then sell Colin's house and buy somewhere together, they knew not where just yet. With the money left to them both by Charles, their savings and the value of two houses they were reasonably well off and were sure that they would find their perfect house.

The first six weeks back after Christmas were pretty hectic and Colin had driven up and down the M1 on five occasions, picking up Maddie's belongings and taking Maddie to meetings with her Estate Agent, Solicitors and Bank. Maddie could drive and owned a very nice little Citron C1 but she didn't like driving long distances or driving inside the M25, so Colin had been given that role. Her car was another issue and she had decided to sell it.

Colin was aware that moving in together was a big step and for him it was something new. He had shared a house with Charles but that was a long time ago and this relationship was very different. He found it strange and scary but he was also under no illusion that it was any easier for Maddie. She was making all the early sacrifices and he appreciated her willingness to 'up sticks' and move back to London.

By mid February, Maddie had set the sale of her house in motion, collected what she needed from Sheffield, arranged storage for everything else and sold her car. She had also transformed Colin's house and turned it into a home. Colin was impressed. Apart from the driving, he seemed to have done very little and was under the impression that he was lagging behind in the sharing stakes. He tried to remedy that with some advice for Maddie as to what she could do with her money from her house sale while they were deciding where and when they would finally move.

With this in mind Colin felt a little awkward when he had to raise the fact that he needed to spend a few days in Swansea. Maddie knew this was coming and she was happy to see him get back to his investigation.

"Don't worry, I have plenty to be getting on with around the house. You won't recognise the place when I have finished with it." She laughed.

"I hardly recognise it now." He replied with a smile.

Swansea was not what Colin had expected. It was a bustling city with a lovely centre, although like most big cities it had its darker, more sinister areas. Colin started with the company where he knew that Louise had worked. He had spoken to them a couple of times over the phone and they were reluctant to give him any information about their former employee other than to confirm that she had indeed worked there. He hoped that they would be more open face to face. He was wrong although they did tell him that Louise had handed in her notice over the phone and never returned. In fact her last months pay check had been returned as the bank account had been closed.

Colin asked about the department where Louise worked and who she was friendly with. Eventually, after a complete charm offensive on the young receptionist, he got a name. Louise had been friends with someone called Pauline and Pauline had been called and was on her way down to reception.

It was after lunchtime and Colin was trying to think where it would be best to have a chat with Pauline but he didn't know the area at all. When Pauline arrived he asked her whether they could meet up after work for a chat about Louise and if she knew of a good place to talk.

"I am out after work but if you want to come through to the canteen we can have 30 minutes or so now." Pauline said with a smile and when Colin nodded she led him through a door and down some steps to a large room that looked more like an M&S cafe than any staff canteen he had ever been in.

"Why are you interested in Louise, is she in trouble? There is not much I can really tell you about Louise leaving other than it took us all by complete surprise. She took some time off work to deal with some personal problems and then called me to say she was leaving. I didn't even get a chance to ask why or to say goodbye." Pauline started before Colin had a chance to ask any questions.

"Has she been in touch since?"

"Nope. Not once in four years and I thought we were good friends. I think she left because of Cliff but I've not seen him about for years either." Pauline answered.

"Cliff? Do you think they left together? Was there an issue between them?" Colin was having trouble keeping up with the speed of Pauline's speech. He was not used to her strong accent. He got out his note book and asked if she wouldn't mind slowing down a little so he could make notes.

"They definitely didn't leave together. Cliff was married and rumours in the gym were that he got into a terrible fight and spent many months in hospital. By the time he got out his wife and kids were gone.

"Which gym? Do you know where he is now? Do you know where his wife went? Colin asked still scribbling into his note book.

"Oh it's my gym. He used to go there and that's where he met Louise. No idea where either him or his wife are now. I think she used to work in a cafe at the end of the High Street though." Pauline was still talking faster that Colin could write and he was still struggling to understand.

"Sorry, what was the name of the gym again? I didn't catch it the first time."

"Thats 'cos I didn't tell you." Pauline laughed. "It's the TrueFitness gym in St Helen's road. You can't miss it, its got a big B&Q next door. You didn't say why you're asking these questions. Is Louise OK? She's not in trouble is she? As well as we got on I always thought there was something very secretive about her. She would often turn up at work on a Monday with bruises on her arms and once even on her face but always blamed it on something in the gym or a fall while she was out running. I never believed her."

Colin again had to ask Pauline to slow down while he caught up with his notes. "St Helens road you said? Do you think she was in a bad relationship? Could Cliff have been mistreating her?"

"Oh the bruises started long before she met Cliff but yes for sure he was mistreating her. He was married remember."

"Where did Louise live? Did she live alone?" Colin looked up and asked after a couple of minutes of completing his notes.

"Yes, she lived on her own in a cottage out towards Gowerton I think. I never went there but pretty sure that's where she lived."

"Well you've been very helpful Pauline, thank you." Colin started to rise from his seat.

"I can tell you loads more about the nights we had out in town. Louise was a great dancer and boy could she drink." Pauline was obviously not in a hurry to get back to work and Colin was far too polite to leave just yet. He ordered a couple of coffees and they sat talking for another 30 minutes before Pauline finally decided the she should be getting back to her desk. Colin thanked her again and headed out.

Once sat in his car he looked though his notes. No direct information on Louise's whereabouts but some extra lines of enquiry. He underlined Cliff, his wife and the gym. He also decided to check in with a couple of Estate Agents to ask about the cottage although first he would need to find the address. So, he thought, next stop the gym.

Pauline was right, the gym was easy to find and as he parked up he decided that he would check up on both Louise and Cliff's memberships. He would at least aim to get addresses from their files and he fished into his pocket for an old police badge that he had kept when he left the force. He hoped he wouldn't need it but decided it might help if they were reluctant to help. As it was, once he finally got to speak to the manager he was told that as both memberships had expired a long time ago he could have the information he was after.

While the manager checked the records, Colin watched through the glass partition at the people working out. He had spent a big part of his life in the navy and had prided himself on his fitness. Now he was getting a little soft around the edges and with regret he realised that he would never be at peak fitness again, he no longer had the will and determination.

"Here we go." The manager gave Colin both the addresses. "Funnily enough they both left in slightly strange circumstances. The young lady just stopped paying and cancelled her bank account. It looks like we tried to trace her but without luck. The man cancelled his membership about the same time and put in a claim to have his last couple of payment deductions returned due to an accident that meant he couldn't train. This is before my time but I do remember being told about this man. He was so badly hurt that the previous manager felt sorry for him and made the refunds without question. Colin thanked the man and left with the addresses tucked into his pocket.

Cliff's address, no luck. New owners who had only moved in recently and had bought the house from an elderly couple. At least two owners since Cliff and his wife had lived there, so it appeared to be a dead end.

226

The Cafe in the High Street, no luck. Amy had handed her notice in and moved away years ago and no one had any forwarding address.

Louise's address. Cottage empty with Estate Agents sign up.

Estate Agent., some interesting information. Colin had called from mobile while sat in his car, parked outside the cottage and was told that the cottage had only recently gone on the market but that the employee who had been involved in the sale of the house over the last four years still worked for them. He was on holiday today but would be back tomorrow. The lady Colin spoke to informed him that there was some strange information regarding the sale. Colin said he would come by tomorrow.

Finally, before finding a hotel for the night, Colin text Rachel and asked her to do some internet research on Cliff Wellow and Amy Wellow. In particular he was interested in their current whereabouts. He then headed back into the centre to look for a hotel.

The following morning he woke to find an email from Rachel. She had found no record of Cliff in the last three years. Prior to that he had kept a Facebook account but it held no useful information. Since then nothing. On Amy, she had found a current Facebook page and it was full of details about a new relationship she was in. Although there were no address details, Rachel had examined the recent posts and pictures and deducted that Amy was still in the Swansea area. She was now going under the name of Amy Davies which Rachel assumed was her maiden name.

After a good breakfast Colin called the Estate Agent and arranged to meet a Mr Paul Cowell at 10am outside the cottage that had once belonged to Louise.

As he pulled up outside the cottage a tall, skinny man got out of the car parked in front of him and smiled a typical Estate Agent smile. He greeted Colin as they walked up to the front door. After a brief tour of the cottage they sat at the kitchen table and Colin asked about the sale four years earlier.

"Well, it's been a nightmare to be honest. I had a buyer all lined up but then the owner just disappeared. After a couple of telephone calls she just stopped calling. I tried all sorts of things to trace her but with no luck. Eventually I had to pass everything over to our legal team as we couldn't progress with the sale without the owner. We have only recently been given the go ahead to sell it now. I'm still not sure where the proceeds of the sale will go. The owner was only a young woman but she just vanished off the face of the earth."

A fascinating story for sure, thought Colin but it was not particularly useful to him. Yet another dead end. Could Louise really afford to just give up the value of her cottage? Was she so desperate to stay hidden? This investigation was not just a case of tracking down a killer but of tracking down someone who was going to extraordinary lengths not to be found.

Colin decided to return to Cliff's old address and speak to a few of the neighbours. Someone might know where either Cliff or his wife were living now. He wanted to get back to Maddie, he was surprised by the feelings he had for her and the pull on him when he was not with her. He decided that he would give himself until 4pm to find out all he could before he headed back to London.

One neighbour was very helpful and was still in contact with Amy but she refused to pass on her contact details, instead taking Colin's number and promising to ask Amy to contact him. Colin stressed the fact that he was only in Wales until 4pm.

He had to wait until 3:45 before he got a call. It was Amy and she wanted to know why he wanted to talk to her. He explained as much as he could to her without giving too many details, he didn't want to scare her off. Eventually she agreed to meet up with him and gave him directions to a cafe in Birchgrove and said she would be there until five.

At least it's on my way home he thought and agreed that he would be there as soon as he could.

The meeting with Amy was very interesting and although Colin was loathe to believe everything she told him, he was building up quite a picture of Louise.

"She was a two faced bitch but I can understand that after how Cliff lied to her. What she did to him was completely unhinged though. And what she did to us as a family is unforgivable. The kids haven't seen their father for over three years. He's gone from being a reasonably good father and husband to being a junkie who cares about nothing except his next bag of drugs." Amy explained. "He was in hospital for months after what she did to him and he lost his mind. The painkillers took over his life and when he left hospital he had to find alternatives as the ones he was given were not strong enough. I knew he cheated on me but he always came back to me and the boys. Now he's gone forever. If he doesn't die of the drugs he'll surely not survive long with his injuries. It's a wonder that the hospital were able to save him at all. They said he was so close to death when they found him in the car park that they didn't think he'd make it."

"I'm sorry to hear that, it must have been a terrible few years for you." Said Colin. "What do you actually know about Louise?"

"Only what Cliff told me and I'm not sure I believe a word that comes out of his mouth. I met her once, just before she attacked Cliff. She had the nerve to come into the cafe where I worked and start a conversation. Of course I didn't know it was her at the time but Cliff told me later. He said she was completely delusional and had fallen madly in love with him even before they.. you know..started the affair."

That's not how Pauline had described it Colin thought.

On his way home up the M4 Colin had plenty of time to think about what he had found out in Swansea but he was still no closer to finding Louise.

How many bloody dead ends can we hit, he thought as he reached the M25.

During 2006, Colin was mostly focused on Maddie. He still held his regular update calls with Rachel but again things had stalled and if it hadn't been for Rachel, Colin believed he would have given up completely to concentrate on his own life. He and Maddie had decided against the need to marry and were now living in the small town of Berkhamsted. It was the first time Colin had lived outside the M25 other than while he was in the Navy and it had been his compromise when Maddie said that she was happy to move south but not to London. Maddie had started working in a local charity shop and Colin had found that he was happy pottering around their large garden and wandering up the road to the local at lunchtime for a pint or two. He still regularly reviewed his Crime Board and updated it with any new information that Rachel provided but it was mostly historical stuff rather than information that would point to Louise's whereabouts.

The year was drawing to a close when out of the blue Colin received a call from Richard.

I started 2006 being very pleased for Rachel. She had got off to a flying start representing her country in the 1500 meters in Stockholm and coming third. A bronze medal in her first International. She was delighted and decided that she would spend more time focusing on her running. She was going to be a very busy girl. Her degree course still had over a year to run due to the change of courses after the first year. That meant that I would leave academia a year before her. It didn't bother her too much but there had always been a sibling rivalry between us and I am sure that a small part of her wished she had found the right course for her, first time.

She also had the investigation to consider and she had found a way to combine this with her studies. She told me that as part of her course work she would prepare a detailed study of the mind of a killer and she would base it on everything she knew about Louise. Her main sources of input would come from both Tommy and Amy and she planned to interview both of them in detail to get a better understanding of Louise's mind. Colin's notes would be her starting point but they had focused on where she was rather than who she was.

I spent most of the first half of 2006 studying along side Hannah as well as helping Hannah arrange our wedding. I took on more of a supporting role when it came to decisions about the wedding but I like to think I had at least some important input into the more important areas such as what wedding cars we would use and who we should choose as the caterers.

As expected Mum and Dad were all over Hannah and gave her all the support that I perhaps lacked a little in. I really had no view on the colour of the bridesmaids dresses for example whereas Mum and Hannah discussed it for weeks before finally deciding. Hannah's parents lived in South Africa and although they were very helpful in many ways they were not close enough to help the way Mum did.

We would graduate in July and had set the wedding date for the first Saturday in September. Dad had suggested to Hannah that we should get married in the same church that they did, in Oxford and we were happy to agree. I had managed to get an accounting job in Oxford and again with Dads help we had found a small house to rent only about 20 minutes walk from their house. Everything was going to plan and we were on course for a wonderful summer.

To make the year even better, in August, just ten days before the wedding, Hannah informed me that she was pregnant. I was delighted but she was concerned about the fact that she would be pregnant at the wedding ceremony. I must admit I laughed when she told me that.

"Don't worry about that. It is fantastic news. We can keep it to ourselves until after the wedding if you like but I can't wait for us to be married and start a family. So, we've got a little head start on the family front. It's no big deal is it? No one these days refrains from sex until after the wedding do they?"

Hannah smiled and said that she hoped no one would notice what she had under her wedding dress and then we both broke down in laughter.

So, by October my life was very different from what I had ever expected and I was over the moon about it all. Just months out of university and I was married, in a new house, working as a junior accountant and expecting a baby. Who would have expected that?

The job was good and the new house was lovely. Hannah was far too good for me and had decorated throughout. We had already decided on names for the baby, even though there would be another six months before we would meet him or her and we had started some baby shopping. The big turning point for me was when in November we found out that the baby was a boy, I started thinking about what fatherhood meant and I started talking to Rachel again about our father, John and the progress of the investigation.

I hadn't really thought too much about it for nearly two years and now as I imagined having a little baby boy looking up at me I had flash backs to when I was younger. To be honest I was not sure if they were memories or just my imagination but I liked to think perhaps they were a little of both. Neither Rachel nor I could remember much about our life before we arrived at Highcliffe House and so perhaps we made up a history for ourselves based on what we found out later. Certainly the photos that we found in Mary's box and her diary entries evoked some sort of memories.

I had copies of all of both Rachel's and Colin's notes and decided that now was the time to revisit them and get myself up to date with the investigation.

CHAPTER 40 - LOUISE, 2006

A big mistake. Louise was fuming with herself as she drove back to Buntingford. After all these years of staying away she had got in touch with her past. Why? Why? Why? She asked herself.

She had cried for the first 30 miles. Seeing her aunt and then Dr Brooks had bought back floods of memories of her parents. Now she had calmed down a bit and had started worrying about whether Dr Brooks would start looking for her. She was fairly happy that he would not know where to start but just by meeting him she may have woken an interest in him about her life. She made a firm decision there and then that she would never again visit her past. Feeling a little better as she drove up the A10 she decided that she needed a drink. It was only 4pm and the pubs in Buntingford would not be open so instead of heading home she took a left and headed towards Baldock where she knew that there would be places to get a drink.

It wasn't until her third or forth vodka that she realised that she had driven there. She now had a choice to make. Drive home slightly drunk now or leave the car and carry on drinking. The latter seemed more attractive so she ordered another drink and looked around the bar. It was beginning to fill up with people who were obviously just popping in for a quick one on their way home from work. The pub was right opposite the bus station and she watched as a young woman walked in ordered a drink, drank it quickly at the bar and headed back out to catch her bus. Louise wished that she had somewhere to rush to but she had nothing to go home for so she again returned to the bar and ordered another drink.

By 9pm she was very drunk but instead of the alcohol inducing a euphoric feeling as it usually did, she just felt depressed. She decided just to get a taxi and head home. No feeling of excitement or need for violence existed today. She stumbled out of the pub, got into a taxi and by 10pm she was being dropped off just up the road from her house. Even drunk she still had the wherewithal to maintain her caution.

As she staggered up the lane towards her home she was suddenly surprised by a pheasant leaving the hedge in front of her. It was a large male bird and it seemed oblivious of her. She knew not why but the bird enraged her and she kicked out at it. She missed and that infuriated her even more. By the time she reached her front door she was so angry that she kicked over a flower pot and when she slammed the front door behind her she screamed. The screaming continue for some time until eventually she collapsed in exhaustion onto the sofa.

She woke the following morning having slept on the sofa in her clothes. She rarely suffered from hangovers but today she had a doozy and she took a couple of paracetamol with a coffee before heading upstairs for a shower.

Once clean, dressed and fuelled by another coffee and some toast, Louise called a taxi, left the house and walked down to where the taxi would meet her. She felt better today and decided that after collecting her car she would go shopping. A little retail therapy would help her although she knew that she needed more than that to remedy the rut that her life had got into.

I need to get a job, start meeting normal people and turn my life around, she thought as she paid the taxi driver and headed towards the car park where she had left her car. She was in a positive mood until she saw the ticket on the windscreen of her car. She had only purchased a two hour ticket the day before and had left her car overnight. She would need to pay a fine. Oh well, she thought, at least it wasn't clamped or towed away. Yes, she was in a positive state of mind.

Louise's idea of retail therapy was to leave Baldock behind and head for Hitchin. She had been there before and knew that the quirky shops would satisfy her shopping needs. A couple of hours later she walk back towards her car with three large bags of clothes and a smile on her face.

Dr Brook sat at the table with Elizabeth eating cake and drinking tea. He could hear Elizabeth talking but he was not listening to what she was saying. He was thinking about Louise. He had no idea what the poor girl had been though over the last 17 years but he knew from those brief moments that they chatted that she was now a strong and determined woman. He had noticed the signs of ageing around her eyes and the hard set of her mouth at she spoke.

He remembered the man who had visited him a few years earlier and asked about Louise. He had not said why he needed to find her but it was obvious that it was not in Louise's best interest if he did. What should he do now? He wasn't sure.

This issue would dominate his thoughts throughout the next couple of weeks and his mind was in turmoil. Louise had not returned as she said she would and Dr Brooks was worried about her mental state. There was very little he could do. He had tried to memorise the number plate of Louise's car as she drove away but only managed to get the first part. Perhaps that would be enough for an expert he thought and he remembered Sergeant Shorwell and wondered if she may be able to help.

Dr Brooks was approaching his 80th birthday and had long ago lost the energy that he had once possessed. He somehow knew that if he were to try to find and contact Louise that it would take a lot of the energy he had left in him and he wasn't sure that he wanted that. Even if he traced her he didn't hold up much hope that he would be able to help. In the end he decided that he would give Sergeant Shorwell a call and leave it to her to decide whether it was worth pursuing. Of course, actually tracing Sergeant Shorwell would be quite an effort.

On a bright Monday morning in early December Dr Brook rose from his bed with a little more optimism than usual and over breakfast he decided that he would go to the local police station and ask if they would trace Sergeant Shorwell for him. He dressed as he always did in a smart tweed suit and headed into town. The police station was busy when he arrived and after speaking to the lady on the desk he sat and waited. Nearly two hours later a young man, probably no more that 20, Dr Brook thought, came over to him and asked him to follow him into a small interview room.

"So I understand you would like the phone number of a Sergeant Janice Shorwell. I am afraid that I have to tell you that we have no one of that name here. When was the last time you saw her? Was it at this station?" Asked the young man in a slightly condescending and irritating manner.

"Young man. I explained to the lady on the front desk that I have not seen or spoken to Sergeant Shorwell for many many years. I am not even sure she is still in the police force but when I last spoke to her it was in Northwood nearly 20 years ago. I am not asking you for her phone number I merely want to know if she is still a police woman and if so if you could pass on my phone number and ask her to call me."

"OK, so you just want to know if she is still a police woman. I am sure I can find that out for you. Please give me your number and if I trace her I will ask her to call you. If I can't find her I will call you back myself. Is that alright with you?"

Again the tone of his voice irked Dr Brook but he gave the young man his name and telephone number and got up to leave but before he had a chance to leave the room, the lady from the front desk knocked and came in.

"Found her." She said. "She's not a Sergeant anymore. Moved up to Chief Inspector now, her number is …"

"Wait a sec," interrupted the young man, "should we be giving out her number like this to total strangers?"

"Calm down Pete, I'm just going to give her office number, it's on general record anyway. And I am sure Dr Brook here has a genuine reason for contacting her, haven't you sir."

Why is everyone in this police station so condescending? Is what Dr Brook wanted to say but he just smiled and said he and Janice were old friends who had lost contact many years ago. He took the piece of paper with the number on it and left.

Once outside, he looked down at the paper and saw immediately that the number he had been given had a Birmingham code. He would call as soon as he got home.

The initial call was answered by a WPC Quarr who promised him that she would get back to him within an hour. Just 45 minutes later she called to say that CI Shorwell was very busy today but would be able to speak to him between 5pm and 6pm that afternoon. That gave Dr Brook time to visit Elizabeth.

The Dr was not sure that Elizabeth would understand what he was going to tell her, it just depended on the day, but he wanted to talk though his actions and his reasons. In actual fact when he arrived he was pleased to see that she was in good spirits and fully functioning in the current world. He explained his decision to try to trace Louise via CI Shorwell and that he would leave it to the CI to suggest what to do next. Elizabeth was nervous about digging up the past and didn't think it was a good idea.

"Do you remember the man who came to see us a few years ago and was trying to trace Louise? Did he say anything at all about why he wanted to find her?" Asked Dr Brook.

"No, you know what my memory is like these days I remember he was a handsome man though, perhaps he wanted to marry her."

Dr Brook realised that Elizabeth was not going to be of any further help. He had been keeping an eye on her for some time now and he knew that there would come a time, probably not too far away when she would have to move into full time care. He said his goodbyes and headed home.

At 5:15 his phone rang and it was CI Janice Shorwell. They exchanged pleasantries and then she asked how she could help.

Dr Brook explained what had happened and also detailed his and Elizabeth's views on what to do next. He did not mention the visit of the complete stranger who was looking for Louise until the end of the conversation and it was only at this stage that Janice, as she insisted he call her, gave some interesting opinions.

"When someone is looking for someone else and asks about them without divulging their reasons, it seems to me that there are either good or bad intentions. It is not for us to determine which but based on what you have told me it appears that Louise is safe and well. Probably best after all these years if you just leave it at that. I tend to agree with Elizabeth that at her age she doesn't need to drag up the past. I will look into the partial number plate for you but I doubt that it will help you decide what to do next. After 16 years you should just be happy that you know Louise is well. She probably has a whole new family and life and doesn't want to be found."

Dr Brooks had to agree and he thanked Janice for her advice. He would try to put the whole issue to the back of his mind and spend more time concentrating on writing his book. He was writing a memoir, not for publication but just for his own enjoyment and it had stalled while his mind was on Louise's visit.

At least he thought he had managed to put the visit to the back of his mind but little things kept bringing it back to the front again. Firstly, when he visited Elizabeth she often spoke about Louise now, even though she often referred to her as a little girl. Secondly, he had reached the stage of his memoir where two of his best friends had died in a car crash and Louise had disappeared. Finally, in early January 2007 he received a call from WPC Quarr who apologised for the delay but told him they had finally managed to trace the car for which he had provided the partial number plate. The car was registered to a Miss Louise Culver who resided at The Willows, Vicarage Road, Wyddial.

Now, Dr Brook had to decide what to do with that information. Louise had obviously, he assumed, got married hence the different surname. Did he want to interfere in her life? He deferred the decision and then deferred again. He wasn't sure at all what to do and the indecision was a problem for him as it played on his mind and affected his thoughts and his sleep.

One day while he was sitting down to breakfast there was a knock at the door. When he opened it there was a young lady standing there with an armful of leaflets. She reached out to offer him one and as she stepped forward she slipped and tumbled. Dr Brook helped her back to her feet but she was obviously shaken by the fall. He invited her in and made a fresh pot of tea. The leaflets were scattered around the front porch and as the young lady drank her tea Dr Brook went and picked them up. When he carried them in he noticed that there was mud all up the back of the lady's bright yellow coat and he offered to clean it off for her. She thanked him and took it off.

"That's my favourite coat so be careful with it please, it's such a lovely bright yellow, don't you think, doctor?" The young lady asked.

"Well I …yes I'll be very careful, how did you know I was a doctor, have we met before?"

"No, no, I just noticed the books on your shelves. Many medical volumes among them." She observed. "I'm sorry to have interrupted your breakfast, I feel a bit silly falling like that. I suppose I should be getting on my way."

"I'm not doing anything this morning so only go when you feel ready and when your coat has dried a little." Dr Brook replied.

"Thank you, you're so kind. How is your book coming along?" The lady asked with a smile.

"What? How did you know I was writing a book?"

"Oh, I can see the pile of paper and took a guess. Besides you look like a writer." she laughed.

"Are you sure we haven't met before?" Dr Brook asked, slightly taken aback by the lady's insights.

"I think I would remember if I had met you." She replied. "I really must be getting on now. Thank you again for your help and for the tea."

With that she got up, put on her coat and together they walked to the front door.

"You've been very kind. I hope you come to a decision on your problem soon." The lady said as she walked down the garden path, and then she was gone.

Dr Brook was confused as he returned to his kitchen. He poured himself another cup of tea and picked up the leaflet the lady had left. He was about to read it when he noticed another piece of paper beneath it. There was a name and telephone number written on the paper in his own hand writing. COLIN COMPTON 07703 262630.

"How did that get there?" He mumbled to himself. "I'm sure that was in the drawer of the coffee table in the living room. Strange, perhaps there is some kind of divine intervention going on here and I should pass on the information I now have about Louise's whereabouts."

He picked up the telephone.

CHAPTER 42 - COLIN, 2007

Colin awoke and looked at the sun streaming in from between the curtains. It was a lovely day for the start of February. Maddie was still asleep beside him and he decided to get up and go for a run while she slept. He quietly got out of bed and found his slippers. He then got his running gear together and still in his pyjamas he crept out of the room. He would get dressed downstairs so as to avoid waking Maddie.

As he stood looking out of the kitchen window trying to decide on this mornings route he felt a pinch on his bum and turned around to see Maddie standing there.

"Pinch and a punch for the first of the month." She said and reached up to kiss him.

"I'm just going for a short run this morning as I want to get the car washed later before it starts to rain. Is there anything you want me to pick up from the village shop on my way back?"

"No. Just don't be too long. As well as washing the car I was hoping you would put up those security lights today." Maddie yawned. "I think I'll go back to bed for a while, I'm still pretty tired."

"I could forgo the run and join you if you like." Colin said with a wink.

"No, I need quality sleep, not what you have in mind." Maddie smiled and turned away. Over her shoulder she added, "You can wake me with a kiss when you're back and showered though, if I'm still asleep."

Colin, put on his running shoes and left the house. It was cold but he was happy that he would soon warm up. As he passed the end of the road and turned towards Chesham, he looked up at a passing bus and stopped in his tracks. On the top deck was the lady from the cemetery in Exeter looking down at him. He was sure of it. She was wearing the same bright yellow coat. He decided that he was no longer focused on his run, turned round and headed home.

He spent the rest of the day thinking about what or rather who he had seen. He washed the car, put the lights up and when Maddie called him he went in for lunch. As he sat at the table his phone rang.

"Hello, is that Colin Compton?" Asked the voice on the other end.

"Yes, who is this?"

"You might not remember me but we spoke a few years ago. My name is Dr Brook. You were enquiring about a patient of mine from 1990. I think I have some information for you."

Dr Brook then went on to tell Colin about the visit from Louise and how he had traced her. Before he would give Colin the details he asked for full details as to why he was looking for her. It was a long conversation and Colin struggled to know what to tell Dr Brook and what to leave out. In the end he just said that she had been involved in an incident that Colin was now trying to clarify. He said that it appeared that Louise must have changed her name on more than one occasion and that she probably needed medical help. He hoped that the final sentence would appeal to the better side of Dr Brook's judgement.

"I will give you the address I have but only if you promise me that Louise will not come to any harm. I may have only seen her once in the last 16 or so years but she was the daughter to some very good friends of mine."

"Dr Brook, I assure you that I am not in the business of hurting people and I promise you that she will be safe."

That promise seemed to do the trick and Dr Brooks gave Colin the information he had.

Wow, thought Colin. After all this time we appear to have a current address. He then thought about what he saw on the bus earlier and another shiver went down his spine. Was it just a coincidence that his sighting of the woman in the bright yellow coat and the call from Dr Brook were on the same day? Were they connected?

Maddie was listening to the call and although she could only hear one half of the conversation she knew what it was about. As Colin hung up she threw her arms around him and hugged tightly.

Colin couldn't control the smile on his face and told Maddie that he had to make a few phone calls. First, was Grant. He knew that Rachel would likely be in lectures on a Friday and that Richard would be at work. Grant was delighted with the latest findings and promised to let Colin break the news to the twins this evening. He asked Colin to make some plans on how to approach Louise and told him to be careful. He had read all the notes about the investigation and it was obvious that Louise was pretty violent and pretty clever. Caution was advised.

Within seconds of hanging up the phone, it rang.

This call was from Richard and having not spoken directly about the case with him for a long time Colin was surprised. Grant had promised not to tell the twins about the latest news and certainly hadn't had time to do so in the few seconds since they had spoken. Why was Richard calling now? Just a coincidence or something a bit more sinister. Again Colin's mind flicked back to the lady on the bus earlier.

Richard spoke at length about his feelings following him finding out that he was to have a son. He was keen to resolve the investigation and had re-read all the notes. He had a few thoughts and had run them past Rachel who had advised him to speak to Colin.

Colin decided that rather than tell Richard about the latest information and then have to retell it all to Rachel that they should all get together to discuss everything. Richard agreed and said he would try to arrange something with Rachel over the weekend.

Sunday morning they were all sat around the table in Grant and Fiona's house. Maddie was there but she felt a bit of an intruder. After Fiona had made coffee and bought in a huge pile of cakes from the kitchen, the two women announced that they would leave the house to the three intrepid investigators and Grant and head out for a walk. The remaining four got to work.

First of all Colin gave a complete update of every bit of information they had. Richard was champing at the bit now that he was back involved and on more than one occasion Grant had to step in and ask him to calm down. Rachel sat quietly listening until Colin had finished and she then produced some first draft copies of her thesis on the mind of a killer.

Rachel had been to Swansea and met with Amy Fellow and she had been to Southend to interview Thomas Appley. The information she gained from these together with extensive research from books and links to articles examining the human mind both included in her course and in addition to it had resulted in a document that she was especially proud of. A two page summary was included and she asked everyone to just focus on that.

Rachel had concluded, primarily based on Tommy's accounts of their time together, that Louise could well have a split personality and most definitely was a dangerous woman. She was an extremely thorough and clever woman who would not easily be bettered and she had made a life's work of covering her tracks. If she was approached she could be become extremely volatile and savage in an instant although appearing very calm and serene until that moment.

Again Richard was keen to move on to a plan of action and wanted them to drive to the address they had been given and corner the woman who had killer their father. Caution was not in Richard's vocabulary, he wanted action. Grant again calmed him down and asked what Colin thought was the best way forward.

A long discussion followed about what the actual preferred outcome would be and then once they all agreed, how they should proceed. The ideal outcome would be that they could present complete and undeniable evidence to the police that Louise had killed John. This was far from likely and even if they could, they would be relying on the police to act swiftly in arresting Louise. Colin needed to think things through in more detail and he promised that he would come up with as fool-proof a plan as he could.

Life for all of them should carry on as normal for the time being and Colin would prepare his detailed plan and then carry out some very careful surveillance to get a lay of the land before anything else was decided.

"This has taken us a long time to get where we are today. It would be silly to waste all that time by charging in now and scaring her away. We know how good she is at disappearing so we are likely to only get one chance at this and we need to get it right. We also need to ensure that whatever we do is either on the right side of the law or at least can not point to any wrongdoing on our part.

When the women got back from their walk Colin and Grant agreed that they would update their respective partners on the discussions but first Richard called Hannah and by the time she arrived preparations for dinner were well under way.

Fiona again produced a feast fit for a king and everyone relaxed and talked about other thing such as the impending baby, Rachel's final year at Cambridge, life in Berkhamsted and the fantastic food. Only Richard bought up the investigation a couple of times and he was quickly closed down by Grant.

CHAPTER 43 - THE PLAN, 2007

Colin received three calls the following day and also had a long talk with Maddie.

When he woke up, Maddie was sitting on the end of the bed and he could see that she was deep in thought.

"Is everything OK darling?" He asked tentatively.

"I am just a bit worried about this investigation. It seems to me that yesterday you were talking about the dangers of approaching this woman and yet you plan to do exactly that. Why don't you just report her to the police and leave it to them. I don't want you getting into a fight or getting into trouble with the police. I'm sure Charlie would say 'leave it to the experts, they know what they're doing.' Surely you can't be thinking about tackling this woman alone."

"I am not going to do anything that puts me or anyone else in danger. That is why I slowed things down and insisted on the need for a full plan before we progress this further. Regarding the police, we do not have enough evidence to ensure a conviction for murder. We just have Tommy's statement but that is not enough. I have a few ideas but I do worry that we will not complete this to Richard and Rachel's satisfaction."

Maddie turned to face Colin and there were tear in her eyes.

"I really never expected to find love again at my age and now that I have I will do everything I can to ensure that you are with me for the rest of my life. Please don't do anything to put our life together in danger."

"Maddie, I promise. I will make sure that no one is in any danger at any stage."

Maddie walked around the bed and hugged Colin. They stayed like that for a long time and then Colin's phone rang for the first time that day.

Colin picked up his phone from the side cabinet and looked at the screen. It was a call from Grant and it was only 8:15.

"Fancy putting the kettle on while I take this call?" He asked Maddie and kissed her on the cheek.

"Good morning Grant, is everything OK? He asked into the phone.

"Yes, everything is fine. I hope I didn't wake you up. Sorry to call so early but I have been thinking about our conversations yesterday and wanted to clarify a few things before you make your plans."

"No, I was already awake. What thoughts have you had?"

"Well the main one is regarding the safely of everyone. I know Richard is so eager to get involved now and I don't want him to get into any dangerous situations. I know your skill sets but again you need to be careful, you're not as young as you once were, and I really don't want anyone to get into trouble with the police. When I told Fiona about our talks yesterday she was quite scared and didn't want anyone to approach this Louise directly. She does sound a bit crazy, especially after what happened to that guy in Swansea."

"I've just had a very similar conversation with Maddie, Grant. I can only really repeat what I told her in that I will ensure I have a plan that does not involve any danger before we take any action, and I assure you that I will not involve

252

Richard, or Rachel for that matter, in anything that is not completely safe."

"I didn't have any doubts Colin, I know you will come up with something. I really just want to point out that Richard can be a bit hot headed sometimes and well, you know, he needs to be as far away from trouble as possible." Colin could hear Grant's concerns in his voice and was struggling to say anything else without repeating himself.

"I'll let you go now I'm sure you have plenty to be getting on with. Pass on our love to Maddie, it was great to see you both yesterday, we need to get together more often."

Colin agreed and then they hung up. By the time he got downstairs Maddie had made coffee and put on some toast. She asked about the call and made a few 'I told you so' noises as Colin explained that Grant's concerns echoed hers.

Maddie worked in the charity shop on a Monday and that left Colin to spend the day in front of his computer coming up with a plan. He spent the first couple of hours rereading all his notes and looking at Google maps to see exactly where Louise lived. Finally he opened a new page in his notes and started typing.

At 11am he stopped and put the kettle on. He was struggling to coordinate a viable plan bearing in mind what he had promised Maddie and Grant. As he finished his coffee and took his cup to the sink his phone rang for the second time that day. It was Richard.

"Morning Colin, how's the plan going? I've got a few ideas to run past you. I have been thinking that you and me together should be able to take this woman down easily. We could force her to make a confession and then take her to a police station. If we just turn up at her door unannounced we would take her by surprise and probably wouldn't even have to use much force."

"Good morning Richard, I've never heard anything so ridiculous. Were you not listening to anything I said yesterday?" Colin growled into the phone. "Force her to make a confession and then walk into a police station! We could be arrested immediately. Please calm down a bit and let me devise a plan that will work. I'm not going to lie, it may take a while to concoct something that is airtight. As I said yesterday, we have to be very careful and not rush into anything."

"But I thought…."

"Yes, you thought but not very wisely. Please just leave it to me for now. I will be in touch once a plan is in place, ok?"

Richard was obviously not ok with waiting but he relented and promised that he would give Colin time to think everything through.

"I want to be involved though. We are talking about the woman who killed our father and Rachel and I want to be part of her downfall, not just sit by while you do it all." Said Richard before they concluded the call.

"Shit!" Exclaimed Colin as he pressed the red button on his phone. How could he involve Richard and possibly Rachel yet at the same time keep his promise to Grant?

He went back to his computer and sat staring at the screen.

By 5:30pm he was no closer to having a plan that would satisfy everyone than he had been eight hours prior.

Maddie returned home and told Colin that she had spent all day on her feet and wanted him to make dinner. He was happy to oblige and hoped that cooking would free his mind from planning.

The third telephone call arrived at 6:30. It was from Rachel.

Colin liked Rachel's approach to things and had been impressed with how thorough she was. Over the last couple of years or so she had provided much information about John, Mary and even Baz that, although not directly useful had helped build up a background picture to the investigation. She had insights that escaped Colin and they worked well together.

"Good evening Colin, how are you and Maddie today?" She started brightly. Then she started on the reasons for her call. "I have had Richard on the phone twice since I got out of lectures. He is not happy. Did you really tell him he is ridiculous?"

"No I didn't say that, I said his idea was ridiculous not him."

"I thought as much. He really is too eager for his own good sometimes. I just want this all to be over with as soon as possible now. We've been looking into who killed John for over four years now and at last we have the lead we've been waiting for but I agree with what you said yesterday, we need to proceed with caution. We need to have a really good plan and above all we need proof which we don't really have. Even approaching Louise will not necessarily give us that proof."

"Yes, that is what I was trying to tell Richard. I've spend all day thinking about it and haven't come up with a good plan yet. It will take time and patience and I'm not sure Richard has that. He really has been galvanised into action since finding out he is going to be a father."

"Don't worry, I will deal with Richard. He may be three minutes older than me but I have always been able to control him." Rachel laughed and seemed very relaxed. "Please don't do anything to raise Louise's suspicions we can't afford to lose her again."

Colin agreed and promised that he would liaise with Rachel throughout his planning phase and before he took any kind of action.

He didn't realise it at the time but Richard was going to become much more frustrated as his planning phase would take much longer than expected due to some unforeseen circumstances.

A few days later Colin was out for his morning run. He had taken to running at the same time and on the same route as he had done the day he saw the lady in the bright yellow coat. He knew it was madness but he couldn't help himself and he carefully watched the windows of every bus that passed. It was while looking up at the windows of a passing bus that he tripped on a rock at the side of the road and fell.

The fall resulted in a break to a bone in his left leg and at the hospital he was told that he would be in plaster for about six weeks but that the break should heal completely. This was both a hinderance and a godsend for his planning. He could not get out and carry out any practical surveillance and he could not help Maddie in the garden or around the house. It did mean that sitting with his leg up on a pile of cushions with his phone at his side and his laptop on his lap he could focus on the plan.

Maddie was brilliant and furnished him with fresh cushions, regular coffees and the all important knitting needle for reaching those itchy places inside the plaster cast. She also helped him down the stairs to the sofa every morning and up the stairs to bed every evening.

Within this environment Colin reached what he thought was a pretty decent plan and he invited everyone concerned to a meeting at his house over the Easter weekend. Although Maddie had agreed that the meeting should be there she immediately went into panic mode thinking about what food to prepare and whether she could live up to Fiona's high standards.

Because of other engagements over that weekend the date was finally set for Good Friday and Maddie was ready to feed seven or seventy. She had spent a week practicing all her dishes and Colin, what with his inactivity and the extra food was feeling extremely overweight as he opened the door to his guests. The cast was still on his leg but he was getting around well now and looking forward to it being taken off, hopefully within the next couple of weeks.

Dinner was going to be served at 1pm and the rest of the afternoon was designated for discussing the plan. By 3:30pm they had finished a lovely beetroot and feta tart, a salmon-en-croute main course and an enormous pavlova and had made their way into the living room.

Colin had prepared printouts of his detailed plan and a summary and handed them out to everyone. This time Maddie and Fiona were not going anywhere.

THE PLAN SUMMARY

<u>Objectives:</u>

- To find indisputable proof that Louise had indeed caused John's death.

- To deliver Louise with that proof to the police.

- To ensure that no-one is at any time in any danger.

- To ensure that if possible no one is implicated in the capture of Louise.

<u>First stage:</u>

- Surveillance on the house Louise was believed to be living in.

- Monitoring of her weekly routine.

- Monitoring of anyone else living at the address.

- Monitoring of neighbours routines and traffic passing the property.

- Ensure complete cover. Louise must not know they are there.

<u>Second stage:</u>

- If possible, search the house, preferably before but if necessary after we have captured Louise and certainly before the police are involved.

- To subdue Louise with the least amount of physicality and in a way that is not harmful to anyone.

- To gather as much information about Louise's whereabouts and her aliases over the last 17 years.

- To deliver Louise to the police together with all information gathered.

- To maintain anonymity wherever possible.

Final Stage:

- To monitor the course of action the police decided upon and if necessary watch Louise if she is allowed bail or is released from custody.

- To celebrate when Louise is finally bought to justice for the killing of John, the suicide of Mary and if possible for the crippling effects on Cliff Wellow and his family.

Rachel had insisted on the last part, having heard from Amy Wellow of the devastating effect on the whole Wellow family.

Everyone, including Richard, agreed that this was a good summary of the Objectives and the Planned stages. The accompanying detailed plan was indeed very detailed and added substantially to the above summary.

Colin asked that everyone read the detailed plan and let him know what they thought. He looked at Richard and explained that for obvious reasons, not least that his wife was due to give birth any day now and because a cool head would be needed, he and his old navy friend Jack would carry out the surveillance and whatever other interactions were required. He could see that Richard was not happy but he also saw the way he looked at Hannah and the huge bump she was carrying and he knew that Richard would see sense. Maddie on the other hand would need a lot of convincing but he felt he could handle that.

Grant again stressed the need for Colin and his mate to be very careful and not put themselves in danger.

Colin was happy that his plan had gone down well with the group and said that he would initiate surveillance once he had secured Jack's services and once his cast was removed.

It was again becoming a habit for Louise to stay in a hotel on a Saturday night in order for her to get drunk, fight or have wild sex with a stranger and to return relatively sober on the Sunday morning. It had also become her habit to buy her weekly shopping on the way home on a Sunday thus avoiding the need to leave the house during the week. She had become a weekday recluse who turned into a weekend excessive.

During the week she would have an early morning run on her treadmill or around the local lanes followed by a daily exercise routine that she had found on the internet and then she would write or draw. She had taken up writing and drawing simply to fill her time but she enjoyed both and one of her spare rooms was now full of paintings and writings that no one else had ever seen. She had a whole shelf of note books filled with her poetry, her short stories and even a novel that she had written. She would have been the first to admit that the quality was not great but she enjoyed it and that was all that mattered.

Occasionally she had to go to the local food shop for basics or things that she had missed during her Sunday shopping but other than those rare occasions she was alone in her house.

One Saturday night whilst very drunk she had met a man who seemed nicer that the usual club goers and who had left the club alone before midnight. She had hoped that following their lengthy discussion above the noise of the music she would be spending the night with him but he was too gentlemanly and had excused himself, saying that he hoped to meet Louise again.

Louise had yearned for a more stable relationship, well any relationship that lasted more than one night really and had changed her routine and returned to the same club a few more times but had never seen the man again.

Weekend after weekend of one night stands had taken their toll and she longed for something more settled but her craving for violence always trumped her other desires and she was always attracted to the wrong men, she thought.

A couple of weeks later she was in a club in St Albans, opposite the hotel she had booked into and she made a mistake. She had managed to persuade two men to come back to her hotel room. She had got very drunk and invited the first back at around midnight, she had then carried on drinking and an hour later had invited the second man back. Now, at 2:30 am as she left the club there were two men waiting for her, both expecting to spend the night in her hotel room.

Louise was in no state to get into an argument about which of the two was to go with her and she suggested that if they both wanted her they would have to fight for her. Both men were also pretty drunk and took up her idea. At the back of the car park they took off their jackets and started fighting. Louise was getting very excited and when the two men started rolling about on the floor she couldn't help herself. She kicked the first man so hard that he passed out immediately and then she started on the second man. When she left the scene both men were unconscious and Louise was in heaven. It was like a drug to her and she made her way to her hotel room alone.

The next morning as Louise left the hotel she noticed that there were a couple of police cars outside the club and she realised that her actions may have drawn attention to herself.

She was sure that no-one could connect her to the fighting men but that didn't stop her worrying. She decided that at least for a couple of weeks she would avoid the town and go somewhere else for her kicks. She smiled at the double meaning of the word 'kicks' and drove towards the supermarket.

CHAPTER 45 - COLIN & JACK, 2007

Colin contacted Jack and as he expected got a positive answer to his request for help. Jack turned up at his house a couple of days later and together they added even more detail to the planned surveillance.

"I'm due to have the cast off next week but we could drive up there today and have a little look around if you like. Just a drive past to give us some idea of what we are up against in terms of the area and roads, what do you think?" Colin asked hopefully. He had been pretty much housebound for over six weeks and was keen to get out. Maddie was at work and he would call her first to let her know that he was going out.

"Let's do it." Jack replied and so Colin made the call.

Maddie was not pleased with Colin but she knew that he needed to be doing something. She again stressed the need for caution and told him to be back before she was due to get home from work at 5:30 otherwise she would start worrying.

It was decided that Jack's old van was again the best form of travel and after getting Jack to help him into the passenger seat they headed out. Colin smiled as they headed up the road. It was not his first time out of the house since his accident but it was the first time in a while that he actually felt he had a purpose. It was going to be about an hours journey and so he sat back and relaxed as Jack drove.

When they pull off the A10 into Buntingford, Colin, having examined the maps, directed Jack through the village and up a small lane signposted Wyddial. Within minutes they were sitting in the van outside the village church, engine off and wondering where Louise's house was. The village was small and they were pretty sure they hadn't passed it but the church seemed to be the end of the village. Jack got out and looked around for someone to ask, there was no one in sight.

"Well, she has certainly moved into the middle of nowhere, seems she doesn't want to be found." Laughed Jack through the open passenger window. "I suggest we drive on a little and see if there is anything further up the road."

Five minutes later they were back at the Church having found nothing. This time they were lucky though as a woman was leaving the church and walking towards them.

"Excuse me Ma'am, we are looking for a house called 'The Willows', do you know where that is?"

"Of course I do, I've lived in the village for over 70 years, there's not an inch of this village I don't know. You know, I was 21 before I even went further than Buntingford. Born and bred here and I will die here too." She smiled a toothless smile and pointed back the way they had just come. "About half a mile in that direction, it's down a small track on the right, can't be seen from the main road but it's there. Every time we get a new postman they have to ask where it is."

"Thank you." Said Jack and Colin in unison and Jack started the van. He drove in the direction indicated and when they found the track, he stopped.

"We can't risk driving up the track. We need to proceed on foot from here, probably park the van a little further up the road and cut through the trees. What do you think? Shit, sorry, I forgot about your leg. I'll leave you in the van and go myself." Said Jack.

"We can't take any chances and if you're seen cutting through the trees you will look suspicious. I suggest you get out here and just walk a little up the lane until you can see the house. At least if you are seen and challenged you can just say you're out for a walk. There is no 'No Entry' or 'Private Property' sign up anywhere as far as I can see." Colin countered. "Don't get too close to the house but note everything you see. Particularly look for places from where we might be able carry out some surveillance of the house without being seen."

Jack nodded and left the van. He was back 10 minutes later and after driving in silence back to the church he stopped and turned to Colin.

"OK, so the house is on the right side of the track, facing left. There are no windows in the side of the house so I could get pretty close without fear of being seen. It appears to be a fairly small house and the track ends just passed it where it widens out with a gate into the woods. There is a car parked there. I got the registration number. No neighbours and no reason for anyone to use the track other than to visit the house as far as I can see. There is a small garden behind the house which has a low fence around it and a wooden shed at the bottom. I didn't go close enough to see much of the garden but there are trees at the bottom and on the far side of the house there appears to be a small field before the woods start again. Again I didn't go over that side because I didn't want to pass any windows." Jack reported.

"That's a great start. There is no other way out from there by car, I assume?"

"No. The gate into the woods might lead to a track out but I don't think it's been used for years."

"Right, if we want to monitor people going in and out then all we need to do is monitor from here where the track reaches the road. We could park up there just off the road but

266

will probably have to change vehicles and positions every day otherwise it might look suspicious."

With that Colin looked at his watch and decided that they should head back into Buntingford and find a pub for a pint and a sandwich.

Jack was in full agreement and said that the next time they come here they should be much better prepared now that they know what they are dealing with.

A week after their first visit Colin and Jack were again in the van and sitting outside the church in Wyddial. Colin's car was parked back in a side street in Buntingford and they had decided to take it in turns to keep watch. Jack had fitted the back of the van with a makeshift bed and had a number of flasks of coffee and packs of sandwiches.

Colin's leg was now out of plaster but he had driven against the advice of his doctor and was beginning to wish he hadn't. The drive was longer than before due to heavy traffic and some roadworks and by the time he parked up and walked to the van he was in a bit of pain. He didn't want to show his weakness to Jack so he climbed up into the van with a smile.

"Right, it's 8:30 am now and we will be in here together until the same time tomorrow morning, after that you can take the day shifts and I will take the night shifts. For today I suggest we just do four hour shifts while the other is resting so that we stay sharp. Toilet breaks need to be taken during the rest period and if we just back into the recess we saw yesterday we should be able to exit and enter the back or the van undetected. It's not as if there is likely to be much traffic out here."

"Agreed, let's get on with it then." Jack replied enthusiastically.

Unfortunately they saw nothing useful during the whole time they watched, no one arrived and no one left and Colin was tempted to walk up the track and have a look around. So at 7am the following morning, while Jack was asleep, Colin left the van and made his way up the track towards the house. He was still 50 yards aways when he heard the front door open. He jumped into the bushes at the side of the road ducked down and waited. He heard running footsteps and once they had passed him he carefully raised his head and watched the back of a woman obviously going out for a run. He quickly returned to the van and woke Jack and they drove back towards where they had left Colin's car. On their way they passed the young woman running and Colin watched her in the wing mirror. Based on the descriptions from Tommy and allowing for a gap of 17 years he was convinced that this was Louise.

"You look like you're struggling there mate, everything ok?" Came Jack's voice from behind him as Colin made his way to his car.

"Yeah, I think I hurt my bad leg when I dived into the bushes, I'm sure it will be fine."

Jack got back in his van and returned for another day of surveillance and Colin drove home. He would be back 12 hours later for the night shift.

For three days the same pattern was followed. Every day Louise left her house around 7am, ran for about an hour and returned home, she then didn't appear until the following morning only to repeat the same.

So as to avoid missing anything, Colin and Jack had switched their change over to 10am and 10pm each day and when they reached the weekend they did a couple of short shifts and switched over. Colin was now on day duty.

Colin was covering up the pain in his leg by taking some strong painkillers and that made him a bit drowsy so doing the day shift suited him better. It also meant that he was on watch when finally the pattern changed. At 8:15 on the Saturday evening Louise drove down the track and turned towards the village. Colin decided to follow her but when she turned onto the A10 towards Cambridge he lost her. The van was too slow to keep up with Louise's Audi TT. He returned to the look out spot and called Jack. An hour later Jack arrived in Colin's car and they swapped shifts again.

Jack's shift was boring again as nothing happened, Louise had not returned home. When Colin arrived at 10am on the Sunday morning they had a quick discussion about whether to go and look around the house but decided against it. Louise could return at any time.

They continued their monitoring for three more weeks and determined that Louise was a creature of habit.

Every day she went for a run at 7am. She returned between 8am and 8:30. Everyday she turned left out of the track and ran through the village and down into Buntingford where she would either turn left along the high street, do a loop of the town and return the way she came or she would turn right, run up to the A10 junction and then return home the same way. The later was the 'short' run and took her 65 minutes give or take, the former was generally about 30 minutes longer. Everyday she remained in her house after her run, except for on a Saturday.

They realised that Saturday nights Louise would go out and not return until around mid day on the Sunday. Jack had managed to follow her on a couple of these outings and noted that the first time she went to a nightclub in Hatfield and stayed in a hotel nearby. She had obviously drunk a lot and did not return to the hotel alone but with a much younger man. They had left the hotel the following morning and gone their separate ways. Louise had then visited a supermarket and then returned home.

On a separate Saturday Jack had followed her to Cambridge where a similar pattern was followed.

By the beginning of May, Jack and Colin had built up a pretty clear picture of Louise's movements and were sat at Colin's kitchen table discussing the next stage of the plan. They decided that the following Saturday they would break into the house and search it for clues. The one problem they faced was Colin's leg. Since the day Colin had jumped into the bushes his leg had got worse. He had revisited the doctor on a couple of occasions and now he was facing the prospect of an operation. The break, although healing well initially had highlighted a weakness just below his knee and as they sat at the table Colin, leg up on a chair, had to admit that he would not be able to contribute much.

Maddie was furious. Initially Colin had not mentioned the cause for the pain in his leg but as Maddie had been so supportive of their surveillance plans and the affect of the shift patterns on their daily life, Colin decided to come clean.

"You get your leg out of plaster and then within a few days you're jumping about in hedges? What's worse is that you tried to hide it by taking strong painkillers. You may have caused permanent damage." Had been her first response but many tirades later she was still far from happy.

Reluctantly, Colin made a call to Richard.

CHAPTER 46 - ME & JACK, 2007

As you can imagine I was really excited when I got the call from Colin asking for help. I had pestered him for updates since they had started the surveillance and was getting frustrated by the time it was all taking.

The birth of Harry William Barnes Hamstead had made me realise that what was most important to me was the future and yet the idea of finding my father's killer was also so important.

Colin had explained about his leg and about the next stage of the plan. He had also mentioned that he had spoken to Rachel and they had agreed to ask me to help. I was a little put out by this last comment and was determined to prove to them both just how capable and calm I could be when required. I agreed to drive up to Colin's house Friday evening to meet Jack and to determine what my role would be.

I was shocked by the sight of Colin when I arrived. He was pale and obviously in a lot of pain despite his medication. Maddie made some tea and I was introduced to Jack and to the plan for the following evening. Jack seemed like a good guy, he explained he was out of work through choice and quite happy living on his own.

"It means I have complete freedom to do what I want when I want." He explained. "When Colin called about that Baz bloke a few years ago I was happy to help. Now, although the surveillance has been pretty boring, I'm hoping things will start moving. You lot have been so patient over the years." Jack told me.

I agreed and saw in Jack a kindred spirit, someone who believed in action. As we drank our tea and discussed how the last few weeks had panned out and how Louise was a creature of habit I was getting excited about the next step. That was until I realised where the conversation was headed.

"So, Jack and Richard, you will head up there tomorrow in time to watch Louise leave. Providing she follows the same schedule the best time to go into the cottage will be during the first couple of hours after she departs. Jack will go up the lane and try to find a way in. It is very important, no imperative, that there is no trace of any break in. I stress we must not give her any excuse to disappear again. Richard, you will sit in the car at the end of the track, Jack will show you where, and you will keep watch for anyone turning into the track, in particular a white Audi TT. Make sure you exchange telephone numbers."

So I was just a look out! I must admit I was hoping for more. I promised to be back at Colin's house by 5pm the next day and headed home.

Saturday morning I spent with Hannah and Harry. My mind should have been on the evenings plan but I was easily distracted by these two. I marvelled at the strength of my little boy and the motherly instincts of my wife. When Harry fell asleep just before lunchtime, instead of getting something to eat Hannah cuddled up next to me on the sofa and we just sat in silence. There were no words necessary and I felt that I was the luckiest man alive.

Although I was only going to be a look out, as I put on my shoes and left the house I began to get a nervous feeling in my stomach. I had been looking forward to this moment for a long time but now I was anxious. Just keep your eyes open and let Jack do his job, I thought as I drove north. I arrived at Colin's by 5pm and Jack and I were on the road again before 6pm.

The ride there was interesting. Jack told me a little about his and Colin's time together in the Navy and for some reason I spent a lot of time talking about my sister and the great things expected of her this summer both in graduating from Cambridge and in representing the country in athletics. I was surprised when Jack pulled over and turned the engine off.

"Right, time to focus. We will be in Wyddial in about 10 minutes. I will reverse the van into the little opening we have used before and we will watch for the Audi to leave. From then on you must keep your eyes peeled. I hope to be in and out in about an hour but it really depends on what I find. Keep your phone in your lap and call me the minute anything happens although hopefully that won't be necessary. If anything needs to change I will call you. OK."

With that he started the engine again and we drove the rest of the way in silence, each concentrating of our own responsibilities.

I was nervous when Jack got out of the van but that was nothing compared to how I was feeling over two hours later. Jack had not returned and I was in two minds whether to stay in the van as I had been told or go and see what was taking so long. My phone rang and I nearly dropped it in my eagerness to answer it.

"You won't believe what I've found here, I have a box of diaries going right back to 1990 and even before that. Every day there is an entry and she does not hold back on what she was up to or what she was thinking. This is pure gold." Jack was speaking very quietly and breathlessly but I could feel his excitement.

"That's fantastic," I said, "bring it with you, I'm sure that will include all the proof we need."

"No. I must leave everything as I found it. I have taken photos of a few pages of the diary and there is also a room full of hand written poetry books and paintings. They really give an insight to this woman's mind. I've taken loads of photos but I've already been here too long. I will be out in five minutes." With that he hung up.

Back at Colin's we again sat around his table deciding what to do next. We had all read the copies of the diary pages and seen the photos of the paintings and we were all convinced from what we saw that Louise was fully aware of her involvement in John's death.

"We now know where all the proof we need is and can move on to the next stage of the plan." Colin said. "I promised Grant that we would not put anyone at risk but now that we know about the diaries I think we need a plan that allows us to isolate Louise, get the diaries, copy them as I am sure we, and especially Rachel, will want to read them all in detail and then somehow deliver Louise to the police anonymously. I'm loath to just go into her house with force. That could have all sorts of repercussions. Any ideas?"

I had been thinking about this on the drive back to Colin's and I had a plan but I was reluctant to say it out loud. I was sure Colin would not accept it. After another hour of us coming up with ideas and then discarding them I decided to give it a go.

"I have a plan," I announced, "but before you interrupt me or discount the idea please hear me out to the end."

My plan was simple but revolved around knowledge of drugs that could incapacitate someone without causing lasting danger. I did not have that knowledge and hoped that someone did.

"Right, we know that Louise goes out every Saturday night, we also know that she gets drunk and tries to hook up with a young man, presumably for a night of sex. That has to be our window for wrapping this whole thing up. A two pronged attack as it were."

"Haha, you're the only young man here so I assume you want to have sex with her. What would Hannah say to that?" Interrupted Jack.

I said. "Let me finish please. I can think of nothing worse than sex with my fathers killer." I stared at Jack and he nodded an apology. "Now, once she is out of the house Jack can do what he did tonight, only this time he needs to get the diaries and any other incriminating evidence he can find to help with a police enquiry. On to part two. I will follow Louise to whichever club she chooses and make it obvious that I am watching her. I will do my best to encourage her to approach me but if she doesn't I will approach her and well, be as charming as I can."

I could see that Jack was again itching to say something but I continued. "I will get her alone, possibly in her hotel room and I will drug her. I will then meet up with Jack and we can leave her and the diaries outside a police station. Ok, I will need help with the drugs part but everything else I am sure I can handle. Right I'm finished, what do you think?

There was a long pause and then Colin let out a hearty laugh. "Not bad, not bad, certainly the best we've come up with yet but it does need a bit of finessing. I can't let you tackle Louise alone. Let me sleep on it and we can discuss it again tomorrow.

CHAPTER 47 - COLIN'S REVISED PLAN, 2007

"I'm torn between finalising this investigation and putting Richard in any harms way." Colin told Rachel over the phone. "I promised your Dad that I would keep the two of you safe and away from any danger but Richard's plan could work and solve this once and for all."

"Right, so if I understand you, Richard will be alone with Louise in a nightclub somewhere. Then if he succeeds to charm her he will be alone with her in a hotel room. He then has to administer a drug that will put her to sleep. These are the dangers zones right?" Rachel summarised.

"Yep, as I see it they are the times he will be in danger."

"Well first off, I do not want to be left out of this so I can follow Richard into the nightclub and watch over things in there. If your leg is up to it, you could follow them to the hotel room and somehow get yourself inside. The two of you should be able to overpower her and drug her, then we all wait for Jack to arrive with the diaries etc. How does that sound?"

"Apart from the bit about you being in the nightclub, it is pretty much what I was thinking. We don't know which nightclub she will choose and we certainly don't know which hotel but we can follow her and I am sure that we can work it out as we go. Are you sure you will be able to keep an eye on Richard? He can be a bit spontaneous sometimes."

"Yes, I can watch them from inside the club and let you know when they are leaving."

"Your Dad would go nuts if he knew that both of you will be so close to a killer. I think we need to be extra, extra careful, I will have a long conversation with Richard before hand. Can you be here by about 4pm next Saturday or do you want to meet us in Buntingford, its not far from you?"

"I prefer to come to yours, early Saturday morning so that we can go over the plan in detail a final time and check for any weaknesses in it. Also, I want to have a word with Richard face to face before we leave for Buntingford. What do we know about drugs though? We need to be sure of both the dosage and the timing of the effect. Ideally something that can easily be administered and will put her to sleep for a number of hours without killing her. Can you write up the plan in detail and send it to me please?" Asked Rachel.

"OK. I've had a chat with Jack and he knows someone in the 'pharmaceutical industry' don't ask, who will be able to give us what we need. I will make sure we are well prepared and yes, I will type up the plan and send you a copy." Colin concluded. "I'll probably get that done tomorrow."

Colin was true to his word and drew up a step by step plan of everyone's required actions for the following Saturday night. He contacted everyone and it was agreed that they would all meet at Colin's house on the Saturday morning to go over the plans and ensure everyone knew their part.

The game was on.

I arrived at Colin's house to find that both Jack and Rachel were already there. Maddie opened the door to me and threw her arms around me.

"You will be extremely careful tonight won't you? I am so worried about you all." She whispered into my ear.

I then went into the living room where I was met by Rachel who threw her arms around me too. If I have the same affect on Louise, tonight will be a doddle, I thought.

Colin and Jack were a lot more reserved and we shook hands and nodded at each other.

We had all read Colin's final version of the plan and we were all in agreement that it was the best we could come up with. There were obviously a few unknowns in the plan such as where Louise would choose to go dancing tonight, where she would stay and what her mood would be. Everything else, we hoped was covered.

Transport was the first topic and we all agreed that Colin and Jack would travel up in Colin's car, with Jack driving. Rachel and I would use Rachel's car.

I was particularly concerned about the drugs we would be using but Colin and Jack assured me that what we had was perfect for what we needed. The only real concern there was the actual administration of the drug. Jack seemed to be, well, a Jack of all trades really. He had sourced the drug, determined the dose and loaded the syringes. He never explained how or why he knew so much about putting someone to sleep but Colin seemed to trust him so the rest of us just followed suit.

Another issue, raised by Rachel was how exactly the diaries and any other compelling evidence would be copied during the evening and early hours of Sunday. She solved this herself by calling a college principal friend at Cambridge who agreed to let Jack have use of some copiers at the Cambridge Press. She also arranged for someone standing by to help Jack copy everything.

After a couple of hours discussion and some coffee and cakes we retired to the living room for a rest. Tonight would be a long night and we needed to be ready. Discussion turned to what we would do once the investigation was complete and, hopefully, Louise was behind bars.

Jack gave the most surprising answer to that question. He had been saving his Navy pension and was in the process of buying a boat in which he planned to sail down into the Mediterranean and visit relatives in southern Italy. None of us, including Colin, had any idea that he had Italian heritage.

Colin and Maddie also planned to do a little travelling around Europe and I think that at one stage they agreed that they would meet up with Jack in Italy if the timings could be sorted out.

Rachel's plans were the grandest of all. The first thing she planned to do was to graduate. She was on course for a First from Cambridge and that would open up a host of opportunities for her. She was expected to be included in the GB olympic team for the 2008 Olympics in Beijing where she hoped to run both the 800m and the 1500m.

In addition to all this she wanted to continue with her thesis post graduation and using the diaries etc that we hoped to gather tonight, she was planning on turning it all into a book. One of her masters at Cambridge had raised the idea of a book after reading her thesis and had offered both his and the college's support. There was no doubt in my mind that Rachel would be a star. I was so proud of her.

My plans were a lot simpler. I just wanted to be the best Dad and Husband I could be. My job was going well and I was part of a very happy and loving family, what more could I want? Well, I did also want a daughter but I kept that to myself as I hadn't even raised the idea with Hannah.

About an hour before we were due to leave the house and travel up to Wyddial, Rachel asked me to accompany her on a little walk to get some fresh air. I was happy to oblige as conversation had stalled a little and my nerves were beginning to kick in. Once outside she revealed the real reason for the walk.

"I wanted to talk to you about your role in tonights action." She began. "Richard I have full confidence in you, you know that, but please don't go off script and do something stupid. Colin has promised Dad that he will ensure we are safe throughout the operation and I know that he is a bit concerned that you will be too impulsive. That is why he scripted your part in such detail. I will be there keeping an eye on you but there is only so much I can do. We are so close to wrapping this whole thing up now, so we have to follow the plan.

I agreed with Rachel completely and told her so. "You don't need to worry Sis, I promise I will follow Colin's guidelines to the letter and not let my feelings get in the way of the plan. Besides, I want this whole investigation over with so that we can all move on with our lives."

At 5pm we started to get ready. With everything we needed packed into the cars, we left Maddie and made our way to Wyddial. Jack backed the car into the parking spot he had used many times before and Colin transferred to Rachel's car with me and Rachel. We then moved back towards the village and parked outside the church. Jack would notify us as soon as Louise left and we would follow.

I had been warned by everyone at least twice to maintain a cool head and stick to the script. I vowed to myself that I would make everyone proud tonight and as we sat waiting in the car my hands began to shake a little. That short period of just under two hours waiting was the worst of my life. There was very little conversation in the car and I think all of us were feeling the strain. Finally, just after 8pm, Colin's phone rang and Jack informed us that Louise was heading our way.

Rachel started the engine and looked over her shoulder at me in the back seat. "Game on!" Is all she said and pulled out as Louise passed.

"Keep your distance but keep her in sight." Was Colin's instruction and Rachel did just that.

Louise was heading east and we guessed that she was heading for either Stevenage or Luton. The former turned out to be her destination and she pulled into the car park of a Premier Inn, parked her car and walked in. Rachel and I again sat and waited but Colin was out of the car in a flash and followed Louise into the hotel. He was standing right behind her when she booked in and was told she would be in Room 215. He returned to us and after 30 minutes we saw Louise leave and start walking towards the Town Centre. This time, Rachel and I departed and together we followed Louise to a night club 10 minutes walk away in the Leisure Park.

The Club Louise had chosen was still pretty empty and I pointed out to Rachel that it would only fill up after the pubs had shut as the price of drinks was pretty high here. That didn't seem to stop Louise though and over the course of the next couple of hours I watched her down at least 10 vodkas. Rachel had moved to the other side of the dance floor and found a table. She was chatting to a couple of girls and although I noticed that she kept looking my way it was not obvious. After a while I watched as Louise got up to dance. She had not spoken to anyone in the whole two hours she had been there and seemed to be in a world of her own. I moved closer and tried to catch her eye. This was the first time I had seen her up close and I was surprised at how old she looked. She was obviously a beautiful woman but she looked old and sad and somehow shrunken as she danced alone.

When the record stopped I finally managed to be noticed and she smiled at me. I smiled back and indicated that I was going to the bar and did she want anything. She understood my question and came over. This was now the key part of the plan we had made. I had to be as charismatic as possible but remain fairly laid back at the same time. Not really my strength. However, although she had drunk more in two hours than I could manage in a whole day, Louise was effervescent and I actually found it very easy to get along with her. We got some more drinks and found somewhere to sit and chat. I noticed over on the other side of the room that Rachel had moved a little closer and I tried very hard to focus on Louise.

I was now sitting directly opposite the woman who had killed my father and believe it or not I was actually finding her very charming. I had to keep reminding myself that I was there for the sole reason of putting this woman in prison where she belonged. The evening was going well and I think I was stepping up to the plate and playing my part. That was until 'Gorilla' turned up. I call him 'Gorilla' because that was my first thought when I saw him.

"Fancy a dance with me, darling." He snarled.

"Piss off, I'm talking." Louise replied catching me by surprise.

"No need to be like that darling, you just look far too good for this punk." He replied, indicating me.

I was about to stand up when one of 'Gorilla's friends arrived. "Don't mind him, he's had too much to drink. Come on mate we don't want any trouble do we."

Louise let out a raucous laugh and shouted above the music. "I told you to piss off. Are you deaf? Listen to what your mate is telling you. My friend here would have you for breakfast."

Shit, I thought, she is not helping matters here. I indicated to Louise that it was time to get some more drinks and I went to the bar. Within seconds of me arriving at the bar Rachel arrived at my side.

"You ok?" She asked. "It looks like you're getting on well there but she is a bit of a handful. Watch out or she'll get you into a fight.

"Don't worry it's all under control." I said although deep down I was a little shaken.

I returned to the table with the drinks. I had lost track of the number of drinks Louise had knocked back and I was monitoring mine carefully. I was drinking water or coke mostly and was remaining alert. 'Gorilla' was nowhere to be seen.

"You'd have taken him easily wouldn't you?" She asked as I sat down. I smiled and changed the subject.

"Let's dance, shall we?" I reached for her hand and we made our way onto the dance floor.

I think I've mentioned before that I love dancing but this night I was out of my league. Louise seemed to have absolutely no inhibitions and flowed around the floor. I tried to keep up but was a little in awe of her fluidity and her carefree attitude. It was now after midnight and I had managed to keep Louise to myself so the opportunity to go back to her hotel room with her was a real possibility. I decided to broach the subject as we returned to our drinks and was surprised by the answer I got.

"Richard, you seem like a lovely bloke but I am not a lovely woman. Go find someone your own age, believe me you'll be better off that way."

"I don't want anyone else, it has to be you tonight." I said and hoped that my meaning was misinterpreted.

"I really don't want to hurt you but if you insist you can come back to my hotel room." With that she unexpectedly leaned over and kissed me.

Her kiss was rough and hungry and I was torn about what to do. I had very little time to think about it so I kissed her back with equal vigour. Her right hand had gripped my knee and she was squeezing so tight that I thought her nails would draw blood through my trousers so I stood up and suggested we leave.

As we made our way towards the doors I took a peak over to where Rachel was and I could see that she was already on the phone.

Outside in the cool air I think all the alcohol that she had consumed went straight to Louise's head. She stumbled and grabbed for my hand.

"Come on big boy," she slurred, "let's get you into bed."

As we walked back towards the hotel I thought of Hannah and little Harry and felt a little pang of regret that I was walking hand in hand with a killer towards her bedroom. I am not a religious person but in that moment I prayed that the next few hours would go as planned and that I would be forgiven for my actions. I knew that Rachel would not be far behind me but refrained from looking round.

When we reached the hotel, Louise led me towards the lift and once inside she again attacked me with a long kiss. I could taste the alcohol on her lips and smell it on her breath but she would not let go and as the lift stopped on the second floor she continued to hold on to me. I thought the lift was going to move onto the next floor but just as the doors started to close Louise stuck her foot in the way and we got out. There was a long corridor ahead and I could see Colin standing at the end, seemingly drunk and fiddling with his room card.

When Louise opened the room door, everything happened very quickly. As I followed her in, Colin stormed past me knocking me aside and rugby tackled Louise to the floor. She let out a small yelp and started fighting back but Colin had used the element of surprise and he had her pinned to the floor with one arm and a hand over her mouth. I closed the door and looked down at Louise. She was wriggling and gnarling and spluttering and immediately I seemed to see inside her head and realised how ugly she actually was.

I took the syringe from Colin's pocket and injected it into Louise's arm. I had no idea what was in the syringe, only that

286

it would put her to sleep and within a few minutes that is exactly what it had done.

The knock on the door startled me and Colin rose to answer it as I seemed unable to get my legs to move. Rachel entered and looked down at the body on the floor.

"She's not dead is she?"

"No, she's sleeping like a baby. Should be out for a few hours now." Colin told her. "Have you heard from Jack yet?"

"Yes, he called a few minutes ago. They have finished copying all the diaries and he will be back on the road soon. He should be here in less that an hour." Rachel reported.

"Great, all going to plan. Richard are you alright? You haven't moved for the last five minutes" I could see Colin looking at me from the corner of my eye but I couldn't take my eyes off of Louise.

"I'm fine." I replied quietly.

"Well I'm fucked. I twisted my knee again when I jumped on her and I'm in a lot of pain." Colin sat on the bed and raised his leg. I could see from his face that he really was in pain and I looked up at Rachel and saw the concern in her eyes.

"I'll pop down to reception and see if they have some painkillers." She said and before either of us could argue she was gone.

An hour later Colin was still in some pain despite the painkillers Rachel had obtained and Jack had arrived with the diaries and copies. Rachel had already taken the copies and was reading through them while we all composed ourselves and made a slight tweak to our final plan. Colin's plan had indicated that he would take Louise in her car and drop her off outside the local police station but with his knee so bad, despite the painkillers, he was not able to drive. I volunteered.

The plan was simple. I would drive to the police station, followed by Rachel, then I would leave Louise asleep in the car with all the diaries plus a well written, unsigned letter that Rachel had put together previously and get in the car with Rachel. Then we would find a telephone box and I would call the police to direct them to the sleeping woman the car outside. Finally we would return to Colin's house and meet up with Jack and Colin.

Unfortunately, it didn't go quite to plan. Getting a sleeping Louise out of the hotel unnoticed was the first obstacle and as the night porter was a male, Rachel was dispatched to distract him. While she made up a story and complained about some noise coming from the next room to hers, me and Jack carried Louise down to her car unseen. I had taken Louise's car keys and we opened up the Audi TT, sat her on the passenger seat and put the diaries in the boot.

I then climbed into the drivers seat and drove off. Yes, see my mistake?

The blood was cursing through my brain and I had set off without Rachel following. Not only that but I had turned onto a one way street and after a few turns I was completely lost.

CHAPTER 49 - GAME OVER

I pulled the car over to the curb and stopped. As I looked at the slumped body in the passenger seat next to me I wondered where the hell I was. I knew that I was in the inside lane of a dual carriageway in Stevenage but having driven without thinking for the last five minutes I was not sure exactly which road this was. I thought I would be able to stay cool but I panicked and now I needed to recover my composure and get out of there......

....I am beckoned into the back seat and as I climb in I can relax for the first time in many hours.

Now that I was safely in the back of Rachel's car, my pulse slowed and my head stopped spinning. Having seen that I had already left the hotel, Rachel did what she does best. She calmly thought about what had happened and whether she guessed or whether she knew where I would go, she found me. I had no idea where I would go so how could she? Luck was definitely on my side.

Rachel had convinced Colin and Jack to return and so as soon as I got in the car she called them to confirm that the plan had been completed. We circled around the town and when I recognised the High Street I directed Rachel to the end where she turned right into Martins Way. There were three police cars and an ambulance surrounding the Audi as we passed on the other side of the dual carriageway and I could see Louise was still asleep in the passenger seat with a paramedic at her side. There was also a policeman holding the box of incriminating evidence. I smiled and let out a deep sigh of relief.

We circled around until we reached the A1(M) and headed back to Berkhamsted.

CHAPTER 50 - 18 months later

Rachel sat in the gallery of the court room and watched as Louise was sentenced to 12 years imprisonment. She had followed the case in detail and even written an anonymous letter to the Prosecution team of lawyers pointing them to damning evidence and acts of evil where she felt they may miss something.

Both Tommy and Cliff had been called as witnesses and based on the diaries another eight people had been found, some of whom had harrowing stories to tell.

Rachel smiled and turned to the person sitting next to her. She reached out to take the hand proffered and squeezed lovingly. Jo was there for Rachel and knew what this moment meant to her. They had been together since about a month before their graduation and Jo had been there when Rachel qualified for the finals of both of her events in Beijing. They had celebrated together on reaching the finals and commiserated together when she didn't manage to win a medal.

Jo was philosophical about this and told everyone who would listen to watch out for the home Olympics in 2012. Rachel, she was sure, would be a force to be reckoned with by then.

Amongst all the excitement of the graduation, the new relationship and the Olympics, Rachel had still managed to find the time to monitor Louise's progress through the legal system and to finish her book on the mind of a killer. The copies of the diaries, as Jack had said, were pure gold and gave Rachel a unique insight into Louise's mentality and thoughts. The book, partly a technical guide and partly a novel, was destined for the best sellers list for 2010.

Rachel got up to leave the Court House and Jo put on her bright yellow coat and followed her. They walked hand in hand to meet Grant and Fiona who had arrived too late for the verdict. The four of them made their way to a restaurant and toasted the successes of everyone involved.

Richard was at home but had kept and eye on the news services awaiting confirmation of the expected sentencing. When he read the news he jumped up and down and was soon joined by Harry who didn't know why his father was so happy but just wanted to be part of it.

Colin, Maddie and Jack were all sat together around a table on the deck of Jack's boat moored in Gallipoli when they heard the news and they too raised a glass to a job well done.

Louise left the court in handcuffs, was bundled into the back of a prison van and returned to the cell that she had already spent many months in. She was smiling as the door to her cell slammed shut, she had no idea why but she was very happy there.

Printed in Great Britain
by Amazon

48048864R00165